Steel Blood

THE STEEL EMPIRES SERIES

BOOK THREE

Steel Blood © 2017
by J.L. Gribble
Published by Dog Star Books
Bowie, MD
First Edition
Cover Image: Bradley Sharp
Book Design: M. Garrow Bourke
Printed in the United States of America

ISBN: 978-1-935738-97-8
Library of Congress Control Number: 2017938994

www.DogStarBooks.org

For my mothers:
Ilona, Nedra, and Iolany

Also from the Steel Empires Series

Steel Victory
Steel Magic

Steel Blood

J.L. Gribble

DOG STAR
BOOKS

PROLOGUE

Change drifted in the air like incense caught in a breeze.

It caressed the back of Zhuanxu Xian's hands, as if a silk scarf trailed across his skin. He heard it in the giggling of his many-times-over granddaughter Zhinu and her handmaids, picking out the melodic sounds from among the murmuring of the others present at court for Governor Yu's announcement. But the lacquered banquet table beneath his fingers remained solid, as unchanging as the tropical humidity.

Yu spoke a few seats away from Xian at the head table. "—And we will welcome our visitors from Britannia with open arms and light hearts. New treaties will once again clear the trade routes in Europa that have long been denied our people, and we are honored by Emperor Zhuanxu Elai for choosing our glorious city for these talks. In turn, we shall honor the emperor by being excellent hosts and diplomats."

Xian huffed in exasperation while polite applause rose from the assorted courtiers, officials, and useless hangers-on attending the evening's banquet. His cousin the emperor, the older and much more renowned keeper of the family name, had chosen the city of Jiang Yi Yue in order to deny any involvement if these trade talks went to hell.

With the governor's announcement finished, the more interesting portion of the banquet could begin. The scent of fresh curries and hot rice reached his nose, and air stirred behind him as servers brought in the evening meal.

His assistant Kyo-Young brushed the back of his right hand with her delicate fingers. "Dinner is being served. Do you have any preference, Master Xian?"

Xian released his hold on the table. "No, no," he said. "The usual will be fine." She directed the servers to fill his plate with his customary choices. The meal would be bereft of the salty dishes he loved, thanks to Kyo-Young's strict adherence to his doctor's wishes, but as always, Governor Yu would pass at least one pork roll his way. Being the favorite uncle had its benefits.

No one dared deny the governor if he chose to share a particular delicacy with his predecessor. Some days, Xian resolved to stay in his replacement's good graces for that favor alone.

Kyo-Young pressed chopsticks into his right hand and lifted his left to the rim of his bowl. He set to eating with determination. The unlucky tablemate on his other side tonight was Minister Chang, and the two men would ignore each other the way they had for the past twenty years.

The bright tones of Zhinu and her maids rose again from their seats at one of the lower tables. "Will the wolves truly send a prince to our city?" asked a voice Xian didn't recognize. Must be one of the newer maids hired within the past months. He hadn't had enough time to learn each of their particular vocal ticks yet.

"Don't refer to them as wolves," Zhinu said. Though Granddaughter reprimanded her handmaid, Xian heard the intrigue in her voice. "And it probably won't be a prince, since the current family is heavier on princesses. But perhaps a duke, or maybe an earl. Those are like our ministers."

Xian frowned, then waved off Kyo-Young's query regarding his satisfaction with dinner. Since when did Zhinu know so much about the titles of British nobility? Perhaps she had been spending too much time in the palace library again. A growing girl should be learning handicraft and courtesies, not the political systems of other empires. In fact, her interest in the trade delegation was out of character for a woman of her position. This would not do.

In predictable fashion, however, her handmaids were more interested in discussing the level of attractiveness of this potential prince or duke or earl, which turned in due course to the levels of attractiveness of the officials and ministers surrounding them in the banquet hall. Xian tuned them out.

The evening's dining entertainment was a quiet harpist, so Xian had no trouble picking apart some of the other conversations that drifted up from the hall. All of them included some variation on speculating the makeup and nature of the visiting British delegation and whether they would be inclined to hear of this or that minister's pet projects and work them into the trade agreements. Dull. This was why he had retired when the complications of his failing eyesight grew too onerous to manage. Politics was a younger man's game, and Yu was still young enough to find it fascinating. His (also many-times-great) nephew had done an excellent job for the last ten years, after Xian's physical difficulties made the job more of a chore than a challenge.

"From the governor, Master Xian." Kyo-Young removed his empty bowl and placed a small plate in his hands. As expected, the pork roll from Yu was delicious and savory. An old man deserved his treats.

With so many people in the banquet hall for the announcement, the room grew warm and stuffy. His robes clung to his torso, and sweat ran down the back of his neck. Since his only other option was lowering himself to speaking with Minister Chang—which would not occur until Chang apologized for his inappropriate comment about Xian's mother—it was time to retire for the evening. He pushed away the second bowl Kyo-Young tried to press into his hands when he finished Yu's pork roll. "No, I'm done," he said, standing before his assistant could try to help him. He was blind, not infirm.

As Kyo-Young led him from the banquet hall, Zhinu's voice again brushed Xian's ears. "Of course, there's a chance one or more of the trade delegation might be a woman.... No, I read that it's even possible for women to be werewolves instead of just men. Can you imagine?" She dissolved into giggles with her handmaids, and then Xian was out of hearing range as Kyo-Young escorted him into the gardens.

Before dismissing Kyo-Young to her own evening meal, he settled at his desk and had her fetch writing supplies. The woman had failed the examinations necessary to enter public service, but was too educated to remain in the serving class and too ugly (so Xian had heard rumored) for a good marriage match. But he needed her eyes, not political acumen or beauty.

But while he and Kyo-Young made an effective pair at managing his own affairs, Xian knew his limitations. Curbing Zhinu's unladylike interest in the upcoming trade delegation was beyond his abilities at this time. However, he knew two people with the perfect combination of skills and experience for this task.

When Kyo-Young indicated her readiness from the other desk near him, Xian began his dictation.

Dearest Sun and Moon,

Within this package is a mercenary contract for a bodyguard detail. You have not worked in the Qin territories for many years, but I am hoping a favor for an old friend and generous compensation will prompt you to make the journey. The body in question is my granddaughter, the princess Zhuanxu Zhinu....

ACT I

Victory considered herself a rich woman.

Rich in life experiences. Rich in family and friends. Rich in material wealth. After over eight hundred years as a vampire, she had found her place in the world. The city of Limani was her home, and centuries of previous mercenary work had been more than adequate to buy and furnish an old plantation manor house at the edge of the city. Though her job of vampire Master of the City was nothing more than titular, her current position as a member of the city council earned her a decent honorarium and she lived well enough off the interest from investments made decades and centuries ago.

But when her sire Asaron swaggered into the library that served as her office and dropped a scrap of paper in front of her, even she blinked at the large sum printed in his neat copperplate.

"You need a loan?" That was a lot of money, with a lot of zeros listed at the end. She'd have to do some creative juggling to come up with that much in cash, but she wouldn't hesitate to do it. The trick would be finding out why Asaron needed the money. He had nest eggs on three continents, and considering he kept his permanent residence in her basement rather than bothering with a place of his own, she knew he didn't have too many expenses.

"No, I don't need a loan," Asaron said, huffing in irritation. He tucked a lock of curly red hair that had escaped its tail behind his ear. "We have a job offer. I figured this would get your attention." He presented another packet of papers.

Victory flipped through the fragile rice paper painted with vertical lines of Qin characters. The rest of the pile consisted of regular paper, computer-printed. The right sides of the pages contained more Qin, but she could read the left-hand column of Loquella text with no problem. It was a standard mercenary contract. The exorbitant fee Asaron had shown her first was indeed listed near the top. Typical bodyguard gig for some princess. Likely, the rate of pay had more to do with the girl's political standing than the difficulty of the job.

She examined the rice paper again. Now she recognized one of the first characters as "Moon," the name she had operated under during her and Asaron's stint in Qin almost two hundred years ago. She scanned to the bottom of the page and puzzled out the signature. "Zhuanxu Xian? He's still alive?" She knew weredragons lived for ages, but even so, the man had to be elderly at this point.

"Apparently so. Job's for his grandkid." Asaron stopped looming and dropped into one of the armchairs facing her desk.

Victory leaned back in her chair. "Huh." She found herself twirling her pen in her fingers and used it to twist her dark hair in a bun. She crossed her arms to stop fidgeting.

"That's all?" Asaron said.

"What do you want me to say? It's a lot of money, but I don't do this anymore."

"There's even a personal time allowance in the contract," Asaron said. "One night a week."

"How modern," Victory said. "Your name's on the contract, too. You can take the job without me."

"You are missing the point," Asaron said. "Max warned me this would happen."

"Oh? And what does Max have to say?" Victory didn't hide the sarcasm that slipped into her voice. Maximillian Asher, the head of Limani's Mercenary Guild, was one of Victory's closest friends. But he was Asaron's best friend, and the idea of the two of them discussing her behind her back was both hilarious and terrifying.

"He says you have empty nest syndrome," Asaron said, "since the kids left."

"I already went through that when they moved out for college," Victory said, dismissing the notion with a flick of her fingers. Her adopted daughter Toria recently began her official career as a journeyman mercenary, and she and her partner Kane had left Limani three short weeks ago on their first job.

"But they're not down the street at Jarimis University now," Asaron said. "They're out of reach in New Angouleme. As far as we know. They could be anywhere by now, depending on where the job takes them."

Victory ignored the chill that crept up the back of her neck in favor of pulling the pen out of her hair. She tossed the heavy locks over her shoulders and shifted forward again. "I have work to do." Bills needing payment waited for no woman.

"You should accept the job." Asaron didn't move from his seat. He wasn't going to let this go.

She pointed the pen at him. Time to play a new angle. "We can't both take the job," she said. "One of us has to stay here and be Master of the City."

"Indeed," Asaron said.

Ha! Since he didn't admit defeat, Victory pushed again. "When I left Limani for the peace talks in Roma two years ago, you were miserable and claustrophobic here. I wouldn't do that to you again."

"This is also true." Before Victory could claim triumph, he continued, "But how is that different from how you're acting now?"

He didn't get it, but Victory wasn't going to argue further. She still had work to do. "I'll consider it," she said, even knowing he could read the lie in her voice. She slid the letter and contract to his side of the desk.

Asaron shook his head, but he collected the papers and left the library.

Victory organized receipts for a few minutes, then abandoned them and settled back in her chair. She stared out at the library, but did not see the dark fireplace, the floor-to-ceiling bookshelves, or her daywalker Mikelos' second-best piano. She saw Xian as she had last seen him centuries ago in the Qin court, tall and dashing in silk robes that did nothing to hide the lean strength of his young body. She saw herself and Asaron fighting by the weredragon's side on a mission from the emperor. Saw herself trading kisses with Xian in the palace gardens in the moonlight.

And now Xian wanted her to protect his granddaughter.

But how could Victory leave Limani when her own daughter was far from home? How would Toria and Kane contact her if they needed help?

She was being silly. She knew that. But a small part of her felt like she was also abandoning Toria if she left Limani, even with Asaron remaining to take her place and protect her home.

She returned to the receipts. Asaron could have the job, and the money. Limani was her home. She belonged here.

When the doorbell rang the next evening, Victory paused mid-jab. The punching bag swung from its chain in the corner of the ballroom appropriated into a gym, and she steadied it while stretching her hearing to the front of the house.

The strains of violin music paused, followed by footsteps as Mikelos left his studio and answered the front door. She heard the door swing open, and Mikelos greet the newcomer, then listened long enough to identify the visitor. But it was just Max, probably here to harass Asaron, and so she refocused on the punching bag and tuned out the men's voices.

When Mikelos entered the gym a few minutes later, Victory was more than ready for a break. Vampires didn't sweat or breathe heavily, but a comfortable ache had settled in her muscles. She finished her combination with a fierce roundhouse kick that sent the bag spinning. She steadied it again before facing the lanky frame of her daywalker.

"Max is here," Mikelos said, all but bouncing on the balls of his bare feet. Though he was multiple centuries old, he still appeared in his early twenties, and his excitement added a boyish cast to his features.

The arrival of Max wasn't usually a cause for such celebration. "Okay?" Victory asked, crossing the room to Mikelos.

"He brought a message for me," he said. "You've got to come see this." He grabbed Victory's hand and tugged her close.

His delight was infectious, and Victory rose on her tiptoes to kiss his cheek. "I suppose I can take a break." The tension in her shoulders had eased with the exercise, and she noted a similar looseness in Mikelos' broad back as he all but dragged her through the house.

The fact that Max had a message for Mikelos sparked her curiosity. Mikelos was a musician, not a former mercenary, and so while she had been drowning her stress over Toria and Kane's departure in combat with imaginary opponents, he had spent more time in his music studio, practicing and composing.

Max and Asaron sat at the kitchen table when they entered. In contrast to the silver that laced his hair and a face lined by weather and age, Max was the youngest person in the room by centuries. But despite his decades, the human still maintained a muscular physique and regularly gave both Victory and Asaron a run for their money on the sparring mat.

Victory dropped opposite them and accepted the cold bottle of beer Asaron pushed to her. A black lacquered chest sat centered on the table, decorated in swirls of inlaid mother-of-pearl. Victory recognized the sigil on the lid at once.

"This is cheating," she said, tracing a finger over the stylized dragon that twisted around the characters of the Zhuanxu name. She should be irritated at Xian for manipulating her daywalker, but she had to admire his initiative.

Mikelos nudged her hand out of the way and lifted the top. Within the velvet-lined box nestled a delicate stringed instrument with a rounded body and long, thin neck. It only had two strings, and came complete with bow and roll of sheet music, tied with a black ribbon. Etched onto the body of the instrument was a smaller version of the Zhuanxu seal. "I don't care if it's cheating or flat-out bribery," Mikelos said. "I love it, and I'm keeping it."

"What's the catch?" Victory eyed the three men before her, all of whom displayed a momentary flush of discomfort. She knew how Qin politics worked. There was always a catch.

"The *erhu* is a gift," Mikelos said. "But I've been invited to perform with the Jiang Yi Yue Provincial Orchestra next month. They want to give a concert featuring both Qin and British music in honor of a trade delegation."

Asaron at least had the grace not to play dumb. "Same delegation Xian wants to protect his grandkid from. Guess he figured he'd need a plan B to get us there."

"What was his plan B for you?" Victory asked.

"There wasn't one," Asaron said. "He knows about Limani and how we operate here. He already knew he wasn't getting both of us, and you know he wants you more."

So many levels of subtext there. "That was a long time ago," Victory said.

"Uh-oh," Mikelos said. "Should I be jealous?" He had stopped fondling his new toy and winked at Victory in amusement.

Asaron laughed. "Xian had a thing with one of his bodyguards, and to cover it up the Emperor exiled him to be the governor of one of the colonies. It was quite the public scandal." He picked at the label on his beer bottle. "But you know he wants Moon the famous bodyguard more than he wants you."

It was convoluted, but it made sense. Xian had been a consummate politician in his youth, and the scandal had devastated his career. Victory had offered to follow him to Dongqu, the continent to the south, but he had sent her and Asaron away rather than risk his reputation further. Xian might be elderly by now, but weredragons had long memories. Xian's risk of further scandal showed how valuable he regarded his granddaughter's life.

The fact that he had dragged Mikelos into this made Victory view the contract with a more critical mind. Max sipped his own beer and watched the conversation flow around him, the amusement on his face as evident as on Mikelos'. With her foot, she nudged the ankle of the heretofore silent member of the table. "What do you think, Max?" Victory asked.

"I think getting a ridiculous amount of money to deliver a box to the daywalker of Limani's Master of the City was an excellent surprise," Max said. He handed a smaller envelope across the table to Victory. "I was going to come over anyway. Zerandan dropped this off this morning."

Victory opened the envelope and retrieved a check made out to Torialanthas Connor and Kane Nalamas. "This is the balance for the job the kids took?" The oldest elf in the city had contracted them for the first job of their journeyman mercenary career—escort his niece Syri to New Angouleme and investigate the state of magic in the world. It all seemed nebulous to Victory, but she had always dealt in more certain prospects when she accepted mercenary contracts. For example, guarding princesses.

"Said he had business outside of the city and wasn't sure when he'd be back," Max said. "Wanted to make sure everything was settled before he left. And as for your question—I'll keep Asaron from getting bored. You know Mikelos wants to go play with new music. Take the job."

"It doesn't strike you as odd that they would hire a musician not from Britannia to play for the British delegation?" Victory asked Mikelos.

"Not necessarily," Mikelos said. He had toured Europa for centuries as a premiere musician, mercenary in its own way from the stories he had told her over the years. "And if they know enough about you to know exactly how to bribe me to get you to go there, then they know enough about me to know I can play whatever music they want." He stroked the *erhu*. "I'm in if you are."

Under the table, Victory stroked the top of Mikelos' thigh with the back of her knuckles. The warmth of his skin seeped into her, grounding her, though she felt the tension in his muscles and knew he itched to go experiment with his new instrument. "Let's go protect a princess."

"Now I'm almost sad I'll have to stay here," Asaron said.

The nights grew longer as summer turned to fall, and Victory filled them with activity. Max sent the signed contract back to Jiang Yi Yue, indicating Victory alone would be accepting the contract. He also included a letter from Mikelos, accepting the position as guest musician at the court of Governor Yu. Then it was a matter of packing for the trip and swearing Asaron onto the Limani city council as temporary Master of the City.

"Don't start any wars while I'm gone," Victory said as they left the council building.

"The treaties with the Romans have held for two years," Asaron said. He snapped his fingers at Victory, and she tossed him the keys to her electric town-car. "You have the tougher job. Don't let the Qin and British have another world war and destroy a second continent."

"I'll be there to protect a young lady's virtue," Victory said. "Mikelos will probably have to play more politics than me." She settled in the passenger seat and Asaron drove them out of Limani proper and back to the manor.

"And he's going to love every minute of it," Asaron said. "Did you know he's bringing three tuxedoes?"

Victory had, in fact, already teased her daywalker for that the night before. "He can't perform in formal Qin robes, apparently. I'm not bringing anything too fancy. Xian already knows what he's getting, and I won't blend in anyway."

"I remember you looking very lovely wearing silk court robes," Asaron said.

"I remember being thankful I didn't have to breathe," Victory said. She also remembered towering a head above the other ladies of the court, who had done nothing but judge her for her muscles and flat feet. The only thing they couldn't find fault with was her pale, unblemished skin. No wonder she had always jumped at the chance to accompany Xian on missions for the Emperor. Far, far away from the central court.

They spent the rest of the short drive in the sort of companionable silence centuries of friendship could bring. Asaron followed Victory into the house and to the gym. The next goal for the evening was to figure out what to pack in the way of armor and weaponry. Though it had been over a hundred years, stepping back into the role of mercenary was like slipping on an old sweater.

They pulled a padded weapons trunk out of the closet and set to work, sharing the occasional wince at the high-pitched whines that emanated from Mikelos' studio on the other side of the house. Whenever he wasn't readying for the trip, he was attached to the *erhu*. Unfortunately for sensitive vampiric ears, he hadn't gotten the hang of playing it yet.

"Damn it," Victory said, surveying the contents of the large cabinet she kept locked in the corner. "I thought Kane told her not to bring it."

"What?" Asaron looked up from where he packed the collection of knives Victory could secret away in Qin formal robes, should the occasion demand it.

"My palm pistol," Victory said. "Toria must have brought it with her."

"They're smart kids," Asaron said. "They'll figure out how to get more ammo without drawing too much attention. Where's that really long knife you have? Mikelos might want it."

"Toria took that, too," Victory said. She met Asaron's eyes and they shared a grin.

"If nothing else, we taught her how to be prepared," Asaron said.

Victory laughed. "Or paranoid."

"No, the Romans taught her that."

Which reminded Victory of another aspect of this job she needed to consider. "What about the Qin?" she asked.

"What about them?"

"What am I preparing for, really?" Victory spread her arms toward the wide expanse of her weaponry collection. "Is this going to be a simple bodyguard job? The tension between the British and Qin never resolved after the Last War—they just stopped dealing with each other. Has enough time passed for these talks? The Brits are now two or three generations removed, but some of the weredragons in charge are still old enough to remember the war." Scenes of fierce battles and bloody wartime atrocities on both sides flashed through her memory. Neither empire had ever held the moral high ground, and both had used nuclear weapons to devastate the interior of this continent to create the Wasteland, destroying the very river they each sought to control, along with so much more.

And then there was the British paranoia about vampires on top of it all. Could this mercenary contract be nothing more than a power play? A way for the Qin to rub her presence at court in the faces of the visiting dignitaries? Was that why Mikelos had been invited to play, not as a talented and famous musician, but because he was her daywalker? She had to trust that Xian knew better, but a person could change a lot in two hundred years.

Victory dropped onto the bench next to the gun safe. She rested her forehead on her balled-up fists, elbows planted on her knees. She could handle a simple bodyguard job. She'd forgotten about more of those jobs than she remembered at this point. But what if this wasn't so simple?

Asaron settled next to her and wrapped a comforting arm around her shoulders. "Hey," he said. "It'll be okay. Even if you have to deal with bullshit politics between the dragons and the wolves, just remember that all that matters is you, Mikelos, and the girl. You're there to do a job."

Victory dropped her hands, but stayed hunched over. She took a deep breath and expelled the air in a long sigh. An old coping tactic, despite the uselessness of the action. As the air left her body, she felt a tiny bit lighter.

She sat up and patted Asaron's hand. "Thanks," she said. He nodded and returned to the pack of knives, with the problem resolved as far as he was concerned.

But as the Master of Limani, she'd spent the last century taking the long view. She wasn't sure she could narrow her focus like that anymore. Despite covering for her the few times Victory had traveled, Asaron was still a true mercenary. The job would always come first for him. "Let's finish here and then see whether Mikelos wants to catch a late movie. He needs a break from his new toy." As if on cue, another screech of strings echoed through the house.

"I like this plan," Asaron said. He moved on to checking her wrist and ankle sheaths, and she confronted the gun safe again.

So many important moments in Victory's life had happened at this dock. She stood outside Limani's customs house and surveyed the Agios River, enjoying the warm late-night summer breeze that stirred her thick ponytail. The passenger ferry that traveled between Limani and the Roman colonies to the south swayed in the water at the end of the long dock. It had been kind enough to delay its departure past sundown for her. While Mikelos supervised the loading of their baggage and his precious instruments, Victory enjoyed a few last moments with her home.

She couldn't hear or smell the city itself from here, but the surrounding forest was just as familiar. The brackish water of the wide, gentle river rushed at the bottom of her hearing, supplemented by the quiet voices of Mikelos and the dockworkers.

This was where she had first arrived in Limani decades ago, escaping the monotony of Roman culture for a fresh beginning. It was the site of the opening battle of the short-lived war with the Roman Empire, for her at least. To the rest of the world, the opening gambit had been when Asaron and Kane were kidnapped two days later, but to her, it was when she and Mikelos boarded a cargo ship and rescued Asaron from accidentally visiting the British colonies to the north. At least the Qin Empire had never had much problem with vampires, though the Qin vampires tended more toward religious monastic lives rather than the political power plays that so entranced the Roman flavor of her species.

Asaron banged out of the front door of the customs house as Mikelos jogged back down the dock. "Ready?" she asked.

"Everything's good to go," Mikelos said. "Our personal bags are in our cabin, the instruments are in the captain's office, and the rest is stowed away until we get to Fort Caroline."

"This is it," Asaron said. He clasped hands with Mikelos, then gathered Victory into his arms. She tucked her head against his shoulder and hugged him back. "Be well, girl."

"We will," Victory said. "Take care of the city for me."

"I will," Asaron said. "Remember that dragonfire burns."

Victory laughed as disbelief crossed Mikelos' face. "What, wait?" he said. "That's a myth."

"Did you think they were giant lizards?" Victory said. With one last wave to Asaron, she grabbed Mikelos' hand and tugged him with her to the waiting ferry.

"Like a normal person, I assumed they were like the wolves and panthers," Mikelos said. He gestured her ahead of him up the ramp to board the ferry. "You expect me to believe differently?"

The peals of Victory's laughter echoed across the dark surface of the river. It wasn't often that she knew more than Mikelos about culture, but he had always had a Europan focus. "Time to tell you everything I know about the Zhuanxu Clan and its five emperors...."

She could tell Mikelos didn't buy her more outrageous stories about Qin dragons, though he did make the grudging admission that he had only met one weredragon in the entire time he'd traveled the courts of Europa and that perhaps he didn't have the best sample size. Some aspects of the different werecreatures contained similarities—ability to change shape, heightened senses to almost match a vampire's, strict hierarchal society structures—but the dragons were a different sort. Legends said they were born from magic itself, in contrast to the lycanthropy virus that had created the original werewolves thousands of years ago and evolved to spread to other species of animals.

Victory and Mikelos spent a single night at a posh hotel in Fort Caroline, the southern capitol of the Roman colonies. What had once been a rural trade town, the entryway to the open expanse of the New Continent, was now a thriving city that billed itself as the gateway to proper civilization back home in Europa. With the colonies restricted from further growth by the Wasteland to the west, corporations and families across the ocean controlled the remaining available land.

The moment the sun set, they checked out of their hotel and returned to the shore district. Mikelos wanted to make sure all their belongings had been transferred from the ferry to the Qin ship. Victory wanted to see Mikelos' face when he saw the Qin transport junk, still constructed in the old fashion. Qin's navy had not suffered when elven magic set back the rest of the world's military technology by almost two hundred years after the Last War.

She had already spotted the sails towering over the district warehouses, disappearing into the night sky. Mikelos had been too caught up with getting to the customs house for the official declaration that they were leaving Roman territory. But after they left the offices, the crowd clustered on the sidewalk brought them up short. There appeared to be an old-fashioned standoff occurring on the street before them.

Three men bristled in the middle of the empty road, two versus one. The first wore plain jeans and a shirt proclaiming him a supporter of a British rugby team. His accent pegged him as British as well. A native even, not the drawl more common in the British colonies north of Limani. He must be a member of the British trade delegation also scheduled to board the ship with Victory and Mikelos that night.

He wasn't a werewolf, though. His posture radiated hostility and fierceness, but he carried none of the furry scent Victory associated with most werecreatures. She shouldn't be surprised. Not everyone in the delegation could be nobility.

Mikelos, however, gripped her arm as he gaped at two Qin men opposite, marked by their tilted eyes and black hair tied in clubs at the nape of their necks. One wore summer-weight silk robes in deep scarlet embroidered with abstract swirling patterns in dusky rose, though the other sported more familiar Western-style slacks and button-up.

But the invectives now pouring from the robed man's mouth surprised even her. They were directed at the Brit before him, who stood with fists balled. "—So why don't you run back to your mangy lord and tell him he'd better show more respect for his superiors than you have shown me tonight." He spoke Loquella with ease, with a clipped accent.

The Brit stepped forward once, crowding the space before the two Qin. "Earl Wallace will show your superiors precisely the amount of respect they deserve. If they are anything like you two scaly bastards, it won't be much respect at all."

"He'll roll over and show his belly before the might of Governor Yu," the Qin said.

The Brit laughed. "He'll lick his arse before the might of Governor Yu." He raised one hand and bit a thumbnail, then flicked his thumb at the robed Qin.

He didn't get the insult, but his friend did. The man in pants threw the first punch, snapping the Brit's head to the side. But the Brit recovered at once and tackled his aggressor. They both crashed to the street in a mess of limbs, leaving the robed Qin shouting above them.

It was like watching a train wreck, exactly the sort of political bullshit Victory had been concerned about dealing with. But she had expected pointed jibes over state dinners and cocktail parties, not brawling in the streets. This was embarrassing for everyone. She passed Mikelos her overnight bag and waded into the fray, shaking off the standing Qin who tried to grab her arm when she passed.

At this point, the Brit kneeled over his attacker and alternated punching him in the face with each fist. Victory grabbed the back of his jeans and hauled him to his feet, tightening her hand on his waistband when he tried to rush forward again. The man on the ground groaned and attempted to staunch the flow of blood from his nose. Her nostrils flared as the aroma permeated the ocean-scented air around her, but she had already eaten that evening. She was too old and too disciplined for such a petty distraction.

She threw her other arm up when the robed Qin tried to approach. "*Stop,*" she said. She didn't know whether it was the snap in her voice or her use of a two-hundred-year-old Qin dialect that brought him to a halt.

But Victory did know she wasn't the reason the man threw himself to his knees, body bowed low and scuffing his robes on the dirty street, nor was she the reason for the gasp that rose through the surrounding crowd.

Victory risked a glance over her shoulder. She stifled her own gasp, instead schooling her face into a mask of studied neutrality.

A sinuous creature the height of a small horse padded down the street on claws the size of kitchen knives. Its iridescent scales shimmered every shade of green under the streetlamps, and its long snout sported both long whiskers and teeth. Its tall ears aimed front, and the intelligence in its eyes missed nothing of the scene before it.

Before him, Victory corrected herself. There were no female weredragons.

Tugging the Brit around with her to face the dragon, she bent at the waist in a show of respect. After her sharp jerk at the back of his pants, her captive followed suit. He grunted in surprise, but did not struggle when he saw what stood before them.

She kept herself low, waiting for the dragon to make the first move. The hair at the back of her neck tingled, but she resisted the urge to look up. She was not the aggressor here, and regardless of how the fight had started, she knew it would be in everyone's best interest to keep it from escalating further.

Victory, survivor of the Last War, tried not to quake in her boots at the fear that the opening shots of a new world war had been fired by ignorant fools on the streets of a Roman city.

Present-day Victory was irritated over the whole situation. When flames didn't shoot from the dragon's throat, the muscles in her shoulders loosened. Present-day Victory could handle this situation.

The dragon spoke, breaking the palpable tension in the street. "My thanks to you, mistress, for keeping these pups in line." His voice echoed on the sibilants, lending eerie secondary tones to his words.

Gasps rose in the crowd around them, from Romans more familiar with werepanthers and the occasional werebear. Werecreatures retained full intelligence when they shifted, except on the nights of the full moon, but couldn't speak any human language in animal form. The dragons were the exception. It had been one of the benefits of working with Xian on scouting missions, all those years ago. She straightened, tugging the Brit along with her.

"My pleasure, sir," Victory said.

"Do you mark fault with either party?"

"I was not present for the beginning of the altercation," she said. "I withhold judgement."

"Do any witnesses volunteer judgement?" The dragon surveyed the otherwise silent street, now packed with people spilling out of the shops and restaurants for the unfolding drama.

But they were all good Roman citizens, with no interest in the petty squabbles of foreigners unless it had a direct benefit to themselves. No one moved.

The light bent, and the air shifted, and in the space between one twitch of the crowd and the next, a middle-aged gentleman stood where the dragon had been. A final mutter of whispers echoed through the crowd, mostly about how the man had retained his clothing through his shift, but people started to disperse now that the spectacle of the dragon was gone. Soon, the only bystander was Mikelos, still clutching the two overnight bags.

The man stood almost a head shorter than Victory, and though the age of a were-dragon was impossible to determine, his lean frame bore wiry muscles. Gray highlighted his close-cropped black hair. He wore simple trousers and a loose shirt buttoned to the neck instead of the elaborate robes Victory had expected. Instead of the dark eyes of the other two Qin, however, his were a brilliant green, evoking the scales of his other self.

He bowed once. "You can only be one vampire," he said. "Victory, I presume? Thank you for intervening here." He still spoke Loquella, and though the sibilance was gone, his use of the common tongue retained the slightest hint of Qin accent.

"Yes, sir," she said. "Brawling in the street seemed to be an inauspicious start to the proceedings, even if we aren't in Jiang Yi Yue yet." She had been in Limani for too long, where the only thing inauspicious about the start of a council meeting was when someone forgot to make the coffee.

"Please, call me Tan," he said. His attention shifted to his two compatriots, standing to the side with heads bowed and backs ramrod straight. His irises darkened from emerald to evergreen with his mood.

The shorter man's nose had stopped bleeding, but blood coated his face and stained the front of his shirt. The other man's robes were scuffed and stained. "Sun, Gao," Tan said, his voice stern with rebuke. "You have failed in your mission to escort Mikelos Connor and his consort Lady Moon to the *Xianfeng*. Return to the ship and await further instruction." The two men bowed and scurried away, down the street in the direction of the docks.

The scent of forest and furry musk reached vampire and dragon at the same time, and Victory and Tan both scanned the street. An older gentleman passed Mikelos without a glance as he stalked forward. "What the devil is going on here?" His gray hair was in desperate need of a trim, but otherwise his three-piece suit was impeccable. He made no secret of inhaling the scents of the street and narrowed in on Victory and the man in her grip, then barked out another question. "Blood on your knuckles, Adam?"

This time when Victory's captive pulled away, she let him go. He dropped to one knee before the newcomer, head bowed to avoid eye contact. "Lord Reynolds. I was accosted by two men on the street—"

The lord waved him silent. "And felt the need to scrap like a commoner. Rest assured that I will be speaking to the earl about this. Thank the nice lady for keeping you out of trouble and return to the ship, please."

Adam rose to his feet, then hesitated. "My errand for Earl Wallace—"

"I will take care of it," Reynolds said.

Bowing again, this time to Victory, Adam hurried away, glancing over his shoulder twice before disappearing around a corner. She hoped Sun and Gao made it back to the ship before he did, so they wouldn't have a repeat of this scene two blocks away.

Now Victory stood in the middle of the street with a weredragon and a werewolf. The last time she had been in this position, near the end of the Last War, both of the werecreatures had ended up dead, and it had been a narrow escape with her life.

Mikelos made his way to her side, and she sensed the tension also radiating from him.

Tan extended a hand to Reynolds. The werewolf might view the action as a threat, the swipe of claws. Victory placed her hand on the hilt of her bastard sword, prepared to intervene again if necessary. She had already stopped one fight tonight, and she wouldn't hesitate to do so again, even against much fiercer opponents.

But Reynolds gripped Tan's hand in a firm handshake.

Victory never thought she'd see the day.

"Excellent to see you again, Tan," Reynolds said, stepping back. "I trust your trip north went smoothly?"

"It did," Tan said. "And your's west, Benjamin?"

"Very well," he said. "We're in the midst of transferring to your ship at the moment, and I was sent to track our errant aide. Sorry about the mess with Adam. I hope no harm done?"

"No lasting damage," Tan said. "I shall now escort our guests to the *Xianfeng* myself." He bowed to Victory again.

Victory watched the exchange with disbelief born of centuries of conditioning. Mikelos nudged her side, and she returned the bow with haste. Another thing she hadn't missed about Qin culture. All the bowing and taking eyes off one's surroundings. "Um, yes," she said. "It would be our honor to accompany you."

Reynolds and Tan exchanged further words, with Reynolds assuring Tan that the British delegation would be ready to go well before the *Xianfeng*'s scheduled departure. Then Reynolds padded away, hands in his pockets and with a bit of a whistle. That left Victory and Mikelos in the middle of the deserted street with Tan.

"Shall we?" he said.

Victory hoped Tan's clenched jaw was an aftereffect of his irritation with his subordinates rather than aggression directed at her and Mikelos. "Lead the way, sir," she said. She and Mikelos fell into step behind him.

After half a block, Mikelos leaned closer to her shoulder. "He was still wearing his clothes when he shifted back."

"He was. I told you, you don't know as much about the dragons as you think you do," Victory said. "Also, he can hear you."

Though Tan gave no reaction to her statement other than a small twitch of his hand, a flush crept across Mikelos' cheeks. That was okay. Victory would prefer embarrassment over claws and bloodshed and mayhem any day.

Victory had ridden the enormous treasure ships before, so she waited for Mikelos' reaction when they neared the Qin junk and he saw how far it towered above the docks. All his previous embarrassment seemed forgotten as he stared up and up. While not as big as the British cruise liners that steamed across the Atlantic between New Angouleme and ports in Europa, this ship still carried a crew of hundreds. Red flags meant to honor the mythical sea dragons fluttered in the evening breeze from the ship's multiple masts.

As Tan escorted them on board, Mikelos made all of the appropriate noises of awe at the ceremonial gun ports and delicate carvings that set the diplomatic vessel apart from the rest of the Qin navy. Victory watched Tan. She had yet to determine whether his standoffishness was due to his nature or due to his dislike of them. It didn't make sense for Xian to send them a liaison who objected to their presence, but perhaps her old friend hadn't known or hadn't had a choice in the matter. By the time they arrived at the fancy suite they would be using for the journey south, Tan appeared to have warmed up to Mikelos, at least, as the two of them discussed the upcoming concert.

At this point, after the drama on shore, Victory wanted nothing more than a stiff drink. She had the feeling the instruments were about to be unpacked, and she wasn't in the mood for Mikelos' amateur screeching at the *erhu*. He'd been a genius at so many other musical instruments for as long as she'd known him that this had turned out to be a shock to her system.

She felt a bit like a third wheel as Tan shared his impressions of the current status of the Jiang Yi Yue Provincial Orchestra. Apparently Tan was an amateur musician himself. After verifying all of her luggage had made it over from the ferry, she left Mikelos to show off the two violins he had brought. She knew the *erhu* would come out next, and she hoped Tan could give her daywalker some pointers on how to play it without sounding like a tortured cat, for the sake of all ears on the ship.

Not much had changed about the internal layout of a Qin junk, and Victory found her way to the officer's lounge without difficulty. She knew from past experience that it would also be the unofficial gathering place for all respected guests, which meant herself and Mikelos along with the members of noble standing in the British delegation. She hoped they weren't too put out by the presence of a vampire, but she wasn't going to let delicate lupine sensibilities keep her from enjoying a drink.

Her goal had been a quiet moment away from strangled stringed instruments, with perhaps some time to soak in more of the Qin language to refamiliarize herself. However, she found Benjamin Reynolds already ensconced in a corner with a tumbler of his own when she entered the lounge.

It would be awkward to leave now. Reynolds had likely identified her by smell while she was still halfway down the passageway—her chilled aura was a striking antithesis to the hot blood that pumped through all other creatures. Though Reynolds had been pleasant enough to her earlier in the evening, it might have been the proximity of her teeth in regards to his underling's neck. No one else was present in the lounge other than the Qin crewmember servicing the bar, and it could be a different game now.

Though she was on excellent terms with Limani's resident werewolf pack, and even counted their alpha Tristan as a good friend, the werewolves of Britannia were another matter. After centuries of tension with the Roman Empire and as the nobility and chief lawmakers of the British Empire, the werewolves were the guiding force behind the complete vampire expulsion from all British holdings.

She intended to leave Reynolds to his own quiet corner and snifter of brandy, but he waved her over after she received her delicate glass of port from the crewmember. His body was relaxed, and he kept his gaze shifted to one side of her rather than a direct stare that would have been a sign of aggression. One hand rested on his thigh, and the other circled his glass, with no emerging claws in sight. She hoped she could accept his friendly invitation at face value.

She would have to deal with the wolves in Jiang Yi Yue, if only to keep Xian's granddaughter safe if trouble broke out, so she might as well start now.

A human gentleman would have stood out of respect when she approached. A werewolf would have done the same, as a show of dominance. But again, Reynolds kept his seat. Curious. Victory settled in the cushioned chair across from him. She sipped her port—a smooth tawny—and ignored the small crease that appeared between Reynolds' brows before disappearing just as fast. The liquid might resemble blood, but he could very well smell it was not.

Victory took another sip, waiting for him to break the silence. If this was a game, she had all night.

After another sip of brandy, perhaps to fortify himself, Reynolds spoke. "My connections in Fort Caroline had informed me the Master of Limani would be arriving during our stay in the city. You can imagine my surprise to learn you would be traveling with us to Jiang Yi Yue. I was under the impression these trade negotiations would be between Britannia and Qin. What interest does Limani have in the proceedings?"

Interesting. Irritation leaked through Reynolds' voice, but Victory sensed frustration at what he didn't know rather than at her presence. But no reason existed for the British to know her true purpose on this ship, and they might even view Xian's actions as a slight against them. She had no desire to ruffle fur. "Mikelos Connor, my daywalker, was invited by Governor Yu to play with the Jiang Yi Yue Provincial Orchestra as part of the scheduled entertainment during the negotiations. We travel together, of course."

"Of course," Reynolds said.

They each sipped their drinks, pretending the air between them wasn't strained. Victory hated politics. This was ridiculous and uncomfortable. He'd gotten his answer, so why bother dealing with this when there was a comfortable seat on the other side of the lounge?

She started to rise, but Reynolds lifted a hand as if to stop her. Still no claws erupted from fingertips, so it was not a malicious gesture. She froze. He met her eyes for a split second before sliding his gaze to the side.

"I'm sorry," he said. "Please sit and enjoy your drink. I apologize for letting my paranoia get the best of me. It's not often I'm surprised."

Victory resumed her seat, twisting the stem of her empty glass. "That is something I can commiserate with." When Victory smiled at Reynolds, she hid her fangs as a matter of tact, and Reynolds relaxed enough to turn up the corners of his own lips.

He lifted his glass, and Victory clinked it with her own. "Another?" he asked.

"The same, please," Victory said.

Reynolds gestured for the crewmember in the corner, and within moments, the empty glasses were whisked away and replaced by full ones. He seemed comfortable with this level of service, something Victory hadn't experienced since she moved to Limani. Adam had called Reynolds "Lord" back onshore. But that was default for most members of the nobility, of which all werewolves in Britannia laid claim. If the Earl Wallace he mentioned was the leader of the trade negotiations, what purpose did Reynolds, an aging werewolf, serve?

Time to do some information gathering of her own. "Have you known Tan long?" Victory asked. A common acquaintance was a neutral enough topic.

Reynolds lifted one shoulder in half a shrug. "Tan is always involved in diplomatic relations between our people," he said. "Though I have yet to discern what point he serves." Reynolds glanced at the crewmember occupied with wiping a table across the lounge, then leaned across to her. In a much lower voice, he said, "Keep an eye out for that one. He's not offensive about it, but he never lets anyone forget he's a dragon. And all the dragons seem to think they're a step above the rest."

That wasn't news to Victory. Pretty much every dragon she'd ever met acted that way. But she'd keep Reynolds' impression of Tan in the back of her mind, just in case. "I appreciate your insight. Since we have established that I am not here representing Limani's political interests, might I be curious as to your own?"

Victory asked. "You can imagine I've had a bit of a long view when it comes to relations between the British and Qin, so this is purely out of academic curiosity, of course." If she had her way, the British and the Qin would stay in their own lanes, maintaining their civil distance, and let the Last War remain the last war in fact as well as name.

"Of course," Reynolds said. "I am here in an advisory capacity to Earl Robert Wallace, who will be leading the negotiations."

"I can't say I'm familiar with this earl," she said. Another neutral enough statement.

Reynolds huffed into his glass. His pupils were dilated—this was not his second drink of the night, or perhaps even his third. Victory couldn't remember whether she had smelled alcohol on him earlier. She shifted in her seat, trying to appear open and empathetic without sliding into flirtation.

He took the bait. "That's because Earl Wallace is young. To tell the truth, the prime minister and her cabinet don't think much of these trade talks, especially since they're happening in a colonial holding instead of the Qin capital. At best, we're looking at some export rights of Dongqu colonial lumber, not major tax concessions toward imports from home."

As far as Victory knew, the Romans appreciated being the "anonymous" middlemen between British and Qin trade goods. Did her former people know how close they were to losing that hold on the world's economic structure?

But Reynolds had only paused for another sip of brandy. "Young Rob is the grandson of the current minister of Finance, who thinks this trip will make the lad shape up and take more of an interest in the family business. So I'm here to do all of the heavy lifting while the earl gets distracted by the useless friend he insisted on bringing along." He found his glass empty again and set it on the table, perhaps heavier than he had intended, before continuing. "The boy thinks he's on a grand adventure instead of a political expedition. With my luck, he'll offend a high-ranking official, fall in with the wrong crowd, and start an international incident."

Victory seemed to have transitioned from "threat" to "sympathetic listener" in the space of a few awkward moments, though perhaps it was the drink affecting Reynolds. "That would be unfortunate," she said to fill the sudden silence.

"And I'm sure he didn't even read the security briefings I forwarded him before we left Londinium," Reynolds continued. "Since he had no idea what a *kitsune* was when I mentioned them earlier."

Kitsune? Victory hadn't heard that word in centuries. The werefoxes of the Nippon isles were a reclusive folk who clashed with the ruling weredragons on occasion. She made a note to get an update on the situation when she made the princess' security arrangements in Jiang Yi Yue.

So along with that issue, she had an inexperienced nobleman, a distracting friend who could be anything from a bootlicking crony to a gold-digging mistress, and an old lover either concerned about the safety of his granddaughter or just looking for an excuse to see her. What a mess.

This was why she had gotten out of the mercenary business. Nothing was ever simple.

Reynolds signaled for another drink, but Victory waved away a refill. Instead, she wished Reynolds a pleasant evening and made her escape.

This trip was going to be amazing.

Mikelos dropped onto the seat under the wide porthole, setting the *erhu* case next to him. Tan sat on the suite's couch, stroking the wood of Mikelos' second-best violin where it rested on his lap. He ignored the bow still in the case in favor of plucking at the strings with his other hand, producing an unfamiliar melody.

Mikelos would hear a lot of unfamiliar melodies over the next few weeks. He couldn't wait.

Tan had done his best to fulfill his duties as host, despite his obvious reluctance to do so. He had shown them around the small set of cabins and explained how meals would be served, including inviting them to the formal welcome dinner for the British delegation later that night. But when Victory wandered away, and the conversation turned to music, the man became almost a different person as he relaxed into his seat. He'd made a perfunctory offer of food or drink, but bemused, Mikelos had declined and allowed Tan to turn the conversation to what interested them both much more.

But there would be plenty of time for lessons during the week-long voyage. "I have to ask," Mikelos said. "Is what we saw on shore common? How dangerous are these trade negotiations going to be?" He knew Victory was anxious enough about the upcoming weeks.

He had lived through the Last War, safe on the sidelines in Roman Europa. He'd been glued to the news coming from the New Continent, but no one in his immediate circle was involved with any sort of combat.

31

Tan focused his startling green eyes on Mikelos, fingers stilling the violin strings.

Most sane people quaked under such intense attention, but Mikelos maintained his façade of innocent curiosity. He'd played this game before, at the highest levels of Europan society. Playing violin with his partner Connor had only been half the job. Playing the crowd itself was the rest. If the Qin thought they had hired a simple musician in order for Zhuanxu Xian to secure Victory's presence, that was their mistake. Acting the simple musician was as much a performance as the music itself.

Tan cleared this throat, covering the moments of stalemate. "I apologize for the scene you witnessed outside. I assure you Sun and Gao will be suitably reprimanded."

Mikelos busied himself with pulling the *erhu* from its case. "I'm sure they will be," he said. "But will that be an isolated occurrence? Or are the members of the entire trade delegation in danger in Jiang Yi Yue?" He waved his hand, encompassing his shaggy brown hair and Europan facial structure in one gesture. His aquiline features marked his heritage as Roman, but to the untrained observer, he fit right in with the Brits. "I do happen to look a bit like them."

Tan's face grew stony once more, shadowed in the lamplight of the cabin. Mikelos hoped he hadn't ruined his music lessons before they started.

"I assure you," Tan said again, lifting his chin, "that the safety of all of our visitors is of the utmost importance to Governor Yu and his court."

"Excellent," Mikelos said. He raised the *erhu*. "And this is even more exciting to me. I'm afraid I've not quite figured out the trick of this yet."

"If I may, you must shift your hold on the *erhu* like so—"

As Tan commenced the music lesson, Mikelos made note to discuss their short conversation with Victory later that night. Though Tan had sidestepped expressing any opinions about the British one way or another, as a high-level member of the Qin side of the trade delegations, his perceptions were worth watching to get a sense of the bigger picture.

After her odd encounter with Reynolds in the lounge, Victory headed onto the main deck. She wanted a last look at the safety of solid land before they sailed south through the Sapphire Isles and on toward the southern continent of Dongqu. She asked one of the sailors preparing the giant red sails for departure to direct her to a good viewing spot out of their way. The lights onshore sparkled, and raucous music from a festival up the beach drifted on the breeze.

Tan escorted Mikelos to join her about an hour later, as the sailors cast off from the docks. Mikelos chattered about his first lesson on his ridiculous new instrument, resting his hand on hers atop the deck railing. Victory managed to nod in all the right places. She started to ask why Mikelos was acting like an over-excited teenage girl, but bit her tongue when he tapped the side of her hand with this thumb three times, indicating news or information he would share with her later. She settled and let the low tones of his voice wash over her as the ship drifted away from the docks.

She kept a portion of her attention on Tan, who stood subdued to the side during the launch. She knew the weredragon was "assigned" to Mikelos due to his position as an honored guest, but she hoped he didn't intend to hover the entire time they were out in public. Victory had always tried to remain inconspicuous during bodyguard jobs, blending into the background and hidden in the shadows unless necessary. An escort by a member of the highest echelons of Qin society would not aid in that tactic.

Even now, the sailors who passed treated Tan with great respect, with more of the bowing she hated. Each of them eyed her and Mikelos with curiosity. She could see it now. Within an hour of landing in Jiang Yi Yue, word of the weredragon's guests would spread, destroying all of her chances of anonymity.

She made a point to return each sailor's curious glance with a demure bow of her own, as befitting a young woman of average social standing. Of course, the image was ruined when each sailor's next astonished look was at the bastard sword belted at her waist, but she tried.

As the lights of Fort Caroline receded into darkness, Victory was struck with a sudden sense of missing Asaron, her mercenary partner for centuries. Not because he would be of any great help on this job, but because it was much easier to stay in the background when the pale foreigner with bright red hair who towered over the tallest Qin caught the attention of all. This time she would have to make due with Mikelos' engaging personality.

The wind strengthened the farther from shore they sailed, and Mikelos shivered next to her. She tucked herself under his shoulder and wrapped an arm around his waist, angling herself to block the wind. She had no body heat to loan him, but the sentiment was there. He pressed a kiss to her temple and held her close as they stared out at the stars reflected off the water, bright in the new moon.

The moment was ruined, of course, when Tan coughed behind them. "Those invited to the welcome dinner should be soon gathering in the officers' mess. Did you wish to attend?" he asked.

"Of course!" Mikelos said, releasing Victory. "Do we need to change?"

Tan examined them, taking in their casual traveling clothes. "I do not believe so. Later meals may be more formal, however." He paused, staring at Victory's sword. He opened his mouth as if to speak, but closed it again.

Victory got the message. "I should leave this in the cabin," she said. "I'm sure more appropriate cutlery will be available at dinner." Tan did not acknowledge her quip.

Still, no need for the vampire to rile up any of the wolves by arming herself for a peaceful meal. They would still smell steel on her thanks to the hold-out knife tucked into her boot, but metal surrounded them on the ship, and it shouldn't raise any eyebrows.

After a quick stop by the cabin for Victory to secure her sword in the weapon chest, Tan escorted them to the dining room reserved for the officers of the highest ranks. Voices poured from the mess, a combination of Loquella and Qin, which fell silent when they entered.

An older officer approached them from between the gathered collection of British and Qin. He was an older human, with leathery tanned skin and a touch of gray at the temples, and he moved with the gentle sway of the ship with the grace of someone who had spent most of his life at sea.

Tan spoke into the sudden quiet. "May I present Lord-Captain Feizi, commander of the *Xianfeng*. Captain, your other guests: Mikelos Connor, guest performer with the Jiang Yi Yue Provincial Orchestra, and his consort Victory."

Feizi bowed first to Mikelos, then to Victory. "Welcome aboard. I trust your quarters are adequate?" His Loquella was accented but serviceable.

Victory resisted the urge to answer, instead returning the bow in silence. If she was to play the part she had sold Reynolds earlier in the evening, Mikelos was the star of this show.

Her daywalker picked up his cue well. "Our rooms are lovely, thank you. I apologize if we've delayed dinner."

"No, no," Feizi said, gesturing for them to sit. "You're just in time, else my master of the galley would have been standing at the door tapping his foot."

Mikelos laughed aloud. The focus of all the British was on them, though Victory sensed more curiosity than hostility. Adam, the young man from the shore, flushed and ducked his head when she met his glance through the crowd, despite the aura of friendliness she exuded. She supposed he and Reynolds had already spread the word of her presence.

The captain sat at the head of the smaller table, with Mikelos to one side and a lanky werewolf passing out of adolescence to the other. Victory and Tan completed Mikelos' row, and across from them sat Reynolds and another young human man. These must be Earl Robert Wallace and his companion Reynolds so disapproved of.

Victory studied the companion while Feizi and Tan handled the introductions. Though Earl Wallace was a strapping man in his early twenties, a perfect scion of British nobility with his caramel eyes and sun-touched blond hair, Sir Guy Olivier was a study in opposites. As a human, he exuded none of the primal life that seemed to emanate from most of the werecreatures Victory was familiar with. Instead, his most striking features were dark eyes sparkling with mirth.

At first glance, the only thing the young men seemed to have in common were their hairstyles, with Guy's black locks pulled back in a knot much like the earl's. A quick appraisal of body language showed the men were friends rather than more intimate, which did much to explain Reynold's irritation at Guys' presence. A lover could be manipulated or dismissed with more ease than someone whose motivations were less clear.

Fascination for Victory and Mikelos shone from the men's faces. To be fair, they might be the first vampire and daywalker the two had ever seen. Even Reynolds appeared amused at the barrage of questions following Tan's explanation that Mikelos would be both performing with the orchestra and conducting one of his own short compositions. Victory kept a weather eye on Reynolds, but though his pupils were still blown, he did not appear any more intoxicated than he had been earlier in the officers' lounge. If he was a functioning alcoholic, at least he wasn't her problem.

"So have you ever played in Londinium?" Earl Wallace asked. "And please, I'm just Rob. Let's not stand on formality."

"Only a few times, back in the beginning of my career," Mikelos said. "That was almost three hundred years ago, of course."

"I bet you both have great stories about the islands from back then," Guy said.

"Probably very different stories," Mikelos said, sharing an amused expression with Victory. "We didn't exactly travel in similar circles."

That was an understatement. The early days of his musical life had involved smaller concert halls and catered performances, whereas the same time period had been the prime of Victory's mercenary work with Asaron. It had been over a century later before their paths first crossed, when Victory attended a concert featuring Mikelos and the first vampire he'd bonded with. She had been guarding a noblewoman in Roma at the time.

"Wait, so you weren't always together?" Rob asked.

Reynolds perked at the question, and looked like he wished he could take notes. Tan and Feizi seemed less interested in the topic at hand, but at least Feizi seemed indulgent at the young men's curiosity. With his pinched mouth, Tan looked like he'd rather be anywhere else.

The arrival of the first course saved Mikelos from an immediate explanation, but Victory sensed him tense next to her. He had dropped the bait, even if had been inadvertent, but Victory wouldn't make him follow up with more discussion of his old life. That's what they did for each other.

She squeezed his leg under the table as he juggled the chopsticks between his fingers for the salad. "No, I'm the second vampire to have the privilege of a life with Mikelos," Victory said. Someone had paid attention earlier in the evening, and the steward presented her with another glass of the port she had chosen earlier rather than force her to decline the solid food. She paused for a sip and hoped she wouldn't become bored with the port over the length of the voyage. She'd have to drop the hint to Tan that she would also enjoy sampling the teas she remembered loving years ago.

"Sadly," she continued, "I've only seen him perform with a major orchestra once, so I'm excited for this trip as well. The local music scene in Limani is lovely, but no professional organizations. I probably saw more of the Londinium you are familiar with. I was a member of the royal guard during part of Queen Jane's reign."

That had been a dull three years compared to the more interesting jobs she and Asaron had taken over time, but the rest of her stories were not conducive to a polite dinner conversation with strangers. Also, it would be awkward to learn an assassination she had carried out had been one of Earl Wallace's forefathers.

During the main course, Feizi mentioned offhand that his family hailed from the northern portion of Dongqu and that he had met Romans while accompanying his father on trading expeditions to the city of Jiao as a child. Though he had fallen in love with the sea, he had fond memories of tasting Europan delicacies.

"Do the Romans still maintain a presence in Jiao?" Victory asked.

"That is not something I pay much attention to when in port," Feizi said. "Except as far as it takes to acquire bottles of a particular sparkling wine my sister likes."

Victory traded a sideways glance with Mikelos. If it was the same wine Asaron had recently acquired a case of in lieu of payment on a recent job in Parisii, it was worth its weight in gold.

"There are less than one hundred Romans in Jiao, mostly tradesmen and their families," Tan said. "They are not permitted to leave the province, so you will be the sole Europans in Jiang Yi Yue."

"Is that so," Guy said, shooting a smirk at Rob.

The earl missed it, focused as he was on Tan. "How receptive is the general public to opening negotiations with us? Some still see us as traditional enemies, but at the same time, the limits on the Romans are also so restrictive. I would think they would be more inclined to continue trading with the Romans than deal with us."

Victory sat back in her seat, twisting the glass of port between her fingers. This was a solid level of perception, at odds with Reynolds' assessment of the earl's political acumen earlier in the evening.

Tan nodded, acknowledging Rob's analysis. "I believe our other guests have the answer to that question."

But the spotlight wasn't on Mikelos this time. "The Roman emperor overstepped his bounds when he attempted to invade Limani," Victory said. "But I wasn't aware the incident two years ago had such far-reaching implications."

"It caused a stir around the world," Feizi said. "Our ships were mustered in defense of all Qin's holdings, in case his expansion efforts extended beyond your little city."

Victory wanted to jump to her home's defense, but Feizi's earnestness made her consider it a translation issue, not an attempted insult, with the size of Limani being referred to rather than its significance. "Understandable," she said. "I'd like to think the updated treaties we developed afterward would have made that less of a threat."

"But the treaties were with the British and Limani and focused on the New Continent," Reynolds said. "There are no such policies in place with the Romans to protect Qin. They are commercial agreements that only reference trade routes and goods."

Rob raised his glass of wine. "So both our nations have similar goals. Let us work to establish direct trade routes between Britannia, Qin, and both our colonies instead of going through the warmongering Romans."

Victory ground her teeth in an attempt not to wince at Rob's artlessness. Reynolds didn't bother hiding his irritation, and she felt for the older man. Reynolds would have his work cut out for him if Rob was this glib during the actual negotiations.

It was Mikelos' turn to squeeze Victory's thigh under the table, but with his other hand he raised his glass and clinked it with Rob's. "Here's to successful negotiations on all sides."

The tension around the table flowed away as Victory and Guy joined their glasses to the toast. Reynolds fumbled his glass last, barely reaching it across the table before draining the rest of his wine in one gulp. Feizi raised his as well, but Tan cupped both hands around his teacup as if shielding it from harm.

Victory needed to give Mikelos a primer on the Qin customs emerging from her long-term memory. Clashing drinkware together in such a barbaric fashion was anathema to the society who had invented porcelain and bone china.

Soup followed the main course. Victory sampled one of the smaller pieces of seaweed in Mikelos' dish. The young men did not seem as inclined to be adventurous, but Feizi and Tan did not seem offended. Victory hoped they would be less picky once faced with formal political dinners in Jiang Yi Yue, and she even exchanged exasperated expressions with Reynolds over Guy's baleful pronouncement that the soup was "slimy."

The rest of the evening's conversation was less fraught with political landmines, focusing instead on the various travels of the members of the group. Rob and Guy were intrigued by Victory's descriptions of the steppes of Rus, whereas Feizi appeared much more interested in Reynolds' descriptions of the lands around his family's manor outside of Oxenafor. After what seemed like hours, the dinner concluded. Rob collected the rest of his British contingent, all human, and they retired to their quarters. Tan escorted Victory and Mikelos back to their own suite.

"That went well," Mikelos said as they wound their way through the passages of the ship. "At least as an initial mixer for the British and Qin."

"No fights broke out at the other tables, at least," Victory said.

Tan quirked a corner of his upper lip, the first indication of good humor he'd shown around Victory thus far, as he bid them a good night and departed. Perhaps her memories of Xian and the other weredragons from her past had softened over the ages, but she didn't remember all of them having such big sticks up their asses. With any luck, Tan's arrogance was specific to him and not to changes in the culture, or else this trip would be a lot more uncomfortable.

After closing and latching the door to their suite, Victory joined Mikelos in a boneless heap on the large bed in the second room. They relished the peace and each other's presence for a few moments, then Victory rolled onto her side and propped her head up with one hand. She used the other to poke Mikelos in the side, and he twitched.

"Stop that," he said, batting her away.

She poked him again. "You had something to tell me about before dinner."

"Oh. Yes, that." Mikelos raised himself up and mirrored her position. "Tan doesn't know why you're here."

"No surprise there," Victory said. "Xian might not want to telegraph his concern for his granddaughter's safety, or know Tan well enough to trust him with the knowledge."

"Do you think we can trust him?" Mikelos pushed a lock of hair out of Victory's face and tucked it behind her ear. "He's a dragon." It was a statement of fact, not an accusation.

"He is at that," Victory said. "I trust he will do his best by you, because you are essentially his job. Since he'll still be with you so much in Jiang Yi Yue, we will have to wait until we meet with Xian to figure out anything more."

"Though I have met one weredragon before today, we never interacted beyond introductions," Mikelos said. "He was another celebrity, and everyone wanted our attention. Tan has that same sense of aloofness, but I don't know how much is personality and how much is a function of who he is."

"Or how much is a function of his age," Victory said. "There's always that weird in-between stage. Past when everyone you knew before is gone but before you realize that the more things change, the more things stay the same. So you might as well have a sense of humor about it all."

Mikelos leaned over to kiss her nose. "Let me know when you catch up to me and find that sense of humor," he said.

In a flash, Victory pushed him back on the bed, straddling his hips. "My sense of humor is fine the way it is," she said.

He slipped his hands under the hem of her shirt and dragged calloused finger pads up her sides, leaving behind streaks of warmth. "Then let's make you laugh."

Five short nights later, the *Xianfeng* arrived in Jiang Yi Yue. Victory would have liked to see the arrival in the port herself—the city clustered along two beaches, with neighborhoods stretching up the side of the mountains. The palace nestled on Tang Mountain. The enormous dragon statue, wings spread in welcome, which perched on a cliff in the mountains overlooking the city. She had seen plenty of pictures and paintings over the years and was excited to experience the real thing.

As luck would have it, of course, the ship arrived midafternoon. Rather than keep her daywalker from the same chance, Victory shooed Mikelos on deck with Tan and Reynolds to witness the arrival and see the views. After checking that all of their belongings were packed for the third time, she paced the cabin. Soon, familiar dockside noises filtered through the porthole, but she couldn't even twitch aside the heavy curtains.

She paced the length of the suite's sitting room in four long strides again.

How much of the anxiety rippling through her skin was stress over sunlight, and how much was nervousness about seeing Xian? At this point, she no longer knew. Sunlight was a familiar foe, but it wasn't every day one saw an old lover for the first time in two centuries. With one's new lover by her side.

Xian's political status meant he had never been her daywalker, but they had still been close. Mikelos, bless him, had not even expressed concern at the full revelation of her relationship with Xian, discussed over the course of the voyage. Then again, he'd also lived multiple lifetimes before they met, and knew the difference between history and current events.

Not for the first time, Victory thanked whatever deities had led both of them to settle in Limani and find each other when they did.

The door to the suite opened, and Mikelos spilled into the cabin with Rob and Guy. A few of the other British delegates lurked out in the passageway. Even Adam, who had gotten over his nervousness at her presence with time. "Come on!" Mikelos said. "We're going to the palace."

Victory forced her expression smooth. At this rate, she would be the first vampire in this history of the world to get wrinkles thanks to the amount of incredulous expressions she made at her daywalker on a regular basis.

She had hoped for some distance from the British delegates in Jiang Yi Yue, but then Mikelos had gone and bonded with them during the voyage. After the last few days, she had to admit that she agreed with Reynolds' assessment—Rob had potential, if they could get him away from the playboy influence of Guy. She had learned through Mikelos that Guy's family had achieved status and wealth a handful of generations ago, but as a third son, Guy would have a sufficient trust fund for the rest of his life without the expectation of going into the family business or fulfilling military service. Instead, he had latched onto Rob during their time at university and reaped the rewards ever since of having a friend with such privilege and position.

Guy's friendship with Rob appeared authentic. Even now, the two young men grinned at her behind Mikelos, standing shoulder to shoulder. "It is ridiculous for you to be stuck on ship until nightfall," Rob said. "Since there's no formal welcome ceremony until we get to the palace itself, I asked whether the ceremony could be moved under cover. Didn't seem fair for you and Mikelos to come all this way and miss the pageantry."

Victory's heart ached for the stewards at the governor's palace who must be scrambling to fulfill the foreign dignitary's wishes. And poor Reynolds must even now be calculating how much political capital Rob had wasted on such a frivolous request and wishing for a stiff drink. She met Mikelos' eyes, and he tilted one shoulder up. No way out of this then, or else Mikelos wouldn't have even let them make it as far as their cabin to fetch her. "That is much appreciated, Earl Wallace."

"Let's go!" Rob clapped his hands once, and what followed was one of the most ridiculous experiences of Victory's very, very long life.

They bustled her through the passageways of the ship as a mixture of Qin crewmembers and Rob's clerks kept ahead of her, using thick blankets to block the few windows they came across. They joined together to create a barrier of blankets to shield her while she crossed the open deck and made her way to the broad gangway connecting the tall ship to a tower at the docks.

Victory tried not to think about how a gaggle of Qin and British young men who thought this was all a grand adventure held her life in their hands. Mikelos would be at her side each moment, watching the proceedings like a hawk. It wasn't often, in their stable, civilized life, that he had to fulfill the traditional duties of the daywalker, but she trusted him with each step.

The blankets fell away when dimness enveloped the group once again. They had arrived at the docking tower without incident, though Victory rubbed her bare arms and told herself the light scent of singed hair was all in her imagination. A Qin crewmember latched the door to the gangway behind them, and storm shutters protected the windows on either side.

Tan and Reynolds awaited them in the vestibule at the top of the tower. Tan's expression was impassive, his usual unflappable self, but Reynolds' gray hair tufted out on one side, as if the werewolf had rubbed his hand through it. Victory caught the dark look Reynolds shot at Rob and Guy, where they congratulated everyone on a job well done. She mouthed a "sorry" to him and emoted as much contrition as possible, hunching her shoulders and ducking her head werewolf-style. While Mikelos had spent much time socializing with Rob and Guy the past five days, Tan following along behind, Victory had spent it with Reynolds and found a fellow cynical soul in the man. Some of the tension eased from Reynolds' shoulders.

"This way, please." Tan led them into a cargo elevator, and Victory and Mikelos clustered in with Reynolds, Rob, and Guy.

Doors shut on the enclosed steel cube, and Mikelos found her hand to squeeze it. When the elevator finished its descent, the doors opened to reveal a spacious lobby. She flinched out of habit, but like at the top of the tower, shutters blocked all of the windows. A stretch limousine, similar to those Victory had seen on the streets of Roma two years ago, sat in the center of the large room. The cavernous space was otherwise empty except for the small cluster of uniformed Qin gawking behind one of the ticket counters. No one in Limani owned such an outrageous town-car. The amount of electricity it took to run must be astronomical.

"The governor has sent his personal vehicle," Tan said with calm inflection, as if refusing to acknowledge how ridiculous this entire adventure had become. "The tint on the windows is adequate protection against the sun for you." He gave Victory a short bow.

"Not to be crass," Mikelos said, approaching the ostentatious town-car and running a finger over a rear window, "but how sure are you of that?" Victory followed him and opened the back door, examining the glass from both sides.

Still unruffled, Tan said, "Last month there was an emergency in the mountains that would have caught a priest out during the day. The governor sent this vehicle then as well, and Brother Shi was retrieved without incident."

If Governor Yu sent his own transportation to rescue wayward vampires on a regular basis, that was good enough for Victory. She nodded at Mikelos, who handed her into the town-car. She slid down the bench seat toward the front of the vehicle, and Mikelos and the Brits joined her. Tan sat in the front passenger seat.

They all gave a startled twitch as the engine rumbled to life. In Limani, the colonies, and most of Europa, only larger trucks used precious gasoline and diesel. Personal vehicles had all been electric for going on fifty years now, once the families and corporations controlling the desert oil fields in southeastern Europa choked their exports to a trickle after the Last War.

Rob's nostrils flared. "Ethanol," he said. "I'd almost forgotten."

"I'm sorry?" Victory said.

"This engine is running on sugar cane," Rob said, exchanging smug grins with Guy.

Reynolds straightened with pride. "That's right. Ethanol is one of the exports for which we hope to establish more rights."

Victory tucked this tidbit in the back of her mind to bring to Limani's city council when she got home. But before she could ask about the cost of shipping the ethanol versus continuing research into developing effective electric engines for larger vehicles, the town-car pulled out of the docking tower and into the sun.

A hiss of pain escaped Mikelos, and Victory eased the grip she had on his thigh. She leaned closer to the window and pressed the palm of her hand against the glass. The town-car fell silent, and she knew the three Brits must be staring at her odd reaction, but she ignored them.

Sunlight.

This part of the city was unremarkable, cast in late-afternoon shadow and indistinguishable from any other major port she'd been in except for the Qin lettering on signs and the people traveling the streets. But her attention trailed up the side of the mountain to the shanty neighborhoods perching above the city. Light dappled the buildings painted a myriad of bright colors from whatever materials the occupants could scrounge. Then the trees and plants farther up the cliffs, shimmering in hues of green she'd never seen outside of a television screen. Green the color of emeralds and the shadow of her foster son's earth magic.

Perched upon the mountain sat a carved dragon, overlooking the city with diamond eyes that glinted in the sunlight. It sat proud on its haunches, with one clawed hand raised in welcome and fantastical stone wings outstretched, embracing the city in its shelter. Though it appeared tiny from this distance, she knew it was over a hundred feet tall, even without counting the base.

"That is a hell of a sculpture," Rob said. He and Guy had been sucked into the sights as well, though probably for much different reasons.

"Jiushizhu Statue," Reynolds said, naming the famous landmark. "Cement and soapstone."

"Ben knows everything, as usual," Guy said, but his voice lacked malice as he also pressed his face to the town-car's window.

The vehicle shifted direction, aiming for the palace nestled on the smaller mountain between the city's two main beaches. And Victory was enraptured again by something else she'd never expected to see in person, despite the protective glass.

The ocean, shimmering light blue in the sun. To her, water was always black, perhaps with sparkling reflections of the moon and stars. Not this blinding expanse of turquoise, highlighted gold by the early evening sun.

A thumb touched her cheek, and Victory turned her face into Mikelos' hand as he wiped away the tear she hadn't noticed trailing down her face. He sucked the smear of blood from his finger. Instead of watching the city, he'd been watching her, and the expression on his face almost made her tear up again. This might wreck her badass vampire mercenary image for Rob and Guy, but she didn't much care at the moment.

"I'd forgotten," Mikelos said. His breath tickled her ear as he leaned close.

Unlike most vampires, her first death hadn't been a choice. Asaron had brought her back from the brink after she'd experienced a traumatic brain injury at the hands of the bandits he'd been contracted to hunt. While most of her had healed in the transformation to vampire, she had no memories of her human life.

This was the first time she had seen the sun outside of a movie or television screen in over eight hundred years. Rob would never know how precious a gift he'd given her as a result of his reckless whim.

She caught the barest glimpse of the governor's palace before the limousine entered an underground parking structure in the depths of Tang Mountain. She knew the estate consisted of towers and pavilions that terraced the small mountain like architectural flowers, a multileveled structure topped by a large garden. Xian had shown her the plans when it was first designed in Liangzhu two centuries ago, after the colonization of Dongqu by the Qin. She couldn't wait to see it in person.

A shiver of mixed excitement and apprehension raised the hair on her arms. She would see Xian soon. He would be an old man. She would be exactly as he remembered her.

The town-car parked amidst a number of other palace vehicles in a service garage, where an escort awaited the small group. Three military members of a rank Victory could not interpret, along with a liveried palace official who conversed with Tan in rapid-fire Qin. Rob and Guy examined a nearby flashy sports convertible while Victory waited with Mikelos and Reynolds with more patience.

Tan turned back to them. "If you will follow us, please. The welcoming ceremony has been moved as you requested, Earl Wallace."

"Excellent!" Rob clapped Reynolds on the shoulder. "Lead the way, sir."

They followed Tan, the silent palace official, and one of the guardsmen. The two remaining guardsmen followed behind the group, but nothing aroused Victory's suspicion. This was a standard honor guard out of respect for the rank of the visitors, not a threat. Reynolds' shoulders were tensed, though Rob and Guy were oblivious—the more experienced werewolf didn't like feeling cornered. Victory touched his arm and tilted her head at their escort, once again attempting to convey emotions through her eyes alone. She was going to get the hang of this werewolf thing whether she liked it or not by the end of the trip.

But Reynolds' metaphorical hackles lowered, and the stiffness in his back eased.

They traveled through the back halls of the palace, windowless servants' passages, without incident. Lower-ranked members of the household such as maids and stewards stopped in their tracks at their approach, bowing in place until the group continued around the corner and out of sight.

The working areas of the extensive palace structure were probably not the initial impression Governor Yu had wanted to give the visiting British earl, but to his credit, Rob appeared at ease with the situation. He returned each bow with a respectful nod as the group traversed the halls and gave nothing more than a nose wrinkle when they passed the entrance to the laundry facilities and a scented wave of bleach assaulted their noses.

They climbed a final set of back stairs, and the palace official held open the door to a wider hallway lined with enameled panels decorated with nature scenes in the abstract style that distinguished much of Qin art. The fragrance of fresh flowers chased the remnants of the bleach from Victory's nostrils, but thick drapes shielded the hall from what would otherwise be sunlight pouring in from a garden.

Tan directed them into an enclosed space, not much bigger than the repurposed ballroom Victory used as a workout studio back in Limani. People packed the room, but their group followed Tan down a cleared aisle to the front where a cluster of robed men stood on a dais. The rest of the British contingent gathered together to one side, and Victory smelled mingled fear and excitement from them. Studying the larger mass of Qin in the room, she also sensed intrigue and excitement. Her shoulders almost sagged in relief at the one thing she did not detect—outright anger or animosity. There would still be time for these negotiations to go to hell and for her and Mikelos to be caught in the crossfire in the coming weeks. But not right at this moment.

The enameled panels on every wall depicted dragons instead of forests and ponds. Stylized dragons in each color of the rainbow, and even some metallic hues such as bronze and silver. Victory had been in a room like this before, back on the Qin mainland. This was a chapel dedicated to the ancestors. Specifically, Governor Yu's ancestors—the dragons of his family line, stretching back to one of the first five dragons said to have established the Qin empire thousands of years ago.

Though three of the men on the dais shuffled and murmured to each other, wearing ornate embroidered fabrics, the fourth stood poised, draped in unadorned white silks. When the group stopped in front of the dais, the vampire priest caught Victory's eyes at once.

She braced herself but held the gaze steady. It wasn't often she met another vampire of similar age and power able to meet her eyes without flinching. He twitched his lips in a miniscule smile. Victory remained at attention behind Mikelos, but let her muscles relax a fraction. One major hurdle passed. This man was the top religious figure of the city, the equivalent of the vampire Master of the City for Jiang Yi Yue. If he had not accepted Victory's presence in his territory, she and Mikelos would have packed for home, concert and mercenary contract be damned.

Releasing Victory's gaze, the priest stepped to the edge of the dais. He raised his arms and the gathered crowd descended into silence.

The priest had probably insisted on being made part of the welcoming ceremony when Rob asked for it be moved inside for Victory's convenience. Otherwise Victory would have had to seek him out on her own later in the evening. This change in plans served double-duty, at least.

Talking with Tan and other crewmembers on the ship had refreshed much of Victory's memories of the Qin language. But the priest performed a blessing in a dialect so old she doubted anybody else in the room understood him either.

Instead, Victory studied the two weredragons behind him. The most elaborate robes, saffron with metallic rainbow thread, must belong to Governor Yu. He was an unassuming man of both middling height and attractiveness, but his aura of intelligence was unmistakable. He made no secret of the fact that he studied Victory's group one by one, though he maintained a closed expression.

The other man caught her attention and held it—an elderly gentleman, with black robes hanging loose on thin but unbowed shoulders. He stared out over the massed crowd, but saw nothing from milky eyes clouded with cataracts. Something about the shape of his jaw and nose was familiar to Victory, but too many people packed the small space for her to glean anything specific by smell. He must be another relative of Xian's for her to see the resemblance. Xian himself must lurk in the surrounding crowd, accompanied by her new charge.

The priest fell silent and stepped back, replaced by Governor Yu. In a clear voice that echoed in every corner of the chapel, he performed a short welcome speech to the British contingent. In the corner of her field of view, she could see Rob remain attentive, though his eyes glazed under the deluge of the Qin language. This can't have been the first formal ceremony he'd participated in, but it might be the first where he had no idea what was going on.

To Victory's surprise, Yu finished his short statement and switched to accented Loquella after a brief pause. Rob perked as Yu repeated his statement.

"On behalf of the people of the Qin Empire and the descendants of the five heavenly ancestors, I hereby welcome Earl Robert Wallace and his companions to the city of Jiang Yi Yue," Governor Yu said. "Though past conflicts still remain in the memories of both of our peoples, it is my greatest hope that this moment will lead to a fruitful relationship between our great nations. Rather than fear and death, we should instead focus on creating a mutually beneficial alliance through the trade of technologies and goods that will only enhance the lives of us all." He bowed low.

Rob returned the bow. "Thank you, Governor Yu," he said when both men straightened. If speaking to the governor from a lower physical level made Rob's inner wolf bristle, the young man showed no sign of it. "On behalf of the British nation and the descendants of the four royal packs, we accept your welcome. It is our sincere hope that the future brings friendship and prosperity to both of our peoples."

Mikelos glanced over his shoulder, as if verifying his reaction against Victory's own. The young werewolf's smooth response to the governor's welcome also impressed her.

The rest of the ceremony was short, though Governor Yu did not mention Mikelos once. Victory couldn't find it in herself to be irritated at Rob's insistence on their presence, however, because the ride through the city in daylight would be seared in her memory for a long time to come, worth any awkwardness. When the crowd dispersed, Tan turned to them. "I am to bring both of you to Lord Zhuanxu Xian's apartment at this time, if that is acceptable."

Butterflies beat against the inside of Victory's chest. "It would be perfect, thank you."

Mikelos took her hand, and she clutched it as they followed the crowds out of the chapel. Instead of leading them through the main halls, Tan escorted them once again through the servant passages. Knowing all of this was here could come in handy, and Victory distracted herself from her sudden nerves by asking Tan whether it would be possible for her to acquire a map of the palace marked with safe routes. He indicated that one would be delivered to her quarters in the palace as soon as possible.

All too soon, he brought them into another main hallway in a different section of the palace, where they approached the entrance of what must be a large set of apartments. Victory squeezed Mikelos' hand once more, then let him go and smoothed the front of her clothing. Tan knocked once. The panel door slid open, and a young woman in plain garb invited them to enter.

Tan motioned for Victory to lead the way, so she entered when the young woman moved aside. The blind man from the ceremony waited in the center of the sitting room, hands clasped before him. Victory stopped short, noting as if from a great distance that Mikelos tread on her heels.

This old man didn't look like Xian because he was a relative. He was Xian.

She knew he would be old. But she hadn't expected this.

"*Moon,*" he said in Qin. Though his fingers were bony and age spots decorated the back of his hands, his voice was the strong tenor she remembered from her vibrant prince. "*Is it really you, my dear?*"

Victory accepted his offered hand, and she didn't remember crossing the room. "Yes," she said, shock forcing her to revert to Loquella. "I came."

Xian lifted his other hand and touched her cheek. "I never doubted," he said, as much at ease with her language now as he had been centuries ago. "And it is so nice to know at least one person in this world still looks the same as I remember."

"How long?" Victory asked. She kept staring into his eyes as if that would force recognition, but none came.

"Have I been blind?" Xian said. "Long enough. It's why I retired. I imagine this is a bit of shock."

"Just a bit," Victory said, her voice cracking. That was an understatement. Did Asaron know? She had a vague memory of him in contact with Xian at one point during the Last War. But she had moved to Limani and retired, leaving that part of her life behind forever—or so she thought. A wave of guilt crashed over her out of nowhere. Their parting of ways had been final, but should she have left it at that?

"Do not fret," Xian said. "I'm fine, otherwise. I enjoy my retirement, with Kyo-Young's help." He raised his hand, almost as if to brush it across Victory's check, but aborted the gesture in favor of waving to the side. The young woman who had greeted them ducked her head once. Kyo-Young's features marked her as from one of the other Qin colonies, somewhere in the large Joseon Peninsula.

"I know you are not here alone," Xian continued. "Introduce me to your new companion." He let go of Victory's hand and stretched it out in front of him again.

Words caught in Victory's throat. Mikelos was in no way Xian's replacement, but everything she had imagined about this moment, fraught with potential conflict, fled from her mind.

Mikelos stepped next to her. He shook Xian's hand once. "My name is Mikelos Connor, Lord Xian," he said, his diplomat's voice smooth and polite. "It is an honor to meet you. I can't wait to hear stories about the famous Moon, and I'm sure you have many." Mikelos winked at Victory.

"I'm sure we can find the time," Xian said. "And I know my court is excited for your performance."

"So that wasn't a ploy to get me to accept your job offer?" Victory asked.

"Of course it was," Xian said. He flicked his fingers, and Kyo-Young sped to his side. With her help, he sank onto the lounge behind him. Victory and Mikelos settled on the other chaise, and Kyo-Young resumed her position next to Tan at the side of the room. "Though even if it had not been necessary, Governor Yu's advisors agreed such an event would help to smooth the relations between us and the wolves."

"I imagine it will," Mikelos said. "Pulling me out of retirement is going to have a lot of cachet for both the governor and Jiang Yi Yue. I have no problem with your bribery tactics, though. Tan has tutored me in the basics of playing the *erhu* you sent, and I'm eager to meet the members of your orchestra and learn from the masters."

"I will be sure it is arranged in addition to your other rehearsal sessions with the provincial orchestra," Xian said. "In the meantime, however, I believe Moon and I have other business to address."

Kyo-Young collected a sheaf of papers from a small writing desk in the corner of the room. She spread them across the sitting table between the two lounges and handed Victory a slim ink pen.

It was a copy of the contract Asaron had presented her in Limani, also in both Qin and Loquella. "I had no alterations to the contract I was sent," Victory said. "Other than to perhaps argue with you about the compensation."

"Nonsense," Xian said. "You'll take it as your due. Zhinu's trust accounts are providing most of the money. Consider me merely the facilitator."

"Fair enough," Victory said. She signed the bottom of the contract, noting it was next to Governor Yu's name rather than Xian's. "When will I meet your granddaughter?"

"Tan will show you to her suite when we are done here," Xian said. "A room has been prepared for you and Mikelos, and you can get acquainted before dinner tonight. Before you leave, however—you spent some time with the British delegation on your way from Fort Caroline. Thoughts?"

"Regarding their threat to Zhinu?" Victory asked. "Or more in general?"

"Either, please," Xian said. "Consider this an informal report I can pass on to the governor."

"Any advantage, huh?" Victory grinned at Xian, then remembered he couldn't see her.

But he smiled back. It appeared that two centuries couldn't dim his knowledge of her voice and its emotional cues. "Always."

"Earl Wallace and his friend Guy are young and impetuous," Victory said. "And have expressed their interest in meeting Qin ladies to me multiple times in the past few days. But they were raised in the courts of the British, where the women have teeth and claws just like the men. The palace chambermaids are in more danger of their advances than Lady Zhinu or any other ladies of the court. And even then, it's the danger of getting their hearts broken, not real physical harm."

"I agree," Mikelos said. "They're rakes, but not dangerous ones. And regarding the negotiations themselves, Lord Benjamin Reynolds is the brains behind the operation. Earl Wallace has the title and the power, but Reynolds is the one with the list of objectives and the real knowledge of what the British are able to provide the Qin, and vice versa."

"I see," Xian said. "Though it aligns with what our informants in Britannia were able to pass along before communications cut out, I still worry that the Brits are hiding their true intentions here."

Tan blanched, and Victory caught the pace of his heartbeat increase. "I'm sorry?" she said.

"Though the arrival of the British was the initial reason for hiring you," Xian said, "there have been other developments in Jiang Yi Yue since then. A rival political faction, led by the *kitsune* of Nippon, is angry about the idea of improved relations with the British and have escalated their petty attacks. Most recently, they have done something to cut communications in the city. The foxes are disavowing knowledge of this, of course, but we are worried that the next steps could include moves against the court itself."

That was a fair assessment, and matched what Victory knew about guerrilla tactics. Over the years, she'd been on both sides often enough.

"So there are no long-range communications outside of the city right now?" Mikelos asked. "Have the elves been contacted?"

"The elves of Dongqu are different than those in the old world, and even on the New Continent where Limani resides. They are less interested in being part of civilization, keeping to themselves in the jungles and mountains," Xian said. "Right now, we are looking at close to two weeks before replacement radio parts can be fetched from Jiao in the north. Never fear, we have backup systems in place."

"What are the chances of these terrorist actions increasing?" This was information Victory would need in order to protect Zhinu with the best effectiveness, both in the palace complex and out in the city itself.

"I imagine that will depend on the outcomes of the trade talks," Xian said. "But at the moment, Zhinu is the tentative heir of the governor's seat here in Jiang Yi Yue, at least until Yu has a son of his own."

"I thought major officials had to be weredragons?" Mikelos asked.

"Zhinu has the genes necessary, despite lacking the ability to transform herself," Xian said. "In fact, if Yu had a son and keeled over dead tomorrow, Zhinu would also serve as the boy's regent if the mother was also dead or not a weredragon herself." He paused. "Not that Yu would ever be permitted to wed a human woman."

There was the weredragon superiority Victory knew and hated. She bit her tongue. That was already an old argument between her and Xian, better left in the past. "So the others would prefer to see another family hold the governor's seat?"

"Correct," Xian said. "A distant cousin who serves in Dongqu City, further inland. His politics also mark him as isolationist, which is why he is stationed elsewhere in the colonies rather than here in the jewel of Dongqu."

"I will need everything you have on the werefox political faction, their leaders, and the man in Dongqu City," Victory said. "I'd also like to meet with the commander of palace security. Today, if possible."

"Of course," Xian said. "I will make sure he is at your disposal after the banquet tonight."

"My priority now should be to meet Lady Zhinu," Victory said. "We will see you at dinner?"

"Yes," Xian said. "I do hope you get along with her."

"I'm sure I will," Victory said. She and Mikelos stood, and Mikelos moved to the door to stand with Tan. But before she joined them, Victory paused to kneel before Xian. "It is good to see you, old friend," she said. It was tempting to press a kiss to his cheek, but the way he held himself back made her reconsider.

"And you as well, Moon," Xian said. "I trust you will keep my granddaughter safe while you are here, especially from the wolves." He bit off the end of the word much the same way he had mentioned the werefoxes.

Victory opened her mouth to reaffirm her position that Rob and Guy were harmless, at least in regards to Zhinu, but cut herself off at the sharp look from Kyo-Young in the rear of the room. She would trust the assistant's assessment about which fights to pick. "I will do my best," Victory said instead.

"I trust your best." Xian patted her shoulder. "Else I would not have called on you to come."

"Thank you, Lord Xian," she said, as much as she hated the reversion to formality that had never before been necessary in her interactions with the man. She rose to join Mikelos and Tan. "Let's go see about a princess."

Though the sun had almost fallen behind the mountains above the city, Tan led them through the back passages of the palace again to be on the safe side. Xian lived in the wing that served the court's bachelors, while Zhinu's suite occupied a more interior section of the terraced palace complex. Governor Yu had gifted his cousin with her own suite of rooms when she came of age two years ago, according to Tan, though her mother lived on the other side of a section of gardens popular with the ladies of the court.

Two of Zhinu's handmaids had been evicted from Zhinu's suite to make room for Victory and Mikelos. To be fair, Victory was much more worried about that than Rob and Guy's good looks or isolationist terrorists. Until proven otherwise, Victory had prepared for the worst of spoiled brats.

"Your belongings should already be transferred to your room," Tan said as they emerged once more into a wide hall. "But I left instructions for the couriers to leave your things packed as they are."

"Thanks," Victory said. "Any advice about Lady Zhinu?"

"It is not my place to comment on members of the governor's court," Tan said. He raised his fist to knock on a suite's panel door, but paused. "It is widely known, however, that the Lady Zhinu is a great favorite of the kitchen staff."

Excellent information. In a complex such as this, with many people of different ranks to keep fed, a special person indeed would stand out enough to achieve favored status in the kitchens.

The panel door slid open, and a young woman in cotton robes appeared before them. Her gaze slid over Tan to land on Victory and Mikelos, appraising both of them. She stepped away from the door, calling over her shoulder in Qin. *"They're here!"*

Victory followed Tan into a sitting room much like Xian's, though perhaps with a more feminine touch. Flowers and nature designs on the wall panels rather than the large military scenes that graced Xian's sitting room. Three more young women spilled out of an interior room, two in cotton robes and one in bright blue silks—obviously the princess.

Instead of waiting for the first handmaid to introduce her, Zhinu strode across the sitting room, hand outstretched. "You must be the mercenary my grandfather hired. Do you prefer Moon or Victory?" Her Loquella was flawless, as was her porcelain skin, the waterfall of straight black hair that brushed almost to her waist, the drape of her embroidered robes—in short, Xian's granddaughter exuded royal class. But fierceness shone from the deep blue eyes that marked her weredragon heritage, and Victory knew this was no average princess. She wouldn't have expected any blood of Xian's to be.

"Either is fine, Lady Zhinu," Victory said, bowing over the princess's hand. "*And I remember much Qin if you prefer.*" Tan had told her on the ship that her accent was old-fashioned but serviceable.

"Nonsense," Zhinu said. "I'd love the chance to practice with a native. And the bowing is kind, but I was trying to shake your hand like a modern woman." She pumped Victory's hand twice, then stepped back. "Welcome to my home." After a quick introduction of each of the handmaids—Lin, Yi-Ting, and An—who lurked nearby, she continued, "I'm sorry that your room is small, but Grandfather assured me you would prefer to be here than in a suite of your own."

"Thank you, he is correct." Victory catalogued this main room, switching to working mode in an instant. One main door to this sitting room, opposite a wall with three large windows draped against the setting sun. One fireplace to the right, and three more doors to the left, to Zhinu's room and those of her handmaids.

Zhinu's personal room was probably along the gardens, leaving the two interior rooms to her handmaids and now Victory and Mikelos. Victory would have preferred to switch Zhinu to one of those, but experience told her that would be a losing battle unless Zhinu's life was in immediate danger. That the exterior of the suite was an inner courtyard within the palace would have to do for now, but she would feel better yet after the promised meeting with palace security.

"I've never had a bodyguard before," Zhinu said, tapping her chin with her index finger. "You had an awful lot of luggage. The servants left it in your room, but were told not to unpack for you." One of the handmaids opened the door farthest away from the gardens, as Victory had predicted.

"Some of the cases contain my instruments and Victory's weapons," Mikelos said. "We would prefer to handle those ourselves."

Zhinu froze, and exchanged glances with the three handmaids who had clustered to the side of the room. Sudden nervousness emanated from all of the young women. "Why wouldn't they have delivered your instruments to your room? You are the violinist, yes?"

"Yes, Lady Zhinu." He extended a hand, and she shook it as if on automatic. "Mikelos Connor, at your service. And I will be staying with Victory."

"That is unexpected," Zhinu said. "And very irregular. This section of hallway is for unmarried women."

"We come as a pair, however," Victory said.

"Does my grandfather know about this?"

"He does." And this was not the first hiccup Victory had expected for this job.

"Well, it'll be interesting when my mother finds out." Zhinu examined them both. "You're married?"

"Close enough," Victory said. Now was not the time to go into the intricacies of vampire-daywalker relations.

"Tell everyone that you are if asked," Zhinu said. "I won't have Mr. Connor's presence sullying the reputations of my handmaids. Part of my responsibility toward them is making good marriage matches, which I will not jeopardize."

"I understand," Mikelos said. "And I assure you that I am virtue personified."

A blatant lie, based on the stories Mikelos had told Victory of his touring days in Europa. But that had been a century ago, and this was a different sort of performance. Zhinu wasn't technically a weredragon, and Victory had never picked up their physical cues the way she could with the werewolves, but she did her best to project reassurance. "I promise we would never do anything to threaten your handmaids' reputations," she said. "I am all too familiar with the importance of a good match."

"Well," Zhinu said. "We must change for dinner. You will be escorting us?"

"Yes, lady," Victory said. "I will be accompanying you as much as possible from now on."

The young woman pursed her lips. "What about during the day?"

"Unfortunately, your daylight activities will need to be altered a bit in order to maintain maximum protection for you," Victory said. "But that is a conversation we can save for tonight."

"We will, indeed." Zhinu clapped her hands. "I am always prompt for dinner. We will reconvene in the sitting room in forty minutes. Please be dressed appropriately." She spun on her heel and disappeared into her own room, her handmaids trailing her like a line of colorful ducklings.

Victory and Mikelos managed to make it to their own room and slide the door closed before bursting into near-silent giggles, sagging in each other's arms. "That was beautiful," Victory said. "I love her."

"Not quite what I expected," Mikelos said, hugging Victory once more before turning to the pile of trunks and suitcases sitting inside the room's entrance. The room was indeed small, more suited to two or three young woman of lower rank than for what might as well be visiting dignitaries. But the room contained a low platform bed that would fit them comfortably, along with two wardrobes and two small desks that must have belonged to the displaced handmaids, which would be adequate to their needs. Lamps gave the windowless room a warm glow, and they even had a private bathroom.

"The room or the princess?" Victory opened one suitcase and dug for garments appropriate for a formal dinner. Black slacks over black boots, fitted black tank top, bastard sword belted at waist, and stilettos strapped to both wrists. She concealed the knives by covering the ensemble with a quilted silk jacket, silver embroidered with Qin-style birds of prey. Asaron had acquired it in the Roman colonies a few years ago, and Victory hoped it wasn't too out of fashion. She would have to speak with Xian about hiring a tailor.

"Both," Mikelos said, knotting his tie with deft fingers. He'd declared back in Limani that he had no interest in fitting in with Qin dress norms. If they were hiring a Western-style musician, they were getting the full exotic package. Victory would never complain about the striking figure he presented in his slim-cut slacks and dinner jacket. He'd practiced eating with chopsticks enough on the ship that he shouldn't drop too much food. "The room is more than fine. I know it's what we were expecting. But that kid is a firecracker. How much of it is show and how much is real?"

"I imagine we'll find out," Victory said. With the time they had to spare, they unpacked a few of their bags and made a laundry pile with clothing they'd used on the ship.

They presented themselves in the sitting room at the appropriate time, beating Zhinu and her ladies by a solid two minutes. All four of them now wore robes with even more elaborate embroidery, hair pinned with flowers and beads, cheeks and lips painted with delicate touches of makeup. Zhinu made no secret of examining Victory and Mikelos. Her gaze lingered on Mikelos, obviously on his unfamiliar style of dress rather than on the daywalker himself. Zhinu's inspection of Victory was much more intent.

"Absolutely not," Zhinu said. "Pants are inappropriate for a woman of your rank. Lin is tall enough. You can borrow something of hers tonight." She switched to Qin to direct one of her handmaids. *"Lin, loan the poor woman something better for dinner."* One of the handmaids scurried to the middle room.

"Wait," Victory said, squaring her shoulders. Lin froze. "With all due respect, Lady Zhinu, what I am wearing is appropriate for my position as your protector. As beautiful as your clothing is, it does not give me the necessary freedom of movement to defend you should the need arise."

Zhinu hummed, low in her throat. "You seriously think I risk attack at a banquet surrounded by my cousin's courtiers?"

"That's not the question," Victory said. "The question is whether I am prepared to defend you if you are attacked." The odds were low, but after Xian's warning about terrorists, Victory wasn't taking any chances until she performed her own security evaluation.

"Fair enough," Zhinu said. "But this jacket is atrocious. *Lin, please fetch the red jacket with silver beadwork, the one loose in my shoulders.*"

Victory shot a glare in Mikelos' direction when he looked outright amused at the whirlwind of activity that followed. Lin and one of the other girls, Yi-Ting, stripped Victory of the offending jacket and replaced it with a style of robe she had never seen before. There was a moment of shock when the stilettos were revealed, but the handmaids moved on when Zhinu snapped that they were already running late. In moments, a garment of thin silk adorned Victory. It buttoned across her chest but was slit up both sides to the waist. The shoulders were still a bit tight, but if the worst happened, she'd be able to rip the buttons and slip out of it in an instant.

When they were finally ready for dinner, the group paraded out of Zhinu's suite to join the crowd streaming toward the main banquet hall. Many of them stared at Victory and Mikelos, trading unsubtle remarks about the unfamiliarity of Mikelos' suit and the objectionable view of her own legs under the slit red robe—evidently the style was worn over more robes. She gave no indication that she understood.

Mikelos was perceptive enough to get the gist of it. He rolled his eyes at her and grinned.

One of Victory's initial worries about accepting a bodyguard gig while bonded to a daywalker had been the split in attention. How could she devote herself to her client if her first priority would always be Mikelos?

Her nerves were shot as the number of people around them, both courtiers and servants, grew. But in a gradual shift, all of her attention turned to Zhinu, where it should be. The handmaids led the way, breaking a path through the crowd for their mistress. Victory followed in their wake, acting as rearguard. Mikelos stayed to her left, opposite her sword hand.

Though her focus narrowed to Zhinu and any potential threats, Victory found that her awareness of Mikelos never faded. He was a solid presence at her side and in the back of her mind. Despite Mikelos' limited combat training, her daywalker was one of the smartest men Victory knew. He'd been around long enough to develop his own sense of preservation, since his first vampire hadn't been any sort of warrior either.

If anything, he would be an asset should trouble arise. As long as his temper didn't get the better of him, Mikelos could get Zhinu out of danger while Victory captured an enemy's attention and defended all three of them.

She would think on this strategy and make sure Mikelos knew of any plans she put together based on the results of her security briefing. But for now, the handmaids escorted them through a tall archway into a cavernous hall. The head table stretched across the front of the room on an elevated platform, and Victory spotted Xian sitting at one end with Kyo-Young as his ever-present shadow. Three more long tables stretched perpendicular to the head table, with space at the other end of the room left open for entertainments.

The girls seemed to have an accustomed spot at the end of one of the long tables, closest to the main dais. Two more young women awaited them, and Victory guessed they were the handmaids displaced from the room she and Mikelos now occupied based on the glare she received from one of them.

Her estimation of Zhinu rose another level when the girl sat on the wall side of the table, directing An to what must have been her previous customary seat. Victory positioned herself behind her. Close enough to keep an eye on each person who passed by, but not near enough to loom during the meal.

Tan materialized next to Mikelos as Victory chose her position next to an alcove holding a tall bouquet of flowers. She made another mental note to ask the alcove be cleared for her use. The blooms were beautiful but fragrant, and Victory didn't want the cloying smell to overwhelm one of her senses that could be put to much better use anticipating danger.

"Sir," Tan said, touching Mikelos' elbow. "Your seat tonight is at the high table with Governor Yu." Mikelos quirked an eyebrow at Victory, but she gestured at the dais.

He deserved the position and honor. Her job was here.

Mikelos followed Tan onto the dais to one of the empty seats in the center of the high table. He towered above the other men and women at the table even while seated and appeared almost drab in his brown dinner jacket amidst the bright embroidered silks worn by everyone else.

The moment Mikelos was settled and Tan had vacated the dais, a hush fell over the gathered crowd as the double doors on the other side of the banquet hall opened. Governor Yu entered, leading Rob, Guy, Reynolds, and a handful of other members of the British delegation. Yu led Rob to the main table while the rest found seats at the third long table on the opposite side of the room.

Victory checked on Zhinu, and was unsurprised to see her focus also on the British men. Though she spent a handful of beats staring at the larger crowd who sat themselves below the main table, her attention switched to Rob as he accepted the empty seat on the other side of Governor Yu.

The respectful silence lasted until the governor sat. After the servants moved to the next empty wine glasses and the courtiers resumed their chatter, though at a more subdued volume. Court politics weren't so different across the world, and Victory was well aware that the majority of the conversation flowing around her included speculation about the unfamiliar guests. Not everyone had fit into the chapel for the welcoming ceremony, and she could hear those who had warranted the privilege share their precious information with their less fortunate dinner companions.

Another set of waiters served Governor Yu, Mikelos, and Rob the first course, then the rest of the table and the courtiers below. By now, conversation had resumed more normal tones, and Victory gleaned snatches of information from the babble around her.

She made yet another mental note to ask Reynolds for one of the Qin language books he had mentioned on the voyage south. Her vocabulary was improving, but picking individual words out of this maelstrom when she could hear each conversation in the hall with her enhanced hearing gave her a headache.

Soon the speculation shifted from the known quantity of the British delegation to the unknown man at the head table. The one who hadn't been introduced at the welcome ceremony, yet still sat in a position of honor next to Governor Yu. Victory had spent too much time with the wolves on the ship south—her own metaphorical hackles rose as more and more people focused on her daywalker.

Servers entered with the next course, and excitement rippled through the crowd when one of the British delegation stood in the midst of eating. As Guy surveyed the crowd, he nodded back at some of the more blatant stares.

Victory stared at him, not alone in the action. If he approached the head table and tried to talk to Rob, Reynolds would have a heart attack.

Instead, Guy sauntered around the opposite side of the hall, away from the dais. The waitstaff gave him a wide berth, but he wasn't interested in getting in their way. He wandered the length of the room, making a show of admiring the flower arrangements in each alcove. As he crossed the open space at the other end of the hall, he stared upward at the carved ceiling beams, paying no attention to the whispers left in his wake. When Guy turned to survey the length of the hall, his notice fell on Victory and his whole face brightened.

He wouldn't dare.

Victory wondered if this was how Reynolds felt all the time when Guy meandered in her direction, once again stopping to examine every flower arrangement along the way. Guy knew why she was there, and was smart enough to realize that where Victory lurked, the princess would be close by. Looked like he didn't plan to wait for a formal introduction.

But instead, Guy parked himself along the wall next to Victory. He ignored Zhinu and her ladies, all of whom stared at him and broke into furious whispers. "The salad they served had more of that seaweed stuff in it," Guys said, as if it was appropriate to make casual conversation with Victory in this scenario.

They weren't stuck on a boat in close quarters anymore. Victory didn't have to be polite. "You are a moron," she said, keeping her attention on the rest of the room and hissing out of the side of her mouth.

"I'm wounded," Guy said, placing his hand over his heart and batting his eyelashes at her. The man had no shame, but she was well aware of that now. "I'm not going to eat the salad, so I figured I'd have a walk, say hi to an old friend."

"We're not old friends." She shouldn't even be having this conversation, but if she continued to ignore him, he would never leave. Better to play his little game and send him on his way.

"Well, the closest thing I've got in this city," Guy said. "By the way, we should find time to continue fencing while we're here. That was great fun on the ship."

"It was a way to pass the time," Victory said. She had beaten him in moments every time, but he'd always come back for more. "We have other things to occupy us here in Jiang Yi Yue. I'm sure we'll be too busy."

"Rob will be too busy," Guy said. "You already know I'm not an official part of the trade delegation. Just Rob's plus one, as it were. And you can't play bodyguard every moment of the day."

"I can when it's what I've been hired to do." Victory had to admit that Guy managed to pout very prettily for a grown man. It was all in the cheekbones.

"So, when are you going to introduce me?" Guy smiled at Zhinu when she glanced over her shoulder at him a third time.

"Never," Victory said. "Your social life is not my responsibility."

Guy slumped against the wall next to her and crossed his arms. "Mikelos is much more fun than you."

"Mikelos has a job to do here as well," Victory said. "You knew what you were getting into."

"Fair enough," Guy said. "I'm just not used to being relegated to the kids' table." For once, his voice had lost all tinges of playfulness.

Guy wasn't pouting anymore. He had none of the showiness that had accented all of his other actions until now. Her voice gentler, she repeated, "You knew what you were getting into. Rob is here to work. You're not in university anymore. He has actual responsibilities to live up to." Was she really consoling him? Apparently she was, at least until he sat the hell back down and stopped making a scene.

"I know," Guy said. "But I'm used to being by his side."

That she could commiserate with. Hadn't she just acknowledged her own angst and discomfort over something similar? She and Guy both stared at the head table, where Mikelos and Rob leaned close to Governor Yu in private conversation. But Guy wanted to be where the action and attention was. Victory just preferred to be by her partner. "So you're being a cranky, spoiled child," Victory said. "I still don't have time for this."

The fake pout was back. "You're no fun."

"Not in the slightest." Victory leaned to the side and bumped his shoulder with her own. "Go eat your dinner. Stop panicking Reynolds."

"Old Ben could use a little fun in his life," Guy said.

"Lord Reynolds could use a little more respect from you," Victory said. "Now go."

Guy heaved an over-dramatic sigh, and Zhinu turned around to glare at him. He shot her a wink before meandering around the outside of the room back to his seat with the rest of the British.

"What a ridiculous man," Zhinu said to Victory. "I do hope the earl is a bit more refined."

"A bit," Victory said. "Either way, he's going to be mortified when he discovers you speak Loquella."

"Good," Zhinu said. "Men should be kept on their toes."

Victory hid a snort of laughter behind her fist, then resumed her stoic pose. "In that we are in agreement, Lady Zhinu."

Governor Yu stood, and silence descended over the diners. Zhinu faced forward again, and though Victory kept scanning the room, she also listened to the weredragon.

"I'm sure most of you are aware by now that the gentleman to my left is Earl Robert Wallace, leader of the British trade delegation," Governor Yu said, and polite laughter echoed around the room. *"To my right, however, is another special guest of this court."*

Governor Yu must have warned Mikelos about this introduction, because despite the fact that Mikelos had learned no more than a few scattered phrases of Qin during the voyage, he stood at Yu's hand gesture and bowed first to Yu, then to the rest of the hall.

"It is my pleasure to announce a formal concert to be performed two weeks from now," the governor said, *"featuring guest musician Mikelos Connor, who is renowned throughout Europa and the New Continent."*

Polite applause broke out across the room. That was a bit of an exaggeration, considering Mikelos hadn't played a public venue bigger than the auditorium at Limani's university in almost a hundred years. Victory stifled a smile when Mikelos sought her face at the edge of the room, because if she laughed, she recognized the expression on Mikelos' face that said he risked losing his composure.

"Thank you for the gracious welcome," Mikelos said, his performer's voice seeking every nook and cranny of the hall. "I am excited to play for you and experience the music of your culture in return."

Governor Yu paraphrased Mikelos' short speech in Qin, which concluded with another round of applause. He made a few other general announcements, and the rest of the meal continued without further incident.

Zhinu declared her intention to return to her rooms for tea and fruit for dessert rather than tempt herself with the heavier fare available in the banquet hall. Tan appeared at Victory's shoulder as the young ladies gathered clutches and handkerchiefs.

"A message, Lady Victory," Tan said. "Your pardon, Lady Zhinu."

"Of course, Tan," Zhinu said.

She and the others clustered around Victory and Tan, and Victory was struck by a sense of being mobbed by a flock of vibrant tropical birds.

"Mikelos has asked me to convey that he has been invited by Earl Wallace to join him for after-dinner drinks out in the city tonight, and that he will return to your quarters later this evening," Tan said.

Victory suppressed an irrational surge of anxiety over the thought of Mikelos in an unfamiliar city without her protection. "Who else will be in the group?" she asked.

"I believe it will consist of Sir Olivier, Lord Reynolds, and a few other members of the delegation," Tan said. "I was also invited to accompany them."

"Oh, you must," Zhinu said. "You don't get out enough, Tan."

Dismay crossed Tan's face, and Victory squeezed his arm. "Do what makes you comfortable." Despite all of Rob's inexperience with the real world, he was still a werewolf, as was Reynolds. Knowing Mikelos would be accompanied by two wolves and a weredragon would do much to alleviate Victory's stress. The combined efforts of Tan and Reynolds should keep them out of trouble.

"I believe I know the establishment that they would find most entertaining." Tan bowed to Zhinu, then to Victory. The handmaids parted, and he returned to the head table.

Victory caught Mikelos staring in their direction and twitched her lips. He broke into a wide grin. Not that he needed her permission to do anything, but life was much easier when they were both on the same page.

The trip back to Zhinu's rooms passed without incident, until they rounded the final corner and Victory spotted a servant lurking outside the suite entrance. She halted the ladies with an outstretched arm and approached the man alone.

"*Can I help you?*" Victory stopped out of reach, keeping her body between the man and Zhinu. He wore the simple robes of a servant, but until she learned familiar faces, caution was never wasted.

"*A message from Lord Zhuanxu for the Lady Moon.*" He slipped a note from a pocket and presented it as he bowed.

Victory unfolded it and scanned the contents, helpfully written in Loquella. Xian had arranged for her to meet with the commander of palace security, and this servant was to escort her once Zhinu and her ladies were settled.

"*Thank you,*" Victory said. "*Please wait here.*" She entered the suite and did a sensory sweep for heartbeats or strange scents. When it proved empty, she waved in Zhinu and the handmaids. "I will return soon," she said. "Please remain here until I return."

"It is our custom to stroll once around the courtyard before we make tea." Zhinu gestured to the gardens. At some point during dinner, the room had been straightened and the drapes along the far wall drawn back. Colored lanterns glittered in a garden, and moonlight streamed through the trees.

"Not tonight, lady," Victory said. "Perhaps when I return in a bit."

Zhinu closed her eyes, as if calming herself. "I'm not used to this, you know," she said. "Grandfather and my cousin seem to think I'm in danger, but I've never been afraid here."

"Things will be more settled once I've gotten a better lay of the land," Victory said. "My job is to keep you safe, not disrupt your entire life. I am used to this, and your grandfather would not have hired me if I wasn't good at my job."

"This I have every faith in," Zhinu said. "Return soon."

"I will do my best." Victory bowed once, which Zhinu returned, then exited the suite and gestured for the waiting servant to lead the way. She would come back when she was satisfied with her meeting with the commander of security, and not before.

Three grueling hours later, Victory returned to her home for the foreseeable future. She slipped into the suite and leaned against the wall after sliding the door shut. The meeting had been brutal, but necessary. She'd done some fast talking to convince Captain Huang that she wasn't questioning his practices or demanding significant changes. The good news was that the captain of the palace guard appeared to trust Victory's assessment of the British contingent. He had been relieved to be able to lessen most of the increased security he'd planned, though she was reassured that he did not cancel the additional guard duties based on her word alone.

But the bad news was that Xian's view of the *kitsune* problem was not also the anxieties of an old man. The captain did not have an official count for how many of the foxes were in the city, because the police force of Jiang Yi Yue had encountered their own trouble keeping up with the activities of the separatist cell. They were sure that no more than half a dozen *kitsune* were in the city itself, but had no more information at this time.

Victory hoped they gathered more intel long before it became necessary. She pushed off the wall and headed farther into the suite. A single lamp lit the main room, shining over the lounge area where Zhinu curled around a book. The princess had changed into a plain cotton robe, and her hair hung loose around her shoulders.

"Welcome back." Zhinu placed her book aside. "Successful meeting?"

"Very much so," Victory said. "I hope you weren't waiting up for me, but do you mind if we chat a bit after I change?"

"My ladies retired for the evening, but I can warm some tea for you." Zhinu made as if to stand.

Victory motioned for her to stay seated. "I appreciate it, but that won't be necessary." She ducked into her room and stripped out of the borrowed robe. Once free, she rolled her arms and did some fast stretches. She was a tad wider in the shoulders than Zhinu, and the meeting had been tense.

Mikelos had not yet returned, which surprised her not in the slightest. She assumed that Rob and Guy intended to take full advantage of their first night back on land.

She packed away her weapons and pulled on her own dressing gown before opening the small refrigerator she had found in the corner earlier. Steeling herself, she drained one of the bottles of chilled blood. That would tide her over for now, and Mikelos could investigate heating options sometime tomorrow.

Victory returned to the main room and settled onto the chaise across from Zhinu. "I apologize for not returning in time for your evening walk."

Zhinu twirled a finger, unconcern evident on her face. She marked her place in the book with a slip of paper and set it next to her on the cushion. "Not a problem," she said. "Though opportunities for exercise grow scarcer the older I get, and I'd hate to turn into my mother." She pointed to a photograph on the mantel, which showed a much younger Zhinu cuddled to the bosom of a plump woman. They showed similarities in facial structure, though Zhinu's mother had the dark brown eyes more common to the Qin. Not a weredragon, then.

"Fair enough," Victory said. "I'd be happy to work some training into your schedule."

Zhinu crossed her arms. "That sounds intriguing. But—I have a schedule, now?"

"More or less," Victory said. "Due to obvious limitations, I cannot accompany you full-time. I've scheduled interviews with Captain Huang of palace security to find appropriate daytime guardians for you. With few exceptions, myself or Mikelos will be with you at all other times."

"I did not realize your… partner was also tasked with my protection."

"He's not. But he'll do in a pinch."

"He does not go about armed as you do."

"No," Victory said. "But he fights dirty, and I trust him more than I trust anybody else on this continent."

"Even more than my grandfather?"

That gave Victory pause. "If you had asked me that two hundred years ago, I would have denied it out of hand." Nothing would be served by sugarcoating things. "But that was two hundred years ago, and as much as I could wish otherwise, even I have to admit I don't know Xian anymore."

"Nobody ever calls him that, you know," Zhinu said. "It's always 'Lord Zhuanxu' or 'Governor,' even though he's retired."

"Nobody ever calls me 'Moon' anymore, either," Victory said. "It's nice, but also odd. Brings back memories of a life I'd left behind."

"A life like this?" Zhinu asked. "Guarding spoiled princesses because overprotective family members see shadows everywhere?"

"Trust me," Victory said. "I've seen spoiled. You barely register on the scale. You've got nothing on my daughter when she was five."

Zhinu did a double-take. "You have a daughter?"

"Adopted, and grown now. A little older than you. She just graduated from college and is off on her own adventures. Journeyman mercenary." Victory cut herself off before she could ramble on too much about one of her favorite topics.

"How wonderful," Zhinu said. But her tone wasn't sarcastic. Instead, a look of longing crossed her face before she schooled herself back into polite attentiveness.

"Not all mercenary contracts involve bodyguard work in comfortable palaces," Victory said. "It's not a glamourous life, but Toria wanted to follow in the family tradition."

"But the college part," Zhinu said. She straightened, tucking one leg beneath her. "What did she study? Was it to learn how to be a mercenary?"

Of all the things to draw the noblewoman out of her reserved and proper shell, this was not what Victory would have expected. But building a rapport with her client was important, and she was always happy to brag about her daughter. "She majored in chemistry, of all things," Victory said. "She added classes later in political science and international relations to help prepare for mercenary work, but her first love has always been science."

"So, she had to take laboratory courses, too?" Zhinu's blue eyes sparkled in the lamplight.

"Yep," Victory said. "Only set a few things on fire, as far as I know. Have you considered college?"

Zhinu heaved a dramatic sign and flopped back onto the lounge. "It is my greatest dream."

"I've heard nothing but good things about higher education in mainland Qin," Victory said. "You're the right age."

"But not the right social rank," Zhinu said. "My job is to look pretty and not cause scandal and wait for the right man to be appointed as the next governor and marry him if Cousin Yu does not produce an heir. Formal education is not to be in the stars for me."

This was all unsurprising to Victory. The noble families in both the British and Roman empires still operated much the same way. "You can't even attend university here in Jiang Yi Yue?"

"I would if we had one," Zhinu said. "I asked to sit for the examinations to qualify for a spot in one of the schools on the mainland, but my family would not hear of it."

Victory kept quiet. Earlier that evening, Zhinu had been preoccupied with what Victory wore and how Mikelos' presence could affect the lives of her handmaids. This was a different side to the young woman.

Zhinu leapt to her feet and paced the sitting room, lapping the cluster of chaise lounges twice before coming to a halt in front of the fireplace. She crossed her arms and faced Victory. "Why do you think you're really here?"

"To protect you from the political faction opposing the governor." Victory drew the words out, but even as she said them, Zhinu shook her head.

"We have an army for that," Zhinu said.

"Then to protect you in case the British visitors to the city have ulterior motives."

"Wrong again." Zhinu paced before the fireplace, her bare feet slapping against the polished wooden floor. "Though I will admit to admiring the young earl from a distance. I wouldn't mind certain ulterior motives."

Victory swallowed a laugh at Zhinu's unexpected crassness, and for a moment, she imagined a reptilian tail whipping behind the girl. Though Zhinu would never have the ability to change her shape, she carried the genetic code for weredragons, and its blood coursed through her veins as much as it did for her forefather Xian.

Zhinu drew to a stop again. Her shoulders heaved as she struggled to control her emotions. "You are powerful and talented, I'm sure," she said. "But you are one woman. You are not here to protect me from threats outside the palace, or even from inside. Your real job is to protect me from myself. From my own goals and ambitions. You're here to make sure I continue to play my part. I'm sure Grandfather has told you to keep me away from the library?"

"That has not been discussed," Victory said. And that was one request she would have dismissed from Xian had it come up. If Xian thought he'd bought an expensive babysitter, he didn't remember his Moon well at all. "So besides access to the library, what sort of physical training are you interested in? There is a lot we can do in the courtyard, but we'll have to move some furniture around in here if you want combat training, since I imagine that won't fly in public."

Zhinu's draw dropped open before she closed it with a snap. "You must be joking."

"Mikelos will assure you I have a terrible sense of humor," Victory said. "Trust me, I'm not here to be another one of your servants. That's not how a bodyguard works. It's in my best interest to give you defensive training in case there is an actual threat on your life."

Resuming her seat on the other chaise, Zhinu leaned forward and mirrored Victory's pose. "That is a generous offer."

"You think I want to follow you and your ladies around while you socialize and knit and flirt with boys?" Victory laughed, remembering too many years of that across the noble houses of the Roman Empire. A female vampire mercenary with ties to nobility herself had been a desirable commodity before she'd gotten fed up with the whole thing and followed Asaron to Qin lands. "I'd rather stab myself in the eye."

"I frequently wish to do the same." Zhinu managed to meet Victory's gaze for a full second before her eyes slid away. She gestured back to the picture on the mantel. "My mother will kill me."

"You're an adult," Victory said. "You live on your own, sort of. You have your household and responsibilities to your ladies. That makes you in charge of your own decisions in my book."

"Yes, but what about my responsibilities to my heritage?" Zhinu asked. "My responsibility to make a proper match and breed more baby weredragons to further the Zhuanxu line?"

"That is a separate issue," Victory said. "As far as I'm concerned, you can live your own life and still have kids. I managed it, and I was a hell of a lot older than you are now."

The princess laughed. "You are the first person I've met older than Grandfather," Zhinu said. "I expected you to be like him. Set in your ways and dedicated to keeping tradition."

"I'm a bit of a futurist," Victory said. "I blame my daughter for that."

Zhinu held her hand across the space between them, and Victory took it. "Thank you, Victory," she said. "You're the first person in a long time to treat me like a person instead of a title, or a womb."

Victory squeezed Zhinu's hand. It was warmer than human average, typical for werecreatures, and she noticed that the girl's fingernails weren't painted blue, but made of a natural enamel the same color of her eyes. Dragon scales, like Xian's. "It is my absolute pleasure, Lady Zhinu."

Mikelos shouldn't have had that third beer. He one hundred percent should not have agreed to the second cocktail Rob had claimed was the official drink of Jiang Yi Yue. Sugar and limes and pure rum made for a delightful combination, but Mikelos wasn't sure whether the room shook from his sugar high or whether he vibrated along to the bass beat of the blasting music.

It was a good idea Reynolds had begged off, claiming such late hours weren't healthy after such a long day and that he had preparations to make for the first trade meeting the next morning. Guy had been plastered before they left the first bar, and Rob was doing his level best to drain alcohol as fast as his werewolf genetics metabolized it. With obvious reluctance, once he saw the amount of alcohol the werewolf could consume, Tan had held up his end of the deal and escorted them to appropriate establishments. When Rob claimed this club his home for the rest of the night, the weredragon abandoned them with evident relief. Mikelos had checked the front entrance an hour ago and found a trio of guards waiting to escort them back to the palace whenever they desired.

Needless to say, Rob and Guy did not yet desire.

A circle of ladies surrounded Guy on the dance floor, drawn to his foreign appearance and charismatic air, even if they couldn't understand a word he said. Mikelos had tired of dancing and retreated to the cluster of seats in the corner where Rob held court. With smiles and caresses, the earl sent away the two ladies who had been urging him to dance through body language. At least, Mikelos assumed they were only interested in dancing.

Rob pushed a glass of clear liquid over to Mikelos when he sat. He tossed it back and came up sputtering. "What the hell was that?"

"Not water!" Rob toasted him with his own glass.

Mikelos took a second, more cautious sip. It seemed they had moved on from the lime cocktails to a more traditional Qin drink of rice wine.

"Worn out?" Rob asked.

"Just needed a break," Mikelos said, sagging amongst the cushions. "Haven't done this in a while."

"I was surprised you came out with us," Rob said. "You and Victory don't seem the type."

"Are you kidding?" Mikelos laughed and sat up, gripping the edge of the low table when the room spun. "I met Victory in a nightclub. She was bartending. Hell, she owned the place."

Rob's expression of surprise grew more pronounced with each detail Mikelos revealed. "The lady has unexpected depths. So do you, buddy, being with her."

"Who has depths?" Guy collapsed onto the cushions next to Mikelos. "Not these birds. One of them kept trying to grope me."

"I thought that was what you were here for?" Mikelos nudged his unfinished drink over to Guy, who repeated the same deep swig and sputtering combination. Mikelos and Rob dissolved into gales of laughter.

Guy glared and waited for them to recover before continuing. "I am here to enjoy the company of the refined ladies at the palace, not be molested by common tramps."

"You're a snob," Rob said.

"And you're a slut." Guy pointed over the table at the earl, still clutching his glass. "How many beds did I drag you out of back at uni?"

"Those days are behind me, I swear," Rob said. "I am a reformed man, here to do a job and represent my country."

"I'll drink to that," Mikelos said. He grabbed an empty glass from the table at random and toasted with the two men.

"Those ladies at dinner, though," Rob said. "What lovely creatures."

"Which ones?" Mikelos asked. He'd barely been able to see into the crowd, thanks to the lighting aimed at the high table. It was fortunate that Yu's Loquella was decent, or else he'd have spent the entire meal wishing he'd been positioned next to Victory. Even if it meant missing the amazing food.

"The cluster by your esteemed lady," Rob said. "Have you met the princess she was hired to protect yet?"

"I have," Mikelos said.

"Please tell me it was the beautiful creature in the blue robes," Rob asked. "I'll never forgive myself if I spent the entire meal pining after one of her maids."

Had Zhinu worn blue? Mikelos searched the alcohol-fueled fog of his memory. "That might have been her."

"Fantastic!" Rob threw both arms in the air. "That's her, gents. That's the woman I'm going to marry."

"You're insane, Rob." Guy pulled Rob's arms back to his sides. "Like you've got a shot with Governor Yu's cousin. She's one of the bloody dragons, remember?"

"No, it's perfect," Rob said. "I'm never going to do better than this back home."

"That's because you're ugly." Guy slouched back in the cushions and nursed his drink.

Mikelos tried to stay focused on the werewolf, who by now was much soberer than him and Guy. "What exactly are you saying?"

"What better way to connect our people and come home a success?" Rob exuded smugness. "The only way it could be more perfect is if it was a noblewoman from mainland Qin itself, but this is what we've got, and it'll be a start."

"So are you doing this for political reasons or because you don't think you'll make a more advantageous match back in Britannia?" Mikelos asked.

"I'm not an idiot," Rob said. "I know Reynolds is here to do all the hard work for the negotiations. But this is something only I can do, so why not give it a shot?" His wide grin made Mikelos worried. "You'll have to introduce us. Work out something with Victory."

Now was not to time to tell the other men that Mikelos occupied Lady Zhinu's suite of rooms. Hell, he should change the topic of conversation, but by this point his brain had bypassed pleasantly drunk and meandered over to the land of exhaustion.

No change of topic needed. Mikelos hauled himself out of the cushions and touched the wall for balance once he found his feet. "I'm tapping out, gentlemen," he said. "Coming back with me?"

"Eh, might as well," Rob said. "Get my beauty sleep before the first meeting." He glanced at his wristwatch. "Which is in five hours."

"Better you than me," Guy said. "I will escort you to luncheon when they release you. I intend to sleep until then."

Mikelos helped pull his companions to their feet, and they stumbled out of the club. Tan had assured him earlier that the bill would be delivered to the palace, but not leaving a tip still sent a twinge of guilt through him.

By the time he made it back to Zhinu's suite, only assisted a handful of times by the patient guard when he stumbled, the set of rooms was dark aside from a single lamp in the sitting area. Though the sun was still an hour away from rising, it did not surprise Mikelos to find Victory sprawled across their bed, body still atop the sheets. It had been a long day and night. A single line of light from the cracked bathroom door highlighted a pale stripe down the arm thrown across his side of the bed.

Gods, she was beautiful.

He was really drunk.

If it had been anyone else, Victory would have launched from the bed in a defensive stance, but their connection meant he could stumble around the bathroom and get a drink of water, then strip off his clothes and leave them in pile without waking her.

She curled around his back when he collapsed into bed, but he remained awake for a few moments longer.

He'd have to tell her about Rob's grand plan tomorrow. Later that day.

Gods, she was going to kill him.

Victory emerged from her room around noon, as Zhinu and her ladies arrived back at the suite for lunch. The first palace guard she had approved for daytime duty bowed once to Victory and reported no incidents. She thanked Sergeant Soon-ja, then confirmed her plans to hold more formal interviews in the evening to round out a five-person contingent.

She reported to Zhinu, who supervised while An and Lin prepared a table for their meal. "Any problems this morning?" Victory asked.

"None at all," Zhinu said. "We observed the opening meeting with the British delegation and came straight back here. Miss Soon-ja seemed adequate to the duty."

"I'll make sure she stays in the rotation," Victory said. There weren't many female members of the palace security forces, but Victory intended to pull the best ones for this detail. It would do well for Zhinu to see women were capable of having both a career and a family. Though Soon-ja towered over even Captain Huang, the sergeant had confessed to Victory the night before that a permanent daytime detail for as long as possible would be perfect, allowing her to be home for dinner with her two children and husband, a detective on the Jiang Yi Yue police force.

"My mother will be joining us for lunch," Zhinu said. "I felt it better for her to meet you sooner rather than later."

As if on cue, a tap sounded at the entrance of the suite. At a gesture from Zhinu, Victory cracked the door and checked the hallway.

"Oh, heavens." An older woman, who matched the picture on the mantel, spread her arms in dismay. *"Has it truly come to this? A woman can't even visit her own daughter without suspicion?"*

Victory checked over her shoulder, but Zhinu rolled her eyes and waved her to open the door. This was not out of character, then. She slid open the panel the rest of the way, and Zhinu's mother swept into the room without invitation.

She embraced Zhinu and kissed her on each cheek before inspecting Victory. *"You must be the bodyguard. Not what I was expecting."*

Victory suppressed the urge to look down at herself. While she would dress in clothing appropriate to the culture when escorting Zhinu in public, she had no problem donning jeans and a T-shirt if the plan was to remain in the suite's privacy. *"I'm usually not, ma'am."*

"Allow me to present the Lady Jinghua," Zhinu said. *"Mother, this is Moon, Grandfather's old friend."*

"Yes, I've heard many stories about you," Jinghua said. *"I do hope you will not be a poor influence on my daughter. Or that your presence will chase away potential suitors."*

"I will do my best, Lady Jinghua," Victory said. *"My goal is not to interfere with your daughter's life in any way, only to protect it."* She caught a whiff of meat and spices before another knock came at the suite's entrance. That must be lunch. She answered the door and stood watch while An and Yi-Ting accepted the platters from the kitchen steward's rolling cart and moved them into the suite.

It was of course at that moment when chaos erupted.

Most likely summoned by the delicious smells, Mikelos stumbled out of their room, still pulling on a shirt and treating all of the Qin ladies to his muscular stomach.

Lady Jinghua screamed.

Yi-Ting jumped, dropping a platter of dumplings. The dish shattered, and steamed chicken buns spilled across the floor.

Mikelos jerked back and brought up his fists as Zhinu's mother shrieked in Qin about the presence of a man in her daughter's suite. He blinked bloodshot eyes a few times, took the better part of valor, and fled back into their room. The door slid closed with a snap.

As the handmaids collected dumplings and the kitchen servant retrieved broken shards of ceramic, Zhinu attempted to placate her mother. By now, Jinghua spoke so fast that Victory had lost the thread of the Qin. She paused for a steadying beat, then approached Jinghua and bowed low. *"My apologies, Lady Jinghua. I did not mean for my husband to startle you."* The noblewoman would appreciate the distinction of marriage over Mikelos' daywalker status.

Jinghua drew herself up in order to face down Victory's greater height as best she was able. *"Your husband?"*

"Yes, lady."

"Remember? Mikelos Connor is the musician Cousin Yu announced at dinner last night," Zhinu said. *"It is only appropriate that they lodge here at the palace together, and Victory's duty is to remain with me."*

Despite Zhinu's greater ambitions, Victory had to admit that the girl knew her politics. Or at least knew how to play her mother as well as Mikelos played the violin. With every word, Jinghua's outrage drained away.

An shooed the kitchen servant out of the suite and returned to the cluster of other ladies in the corner. Mikelos poked his head out of their room. "Victory?"

"Come on out," she said.

When he emerged a second time, she noted that where he had before been dressed in pajama pants and a T-shirt, he had made the wise decision to change into more formal slacks and knit top. Mikelos moved to her side and bowed to Zhinu's mother. *"Honored lady,"* he said in his accented Qin.

Jinghua sniffed. *"I should have you ejected from the palace for your impertinence."*

Mikelos glanced at Zhinu for a translation. With an exasperated sigh, the princess said, "She's mad you're here, but she can't kick you out since you're an invited guest of the governor."

Victory saw the wheels turn for a moment in Mikelos' brain. She was unsurprised when the next words out of his mouth dripped with charm. He had to know the lady did not speak a word of Loquella, so he made do with posture and tone of voice. Her daywalker didn't the play the part often, but here was the man who had charmed his way across Europa for two centuries.

"Please assure your mother that my only intentions are to provide the court with entertainment and that my desire to remain by my partner's side is a failing of my own and not meant to impinge on the honor of her daughter or her daughter's handmaids." Mikelos bowed again, staying low.

Zhinu turned to her mother and said, *"Mama, he's married. Calm down."*

"Very well." Jinghua dismissed Mikelos with the toss of one hand and assumed a place at the low table the handmaids had prepared in the center of the suite. *"I assume he will not be joining us for lunch."*

Even as Mikelos cast a longing look at the array of food, Victory heard his stomach rumble with her sensitive ears. Part of her wanted to insist he join them, and she could see the speculative expression on Zhinu's face that might indicate the same, but best not to borrow trouble. "She wants you to go," Victory said, maintaining her pleasant, neutral expression.

"Ugh," Mikelos said. "You have no idea how hungover I am."

"Oh, I can guess," Victory said.

"Get someone to point you in the direction of the main hall," Zhinu said. "Usually there's a spread out for those who want to grab something on the run. Can you keep yourself occupied for a few hours?"

"I'll hunt down Tan and see if I can find a place to practice for a bit," Mikelos said. He fetched one of his violin cases from their room and pecked Victory on the cheek on the way out the door. They all pretended to ignore Jinghua's loud sniff of disapproval. "Have fun, ladies."

"It will be thrilling," Zhinu said. Once Mikelos had left the suite, she motioned Victory toward the food. "Shall we?"

"I don't have to join you," Victory said.

Zhinu led Victory over to the table with a firm grip on her arm. "I insist."

So that's how it was. Victory settled between Yi-Ting and Lin and allowed herself to be served token samples of each dish while An poured her a generous amount of tea. It wouldn't hurt to allow herself to be used for Zhinu's ulterior motives as long as she still performed her primary function as bodyguard.

For the first ten or so minutes, the conversation was as inane as Victory could stand. Jinghua commented on Zhinu's hair, Yi-Ting's choice of eyeshadow color, the number of dumplings An consumed, and even Victory's rude refusal to eat. None of the comments were favorable, though the woman always stayed on the edge between criticism and insult.

"My pardon," Victory said, before Zhinu had to come up with a polite response. *"I do not require solid food. But the tea is a delicious treat."*

"I see," Jinghua said, drawing out her words. *"Dare I ask what you are eating while you are here?"*

Zhinu gasped. *"Mama!"*

"My contract specifies that the appropriate food will be provided to me during my stay here in Jiang Yi Yue," Victory said, keeping her phrasing as delicate as possible. She knew from past experience in Qin lands that some people tithed blood to the vampires who followed religious paths, and Xian must have made a deal to funnel some of it her way.

"It's good to know the kitchen maids will be safe." Jinghua sipped her tea.

"Oh gods, Mother." Zhinu covered her face with her hands.

Victory did not rise to the accusation, though she bristled inside. *"I assure you I do not acquire my meals from unwilling subjects."* She placed her hands flat on the table. Next to her, Yi-Ting relaxed at her declaration with a visible heave of her shoulders.

Zhinu looked at the ceiling, as if summoning patience. *"Mama, what did you think of the opening negotiations this morning? Where were you sitting?"*

"I was not sitting anywhere," Jinghua said, *"because I did not attend. I have better things to do with my time than listen to prattling bureaucrats."* She eyed her daughter over the rim of her soup bowl. *"I take that to mean you attended, rather than practice your embroidery with Lady Nozomi?"*

"Yes, Mama," Zhinu said. She selected another dumpling from the main platter.

Not offering an immediate excuse was a solid opening gambit to the ensuing argument, and the way Zhinu handled her mother once again impressed Victory.

"You will never finish your gown at this rate," Jinghua said. *"It will go out of style before you get a chance to wear it."*

Zhinu did not rise to the bait. *"The British ambassador spoke very well."*

Reynolds? Why would Zhinu care about—oh. Victory wanted to ask the gods for patience as well.

"Earl Wallace is a handsome young man," Zhinu continued. *"He must be respected among his people to be their chosen representative to Jiang Yi Yue."*

Victory bit her tongue and busied herself with pouring another round of tea. This would have been so much easier standing along a wall acting as part of the décor. At least staying out of the conversation seemed like a valid option, based on the silence of the handmaids.

"He must be very intelligent." Zhinu gave up all pretense and faced her mother straight on. *"He probably attended the best universities the British Empire has to offer. Though I imagine they pale in comparison to the schools in Liangzhu."*

"We are not having this conversation again, Zhinu," Jinghua said. Now both women stared at each other across the table. They might as well have been the only people in the room. *"Furthering your education will not help you in your goals. You have responsibilities to your family. This Earl Wallace is not helping his family by putting this silly diplomatic exercise across the ocean above what his duties to them must be."*

Zhinu exhaled through her teeth, and blue eyes flashed. *"But Mama—"*

Jinghua rose from the table and stared down at her daughter. *"No,"* she said. *"I forbade you from speaking on this, and you have intentionally disobeyed me. Good day, ladies."* She left the suite without an additional word.

Groaning, Zhinu leaned forward until her face rested on the table. An placed a gentle hand on her back. "I deserved that," Zhinu said, her words muffled. "I'm sorry you had to see it, Moon."

"Not a problem," Victory said. "Your mother is a force to be reckoned with."

"That's an understatement." Zhinu stood and stretched. *"Looks like we were done here anyway. An and Lin, can you please clean up? Yi-Ting, can you please search for Mikelos and let him know he can return from exile? I think I will rest in my room for a bit."*

Victory bowed with the other handmaids, who then scurried to do their lady's bidding. For lack of anything better to do, she selected one of the basic Qin language texts Xian had had delivered to the suite at some point that morning. The language, with its updated modern dialect, was coming back to her at a decent clip, but a grasp of the written text had never been in her skill set to begin with.

Her hand darted for the dagger at her ankle when the door to the suite slid open, but she relaxed when Mikelos popped in. "Just us," he said, followed by Yi-Ting.

Victory checked the clock and saw most of an hour had passed. "Were you hiding?"

"No, had to finish an impromptu concert before I would let Lady Yi-Ting drag me back here." Mikelos bowed to the handmaid, who blushed and disappeared into her own room. He placed his violin case on a side table, then dropped onto the chaise next to Victory, squeezing her to the side so they both fit.

She draped one leg over his and hoped none of the handmaids came out. They would be scandalized. "Have fun?"

"Fun enough," Mikelos said. "I'm still a novelty. Tan showed me a place I can practice in private so that the shine doesn't wear off before the big concert. Rehearsals with the provincial orchestra begin tomorrow morning. Needless to say, I will not be drinking tonight."

"I'm surprised you were able to play today," Victory said. "Your eyes are still red."

"I've performed with worse hangovers than this," Mikelos said. "About last night, though. We have a problem."

Victory tensed. "What happened?"

"Rob has apparently developed a grand plan that has nothing to do with the formal negotiations," Mikelos said. "He's going to sweep Zhinu off her feet and marry her, returning triumphant to Britannia."

A female gasp sounded behind them, and Victory and Mikelos untangled themselves. But when they rose to their feet, Victory didn't see a blushing handmaid, but an intrigued princess.

"What, exactly, did the earl say?" Zhinu asked. She stared down Mikelos with all the intent ferocity of her grandfather in dragon form.

Victory did not like the gleam in her eye.

The next two weeks sped by in a blur. Victory and Mikelos were ships passing in the night, as he rose early to attend rehearsals with the orchestra and she escorted Zhinu to all her evening and indoor afternoon activities.

To tell the truth, Victory could have used Mikelos as backup more often than not to keep Zhinu and Rob at a distance from each other. How was it possible for two people who had never had a private conversation to conspire with each other this well?

The logic was so simple. Rob wanted to marry Zhinu as his contribution to the growing alliance between the British and Qin empires. Zhinu wanted to marry Rob and run away to Britannia where she would be free to further her own education and a life free of the stifling binds of tradition and expectation into which she had been born.

The private conversation with Zhinu, late in the evening after her maids had retired, about the ridiculousness of it all had not gone well:

"Lady, you don't even know this man," Victory said. She leaned over the backrest of a chaise and tried not to squeeze so hard that she burst the furniture's stuffing. "The earl doesn't view you as a person. He sees you as an object of power, a way to solidify his political position back home while doing the least work possible."

Zhinu lounged across from her, the picture of disaffected relaxation. "How is that any different from the men here? Who look into my eyes and see only the dragons I will breed?" She picked up the book Mikelos had smuggled out of the library for her earlier that afternoon, when they had discovered Xian's declaration that she had read enough books on world history for one lifetime. "Now if you'll excuse me, I have to make it through the history of Grecian colonization by dawn. I expect I will have questions for you about Limani's economic history tomorrow evening."

A joint confrontation with Mikelos versus Rob and Guy in the earl's private rooms had been equally useless:

"You can't keep trying to maneuver a meeting with her," Victory said. "Her grandfather is already suspicious of your intentions here, and if I have to hear from Zhinu's mother about the appropriateness of your speaking with her daughter one more time, I might scream." She paced the length of Rob's sitting room once more before collapsing onto a couch next to Mikelos, accepting the drink Guy handed to her. She had only been awake for six hours, but those six hours had been filled with a full tea ceremony and mind-numbing embroidery lesson.

Mikelos toyed with the end of her long braid, and she leaned into him. Oddly, Rob and Guy were the only people on the continent they could be around and still act themselves. When had that happened?

Rob nursed his own drink and stared across the gardens outside his suite. Bursts of color from the lanterns outside played across his face. "I am useless here," he said. "Do you understand that, Victory? Ben is doing all the real work. I sit there and look decorative and say pretty things to distract the governor and his advisors from the fact that Ben is still asking for more than they are comfortable giving." He rubbed the back of his neck. "Marrying this girl is the only thing of real value I can do."

"You sell yourself short," Guy said. He busied himself fixing another drink. "Refill, Rob?"

"No, thank you. I have an early session with Ben tomorrow. I'll bid you three a good night." He shut himself away in his room without another word.

Guy sat on the sofa across from them, holding up one hand in defense. "Don't look at me. I'm just the best friend and confidant."

"Exactly," Mikelos said.

The next day, at an after-dinner reception celebrating the birthday of one of Governor Yu's advisors, Victory turned her back for *one single second* to answer a question from An regarding the next morning's security detail. Suddenly, Zhinu was nestled in a decorative alcove. Speaking with Earl Robert Wallace. They stood less than a foot apart, and the flirtation in their postures sent warning bells clanging through Victory's mind.

Lady Jinghua, as if sensing a great disruption in How Things Should Be, saw this at the exact same moment.

Ignoring the gasps as Victory crossed the room at vampiric speeds, she beat Zhinu's mother to the alcove. In the distance, she noted how Mikelos cut Lady Jinghua off. She would owe him for this one, since there was still no love lost between the two.

"Pardon me," Victory said. She bared her teeth in a false semblance of a smile, flashing enough fang for Zhinu and Rob to shrink back from her—and away from each other. "Lady Jinghua requests the presence of her daughter."

Zhinu's attention shot across the room over Victory's shoulder, and her entire face drained of blood. She cursed in Qin, and though Rob might not know the language, he more than recognized the inflection of her voice.

"We will speak again—"

Victory interrupted Rob. "You will *not*," she said, all but snarling.

"My pardon," Zhinu said, as if neither of them had spoken. After a short bow to Rob, the right depth for a noblewoman to give a passing acquaintance, she brushed past Victory.

Rob grabbed Victory's arm before she could turn away. "What the hell, Victory?"

"Let's get one thing straight," she said, keeping her voice low to avoid attracting any more attention than they already had. "I am not your friend. I am a hired mercenary, and she is my client. Her family doesn't like you, so I'm supposed to keep you apart. You do yourself no favor by making my job harder." She pulled her arm from his grip and stalked across the reception hall to resume her position behind Zhinu.

The atmosphere in Zhinu's suite was chilly that night, even for a vampire who didn't notice things like exterior temperature. Zhinu sent her handmaids to their room with a single word, and Mikelos disappeared without even needing that, leaving her alone with Victory in the main room.

"What was that about tonight?" She whirled on Victory, fists balled at her sides.

"My job," Victory said. She stood her ground and resisted the urge to cross her arms in a defensive posture. She'd done nothing wrong.

"Your job is to protect me from physical threat," Zhinu said. "I read the contract when I had breakfast with Grandfather the other day. Your only job is to protect me from the terrorists in the city, not that I've been allowed to leave the palace complex since you got here. Not to protect me from visiting diplomats!"

"Your family has made it clear to me that they disapprove of any interaction between you and Earl Wallace." Victory kept her focus somewhere over Zhinu's left shoulder, as if she reported to a military superior. This entire situation was as frustrating to her as it was to Zhinu.

"I'm not a child anymore," Zhinu said. "What happened to me being my own woman? What happened to physical training? You sang a different tune when we first met."

"I know," Victory said. Zhinu drew up short, as if she had expected Victory to disagree with her. "I know," she said again, gentling her tone. "Trust me, I still believe you should make your own future. But running away with a visiting nobleman from an empire your people once started a world war with is probably not the best future for anybody."

Zhinu threw up her hands. "I'm done," she said. "I can't deal with this tonight. If I can't even have one conversation with the earl without everyone losing their minds, I'll have to figure out something else." She stalked into her room and slammed the door before Victory could even begin to ask what she meant.

Victory shut off the lights in the sitting room before returning to her own room. Mikelos sat on the edge of the bed, resting his elbows on his knees. He'd gotten as far as removing his shoes. "I'm guessing you heard all that?"

"I can't say I disagree with her," Mikelos said. "Honestly, I'm surprised at you."

Victory sat next to him and fell back. She stared at the paneled ceiling, heedless of the wrinkles no doubt forming in her brand-new silk overcoat. "I didn't expect it to be this hard."

Mikelos caught her hand and rubbed his thumb over the back of her knuckles. "What?"

"Doing this again," Victory said. "Being a mercenary. Putting the job first. I was my own woman for too long."

"It has been odd," Mikelos said. He leaned over her and pressed a kiss to her forehead. "Having a different schedule. Being up more during the day instead of spending nights with you. Not being first in your life anymore." But he said that last bit in a teasing tone and pressed a kiss to her lips.

"Everything is different now," Victory said. "I used to live for the job. Everything was by the contract. Even consideration for Asaron or my progeny was second tier after that. But now… now I have a family instead." She laughed, and the sound was harsh in their small, dark room. "Now I have a whole damn city. And the life and drama of one woman is petty is comparison."

"So what are you going to do?" Mikelos asked.

"Abide by the contract," Victory said. "Make it through this. So we can go home."

"The concert is tomorrow night," Mikelos said. "How much would it cost you to break the contract so we can bail?"

Break a contract? Perish the thought. However tempting the idea was at this particular moment. "Not much, in the grand scheme of things," Victory said.

"But I'm still a full member of the Mercenary Guild. That sort of thing goes on your record, and it affects how much you can charge later."

"But you're not a mercenary anymore," Mikelos said. He got up to change for bed, not meeting her eyes.

"Aren't I?" Victory propped herself on her elbows and watched him. "What the hell am I doing here, then?"

"Reliving your youth? Distracting yourself from worrying about Toria and Kane?" Mikelos threw up his hands, shirt hanging unbuttoned. "Pick one!"

They stared at each other for a beat, before Mikelos turned away to hang his sweater.

"Do you think my life with you has been some sort of vacation?" Victory asked, her voice low. "That being the Master of Limani was something to keep me occupied before I took off again?"

"I don't know," Mikelos said, hurt clipping his words. He carried his pajama pants into the bathroom with him.

Fingers of fear clawed at Victory's chest. They hadn't been body-conscious in front of each other in decades.

She rose from the bed and hovered in the entrance to the bathroom. She stared at Mikelos' reflection in the mirror. She knew he saw a shadowy mirage of her in return, but he looked to where her eyes would be while he brushed his teeth. "I'm sorry," she said. "But do you really think we should be supporting the uninformed notions of a couple crazy kids?"

Mikelos spit toothpaste and rinsed out his mouth before replying. "I haven't read the all-powerful contract," he said, "but I didn't think it was your job to be Zhinu's mother. You are nowhere near bitchy enough, for one."

A bubble of humor rose through Victory at that, and for a moment, the tension faded. Mikelos turned and wrapped her in his arms. She tucked her face into the curve of his neck. "We can go, if you want," Victory said, her voice muffled against his skin. "Tomorrow night, after the concert. Just disappear and go for the docks. Figure out a way home."

"I know," Mikelos said. "But I know it isn't what you want."

Victory flicked out her tongue and drew a line up the side of Mikelos' neck, and he shuddered around her. She drew away from him and unbuttoned the silk coat. Leaving it in a heap at her feet, she pulled off the lacy camisole she wore underneath, where it followed the coat. She took Mikelos' hands and stepped backward until they both collapsed onto the bed. It squeaked, and they froze. But when no sounds came from the handmaids' room next to them, Victory entwined her limbs with Mikelos' and nibbled at his neck again.

He moaned into the bedding and ground against her.

Later, Victory sprawled in bed, staring into the darkness as Mikelos breathed deep in slumber next to her, his naked legs tangled with hers. The conversation wasn't finished, and nothing was resolved. She had distracted him for now, but once the concert was over, she would have to do some serious examination regarding whether to stay in Jiang Yi Yue any longer.

Maybe she couldn't be Victory, the vampire Master of Limani, and Moon, the famous mercenary, at the same time.

To be fair, at that particular moment, she couldn't remember what had been so great about being Moon to begin with.

"Are you kidding me?" Victory stared at the array of gowns Zhinu and her ladies had displayed around the sitting room. Identical sets of purple robes, down to the blue and teal embroidered birds. "This is not a fairy tale. This is not happening."

Tonight was the big concert, and Mikelos had been gone when she awoke that afternoon. When she checked, his best tuxedo was missing from the wardrobe, so she assumed he planned to dress with the rest of the orchestra. Either he was making good use of time, or he was avoiding her after their conversation the previous night.

But at the moment, she had bigger problems to worry about than her strained relationship with her daywalker. Such as the fact that the ball after the concert tonight was a masquerade, and Yi-Ting had just entered the suite balancing a collection of matching half-face masks, decorated with peacock feathers, on each of her arms.

"But these have been in production since we first heard about the ball," Zhinu said. "Before you even arrived in Jiang Yi Yue."

"And they look lovely," Victory said, trying not to grit her teeth. "But like I said, this is not a fairy tale. I can't keep track of you if I can't tell you apart from five other women."

"Don't you have enhanced senses?" Zhinu asked. "I can put on a different perfume. You can know me by my smell."

"Until someone else in the hall wears the same scent. Or you dance with people who then smell like you, too," Victory said. "Yes, I can track a person by their scent, but not in these circumstances. Not well enough to do my job."

"But there is not enough time to prepare another outfit for me," Zhinu said. "I had no idea this would be an issue."

Victory picked up one of the masks Yi-Ting had arranged on one of the chaises. "You're not that stupid, Zhinu. And I know this wasn't the original impetus behind the costumes, but don't think you're fooling me. Befuddle the poor merc with six matching women so you can sneak off with Earl Wallace for a private moment." Gripping the three peacock plumes that cascaded down the side of the mask in her hand, Victory ripped the feathers out in one sharp yang.

Yi-Ting shrieked unaware of the content of the conversation between Victory and Zhinu. She snatched away another mask before Victory could touch it.

"No, let her," Zhinu said. *"All but one. I'll wear the feathers."*

"Thank you, lady." Victory proceeded to alter the remaining four masks to her satisfaction. Yi-Ting brought the survivor to Zhinu.

"I'm not an idiot either," Zhinu said, caressing the feathers. "You should go change. Do you have anything appropriate?"

From the tone of her voice, Victory didn't think Zhinu cared much about Victory's response, which was in stark contrast to her reactions to Victory's wardrobe in previous days. "Yes, lady. A formal gown in the style of Limani, since Mikelos is also not wearing Qin clothing."

"That is acceptable." Zhinu sailed into her room, still holding the mask. Yi-Ting shot Victory a final glare before following. Zhinu paused at the entrance to her room. "Also, I might hate you a little bit right now."

Victory bowed once in acquiescence before heading to her room in silence. But she leaned against the inside of the door after she slid it shut. "You're not the only one, kid."

Though she had no idea how angry or upset Mikelos might be with her, Victory did know one thing. Her daywalker was a true professional. He charmed the audience, consisting of Governor Yu's court and as many palace servants as could fit into a gallery above the theater, and told jokes and stories about the music the Jiang Yi Yue Provincial Orchestra played, translated by Tan from the side of the stage. He hit each note of his many violin solos. He dedicated one ballad to the ladies of the court, and another to the beautiful city itself.

If nothing else, Victory would never tire of hearing Mikelos make beautiful music. This entire blasted trip was worth it to see Mikelos in his element. Performing for a crowd of hundreds, accompanied by a professional cadre of musicians. And even though she knew that he couldn't have seen her in the dark theater through the glare of the stage lights, he smiled directly at her once.

Maybe things weren't as bad as she thought.

After the performance, the crowd streamed to the banquet hall. Victory followed in Zhinu's shadow, as usual, while she and her ladies procured glasses of wine and finger-sized delicacies from the long tables now arranged on either side of the room and piled high with sweet and savory dishes.

Victory spotted Rob, Guy, and Reynolds, clustered with other members of the British delegation, on the other side of the room. Despite the colorful Qin masks each man wore, they stood out like crows in their black tuxedoes. Rob caught her staring, but made no move to approach Zhinu. Perhaps Victory had scared him back to reality the night before.

Part of her doubted it.

Applause rippled across the room as Governor Yu entered, accompanied by Mikelos. The two men mounted the main dais and at the governor's urging, Mikelos bowed again before the assembled crowd.

Victory cheered along with a few other exuberant voices, ignoring the pained expression Zhinu shot over her shoulder. She didn't care. She was proud of him.

When everyone settled, the governor stepped forward. *"In honor of this evening's phenomenal performance, I hereby grant a royal favor to Mikelos Connor. For his expertise in sharing unfamiliar music to this court, he has the thanks of this city, this court, and myself."*

As Tan whispered a translation into Mikelos' ear, the governor pulled a gold silk handkerchief from within his robes and presented it with a short bow.

Mikelos accepted the token with a bow of his own. *"Thank you, Governor Yu."* Tan escorted him off the dais accompanied by another round of applause.

Next, in a move that must have been choreographed ahead of time, Rob bounded onto the dais next to the governor. He waved to the assembled crowd, then greeted the governor with a bow. The room was silent, but Rob didn't let his enthusiasm falter.

The governor did not let the silence affect him either. *"I have more good news, ladies and gentlemen! It is my pleasure to announce that the negotiations with Earl Wallace and the other British representatives are proceeding well. Much progress has been made on trade deals beneficial to both our peoples."*

There was some scattered polite applause, but not enough to cover the low roar of murmurs from the crowd. Victory's ears perked at once. The low mutterings contained an undertone of anger and disagreement. She did not wear her sword with her gown, but her fingers twitched in a semi-conscious desire for the sharpened pin holding the heavy mass of her hair. Or the dagger strapped to her upper thigh, accessible through the high slit of her dress that allowed adequate range of motion if necessary. For Victory, dressing to kill wasn't a metaphor.

Though she received regular updates from Captain Huang regarding issues with the terrorist group who had knocked out the city's communications (which they continued to deny, of course), she had no real idea how much support these trade negotiations had from the rest of the governor's court. Zhinu's interactions with other palace residents involved more social conversation than political intrigue.

Mikelos slipped through the crowd and stood next to Victory as the governor concluded his speech about improved relations and an expected influx of British trade goods. "Hey," he said in a whisper. He slipped his hand into Victory's left.

"Hey," she said, squeezing his fingers in her own. Governor Yu finished speaking, but neither of them joined in the token applause. The enthusiasm level was nowhere near what it had been for Mikelos.

Zhinu returned to her conversation with her handmaids, but Victory and Mikelos kept their attention on the surrounding people. The buzz of voices around them had resumed, but there was something darker, sharper about it.

"You hear that?" Mikelos asked. "Sounds like Yu doesn't have as much support for these trade deals as he wants everyone to believe."

"Maybe Xian is on to something about the danger Zhinu is in as Yu's successor," Victory said. She and Mikelos trailed behind as Zhinu and An broke off from the others and headed to one of the food tables.

"It sounds like we have more work to do here," Mikelos said. He plucked a candied fruit from the table and popped it into his mouth, then leaned over to kiss Victory.

Victory licked her lips and tasted mingled sugar and sharp citrus. "We just might."

"Do you mind if I go keep Rob occupied so he doesn't get any crazy ideas like last night?" Mikelos asked.

"That would be helpful," Victory said. "Thank you."

Mikelos placed another kiss on the back of her hand before winding through the crowd to where Guy and Reynolds awaited Rob near the bottom of the dais. This was all a bit of a turnaround from Mikelos' attitude the night before, but she wasn't about to question it now. Not when every voice of dissent was a potential threat to her client's life.

She surveyed the shifting mass of bodies as she followed Zhinu around the room while the princess played courtier. Ten minutes ago, this job had been a lot more boring.

Mikelos needed close to an hour to cross the length of the banquet hall to Rob and Guy. Without Tan to translate for him, it seemed the most popular method of congratulating or thanking him for his performance was having a drink with the visiting performer. He lost count of how many glasses of wine or small shots of liqueurs he shared with various courtiers of all ages.

Finally, he made it to where the other two men lurked near a wall. The rest of the British delegation had scattered through the ballroom, but the two close friends appeared content to watch the passing spectacle.

"The man of the hour!" Rob clapped Mikelos on the shoulder as he joined them. "Well done, sir. Your reputation does you justice."

"Thank you, Rob," Mikelos said, accepting a handshake from Guy as well. He snagged another glass of rice wine off a passing waiter's tray. "The orchestra could have used another day or two of practice, but they did well considering the unfamiliar style of music."

"Trust me, we couldn't tell," Rob said. "And at least I have something to tell the grandkids after you go back into retirement for another century."

"Maybe it won't be for quite so long this time," Mikelos said. If Victory got back into the mercenary game, he could insist on resuming his own career as well.

Guy laughed. "Don't tease."

"I'll do what I want." Mikelos aimed a mock-punch at his arm, and they scuffled without spilling a drop of their drinks.

"At least some of us can do whatever we want." Rob heaved an overdramatic sigh and placed the back of one hand across his forehead. "I'm afraid to leave this corner of the hall for fear that your lady will jump down my throat again. Better to hide here than let her assume I have ulterior motives."

"But you do have ulterior motives," Guy said.

"Well, yes, that's beside the point," Rob said. "There's no need to be blatant about it. That's the opposite definition of ulterior."

While the two Brits rambled on about less than ulterior moves made in their respective pasts, Mikelos studied the crowd around them. Victory was easy to spot across the hall, thanks to her height and the vibrant sheen of her silver gown. She should have been plain amongst all the embroidery worn by those who surrounded her, but instead she glowed bright as a star.

A lock of her hair had escaped its intricate knot, and it curled around her face. If he'd stood next to her, Mikelos would have pushed it behind her ear and followed up with a kiss to her cheek. At least, that's what he'd normally do.

Tension had still undercut their interaction earlier in the evening. Despite their lovemaking the night before, the conversation hadn't ended. Of course he knew Limani was home and that Victory wasn't about to traipse around the world as a mercenary anytime soon. But that didn't rule out using Limani as a home base and taking jobs as they arose, especially if she and Asaron traded time as official Master of the City. As much as Asaron claimed sheer boredom every time he was left in charge, Mikelos knew what sort of trouble the older vampire still managed to find close to home.

Daywalkers were sometimes referred to as human servants, but there had never been any element of servitude to his relationship with Victory. She had saved him from a painful death, and their quick friendship had deepened into love. Even his bond with Connor, the first vampire to which he'd bonded as a daywalker, had been a partnership. So there was no way in hell Mikelos would be content to follow Victory around while she either caused trouble or fixed it. He had a career he could revive, too.

Rob meandered in the direction of the food tables, so Guy leaned against the wall next to Mikelos. "You're a million miles away. Coin for your thoughts?"

"Nothing important," Mikelos said, not about to get into such intricacies with a man a fraction of his age with no real relationship experience. "Pondering the future."

"We are at a party," Guy said. "There is no future beyond the next drink, the next dance, and the next snog." He and Mikelos traded their empty glasses for two full ones via another passing waiter.

"I'd like to see you try to kiss any of the ladies here," Mikelos said. "I know for certain that you have had no luck within the palace." His light dinner before the show and his taut nerves were getting the better of him, and the alcohol of the strong rice wine coursed through his bloodstream. Had there been this many people in the room before? The air pressed in close, and the bright lantern light pierced his eyes.

"Good thing we rented a townhouse down the hill in the city." Guy waggled his eyebrows when Mikelos turned to him in surprise. "You think I've been moping about here while Rob has been in meetings and you've been in rehearsal? I have been experiencing all that Jiang Yi Yue has to offer, my friend. While Rob has been trying and failing to seduce his weredragon girl, I have been having much better luck with a class of less noble ladies."

"Prostitutes or commoners?" Mikelos asked.

"Bite your tongue," Guy said with a smirk. "I've never paid for sex in my life. But we have to do something about Rob. His heart is set on Zhinu, and I can't even tempt the rest of him with anyone else."

Mikelos pretended that he leaned against the wall rather than letting it hold him up. "There's nothing wrong with monogamy." Hell, for all intents and purposes, he'd been married for the past hundred years and didn't feel less for it.

Guy scoffed. "You sound like the bloody wolves."

Rob slouched against the wall on Guy's other side in time to hear their last exchange. "The bloody wolves see no problem with dedicating themselves to one person. And it might be an artifact of the past, but chivalry is not dead."

"Well, you're looking at a losing war with your princess," Guy said. "At this rate, you'd have a better chance of getting lucky with the uptight bodyguard."

Mikelos didn't think he made any outward reaction to his comment. In fact, as he drained his glass, a pleasant sort of numbness had spread through is body. But the prick of nails at his palms made him realize that he clenched his left hand into a tight fist at his side. The tension radiated into the permanent knot in his shoulder blade, which flared in pain.

Rob touched Guy's shoulder. "You should stop talking now, Guy."

If the alcohol affected Mikelos' much larger frame, it seemed to have snuck up on Guy as well. "The only way you're going to get near the damn princess is if Victory is out of the way." He waved his empty glass at the crowd. "So here's a thought," he said, his words slurring. "In order for you to get a shot at the princess, both Mikelos and I will take care of the vamp. I bet she's old enough to have a few tricks—"

Mikelos punched him the face.

He didn't remember moving, but a matching sharpness in his knuckles after they connected with Guy's nose joined the pain in his shoulder. The other man's head snapped back, and his glass shattered on the floor.

Guy yelped in pain and drew his hands to his bloody nose. "Whadda 'ell?"

He should have backed away, apologized, but instead Mikelos grabbed Guy by the tuxedo lapels and shoved him against the wall, lifting him off the ground. "You don't get to touch her."

With an iron grip, Rob pulled Mikelos away from his friend. But he grabbed Mikelos' shoulder, and though it was inadvertent, dug his thumb into the spot where he was already in pain. When he yanked himself out of the werewolf's hand, he overshot and crashed back into the crowd of onlookers who had turned at the commotion.

A Qin nobleman shouted in surprise, and one of his friends shoved Mikelos at Rob. This time Rob grabbed his upper arms to steady him, and Mikelos sagged in his grip as the world spun around him.

Perhaps assuming that Rob held Mikelos ready for him, Guy pushed himself off the wall with a bloodied yowl of rage. All three of them crashed to the floor in a heap.

There went his bad shoulder. At least the drunken haze made all his movements feel like they were underwater, insulating him from the worst of the pain.

He kicked and flailed with his remaining good limbs until he untangled himself from Guy and Rob. But his bad luck continued, and he rolled right over Guy's broken wine glass. He plucked one shard out of his cheek, where it had barely missed his left eye, and stared at the palace guardsmen who loomed over him.

Two other sergeants were in the process of helping Guy and Rob to their feet. Rob merely looked disheveled as he pulled away from them and disappeared into the crowd. Guy was a sight, with blood coating half his face and staining his white shirt, and he leaned heavily on the guard. The three men above Mikelos, however, made no move to help him.

Mikelos raised his hands in mock surrender. Was it three men? The room spun, but at this point he had no idea whether it was the alcohol or if he'd conked his skull on the floor in the commotion.

One of the guardsmen gasped and snapped something in Qin to his partner, who ducked into the crowd. What the hell were they so frightened by?

He moved his hands again, and pain lanced through one of them. He turned his palms up to see the broken stem of Guy's wineglass emerging from the left one. "Oh, shit," he said.

At least every time he managed to get into a stupid fight and mangle a hand, it was his left one.

The scent of blood crossed her nose, and Victory ripped the sharpened pin from her bun. As her hair tumbled around her bare arms, she wrapped her empty hand around Zhinu's wrist and hauled her to the nearest exit.

"Wha—?" Zhinu stumbled along in her wake. "Victory?"

That's when the screams began, and Zhinu at least had the sense to meet Victory's pace and keep her head down. "I don't know," Victory said. "But we're not staying to find out."

Worst-case scenarios shot through her mind, topped by the image of isolationist rebels attacking the palace while the majority of the court gathered in one place. The palace corridors they rushed through were empty except for the occasional servants, all of whom jumped back in fright at the vampire storming the halls, brandishing a slim knife, with the princess tugged along behind her.

By now Victory had a mental map of the palace in place, and they arrived at Zhinu's suite in less than two minutes. She hadn't thought of it as a defensive position at first, but after pouring over the blueprints Xian provided her, she'd learned that its position near the center of the palace provided excellent coverage. And if the palace was under siege, she already knew the best way out of the complex using a mixture of servant's passages and rooftops, depending on whether it was day or night.

As Zhinu paced in the center of the sitting room, Victory latched the door shut. Not wasting a moment, she dashed into her room and tugged off the fancy dress and kicked away her heels, replacing them with more sensible pants and shirt. She shoved her bare feet into boots and grabbed her sword belt before returning to the main room.

Zhinu perched on the edge of a chaise, arms wrapped around herself. She looked up when Victory switched on a lamp. "What's going on?" Her mask rested in her lap, peacock plumes brushing the floor.

"I'm not sure yet," Victory said. She checked the latch on the door again before crossing the room to pull the heavy drapes across the windows. She also made sure the lights were off in Zhinu's room, and that the door was closed. "We'll wait here for news, but keep your ears open. If we hear any sounds of combat or weapons fire, we're going to evacuate. You should change clothes while we have the time."

"What about my ladies?" Zhinu placed the mask on an end table and stood, smoothing the front of her intricate robes. "We can't leave them in danger."

Victory injected as much patience into her voice as she could. "I'm sorry, lady, but you are my primary concern."

Zhinu pressed her lips together and brushed past Victory toward her room. "I know, I'll keep the light off," she said.

"Thank you." Victory buckled on her sword belt and kneeled to lace her boots. But then—footsteps in the hall. One set, low-heeled shoes. She shoved the untied laces into her boots and ghosted next to the door.

The mystery person stopped in front of Zhinu's suite instead of passing by. Victory drew her sword and held it ready. Rather than the sound of a turning key or rattling latch, however, the person knocked on the door.

Zhinu lurked in the doorway of her room and pulled her dressing gown closed.

"Who's there?" Victory said, pitching her voice to be heard through the door.

Muffled by the wood, she heard, "It's Rob."

Suppressing her initial sarcastic instinct to say, "Go away, we don't want any," Victory instead called back, "Why are you here?"

"I saw you haul ass out of the ball," Rob said. "Wanted to let you know that everything is okay. No emergency."

This could all be an elaborate plot, but why send the most high-ranking member of the British visitors? After the entire palace must know by now how Victory had ripped him a new one the night before? "What happened back there?"

"There was a bit of an altercation," Rob said. "No external threat, just a dumb brawl between friends." Now he jiggled the door latch. "May I please come in? I feel ridiculous shouting from the hall."

Zhinu emitted a small squeak and disappeared into her room. It was a noise of excitement, and Victory figured the girl wanted to reevaluate her clothing choices. She weighed the irritation of dealing with Rob and Zhinu in a room together against her desire for more information. Rationality won out, and she unlatched the door and slid it open.

As promised, Rob stood alone in the hall. His tuxedo jacket was unbuttoned, and his bow tie hung loose around his neck. His attention shot straight to Victory's sword and he backed a few hasty steps away from the door. "Whoa, lady."

She returned the bastard sword to its sheath. "You might as well come in." She stepped away from the entrance, but kept her hand on her sword hilt. Not that she had any intention of using it on a member of British nobility, but Rob would do well to remember he was here on her sufferance.

He soaked everything in as he entered the suite, from the collection of photographs above the fireplace mantel to the set of elaborate silk-screened wall hangings decorated with swirling blue dragons. Stopping in the center of the room, his hands fidgeted with the hem of his jacket, as if unsure what do next.

Victory closed and locked the door behind him, just to be on the safe side. "Talk, please," she said, crossing her arms and leaning a hip against a chaise. "What happened?"

Rob fluttered the fingers of one hand. "Nothing, nothing," he said. "Like I said, a scuffle between two friends."

"I smelled blood," Victory said.

"Looked like a broken nose to me," Rob said. "No permanent damage to anyone."

His voice was clear, and though he didn't keep his focus on her, it darted around the room in interest of his surroundings, not in evasion. Victory heaved an unnecessary sigh to show Rob how irritated she was by all of this. "Thank you for keeping us informed. I will apologize to Lady Zhinu for cutting her evening short."

"No, no, it's okay," Zhinu said, leaving her room. She wore more casual clothing than Victory had ever seen her in—knit leggings and an over-large top that hung off one shoulder. Her black hair cascaded down her back in loose waves, free from the intricate hairstyle she had worn for the masquerade. She clutched a tea tray between both hands, and the smell of oolong filled the suite. "Would you like to stay for tea, Earl Wallace?"

Victory held up her hands. "No—"

"It would be my pleasure," Rob said, interrupting Victory and bowing to Zhinu. "Here, let me help you." He accepted the tray from Zhinu and placed it on the table between the chaises where she indicated.

This was awful, but Victory had to admit she'd brought it on herself. A sudden idea struck her. What if she had been handling this the wrong way? Zhinu was a young woman with a strong personality. Though Rob had been raised among werewolf noblewomen, she had never been struck by the sense that Rob wanted a partner, but a trophy with which to return home triumphant. Maybe a real conversation, without the added titillation of secrecy, would be what both of them needed to realize this was not a match made in heaven.

Victory parked herself on one of the giant cushions next to the fireplace, as unobtrusive as possible while still in physical view, to remind Rob that she watched both of them. She opened the Qin language primer she had left earlier, with half an ear on the conversation drifting around her.

In other circumstances, it might be cute. The way Rob complimented Zhinu on her tea, her grasp of the Loquella language, the suite's décor. The way Zhinu blushed and sipped her tea, in turn asking questions about how Rob enjoyed life in the palace and his impressions of Jiang Yi Yue. It almost reminded Victory of eavesdropping when dates had come to the house for the kids, back in high school when they still lived at the manor.

But this was a different set of circumstances. It wasn't cute, it was nerve-wracking. Victory hoped Zhinu's handmaids returned to the suite soon. At this point, she would even welcome an appearance by Zhinu's mother.

Thirty minutes later, Victory reevaluated every decision in her life that had led her to this moment. Zhinu peppered Rob with questions about his time at Oxenafor, and while Rob might assume it was just an effort on Zhinu's part to make conversation, Victory knew better. In turn, Rob flirted back, making pointed comments about how none of the women he had attended school with were a match for Zhinu's beauty and intelligence. Victory wanted to pull her hair out.

She had heard more footsteps in the hall during this time, but ignored them now that she knew the supposed danger in the ballroom had been a false alarm. This time, however, it was a much larger group, and she recognized the voices. Mikelos, his footsteps heavy, was assuring any number of Zhinu's handmaids that he was fine as they cooed over him and stepped in dainty slippers.

Rob also heard the commotion, breaking off his conversation with Zhinu and standing when Victory hauled herself to her feet. She darted to the door ahead of the werewolf, unlatching it and sliding it open as the group approached the entrance to Zhinu's suite.

Mikelos stood before the door, staring around with glassy eyes. "Hi," he said. The whiff of alcohol on his breath mingled with the sharp scent of his blood. Dried blood streaked the side of his face from a nasty cut on his cheek, and when he waved, she saw the bloodstained handkerchief wrapped around his hand.

"Oh my gods, Mikelos," Victory said. She grabbed his uninjured hand and pulled him into the suite. Then she whirled on Rob. "Did you forget to mention one important detail?"

Rob's voice was unrepentant. "The brawl may have been between Mikelos and Guy. They were a bit inebriated."

"An' you left us," Mikelos said, staggering against Victory until she settled him onto the chaise Rob had vacated. "Tan an' Reynolds an' the security guys yelled at us a lot, an' you were here the whole time?"

"I saw Victory escort Lady Zhinu from the hall and wanted to assure them there was nothing to worry about," Rob said.

"The old British man found us leaving the hall to search for Lady Zhinu and asked us to escort Mikelos home." Yi-Ting glared at Rob as the other handmaids clustered around Zhinu. In blatant disregard of the drinks laid out and what

Zhinu already wore, Yi-Ting said, *"Victory, please ask that man to leave so we can assist Lady Zhinu in her nightly routine and prepare our evening tea."*

"With pleasure," Victory said. "Earl Wallace, I believe it is time to say good night." As much as she wanted to examine Mikelos' injuries further, she still had a job to do. From the way Mikelos leaned to the side on the chaise, at least the amount of alcohol he must have consumed that evening still worked as an effective painkiller against his wounds.

Zhinu leapt to her feet. "Victory—" She almost, but not quite, managed to keep the plaintive note from her voice.

"No, she's right," Rob said. He turned to Zhinu and favored her with a stylized bow more common in Britannia, extending his arms in a flourish. "I will bid you sweet dreams, and call upon you at a more civil hour tomorrow."

Not giving Victory a chance to protest, Rob bowed to the handmaids, then Victory, and exited the suite.

Zhinu knelt before Mikelos. She raised his injured hand and pulled back the handkerchief. *"An,"* she said. *"Fetch the first aid kit. We might have to summon Dr. Adachi depending on what's wrong."*

Mikelos tried to push her away. "Stop," he said. "I'm fine. Just need Victory."

Zhinu hissed through her teeth at whatever she saw under the bloodied fabric.

In a burst of speed that made the handmaids gasp, Victory crossed the room and kneeled next to Zhinu. Ignoring the stares of the women surrounding her, she dipped a fingertip to the blood-soaked cloth and licked it. Information about Mikelos' injuries hit her like a wave.

She ignored the muscle knot over his left shoulder blade and the bruise on his neck as a matter of course. Those injuries were permanent facets of his being after years of violin. The cut on his cheek was already healing, and aside from a few other bruises on his back, nothing else stood out as needing immediate attention.

The alcohol coursing through his bloodstream didn't register as an injury, but the rice wine did lend an interesting cast to the taste of his blood. At any other time, she would have rolled her eyes imagining how much he'd had to drink for her to be able to taste it with this much distinction.

But his left hand. The one he'd needed reconstructive surgery on two years before, when he'd been beaten past even her ability to heal him. She clenched her teeth as she finished removing the handkerchief.

"Oh, Mikelos." Victory examined the injury. He'd managed to impale himself on something sharp and narrow. Despite the copious amounts of blood, the entry wound was small. When she lifted his hand, she saw no matching exit wound on the other side. "Make a fist for me."

"That's gonna hurt," Mikelos said. He stared at the ceiling, as if unwilling to face the damage he'd incurred.

"I don't care," Victory said. "I need to see how much muscle damage there is."

"Should I get the doctor?" Zhinu hovered next to them, now clutching a small red case.

"Hold on," Victory said. "I might be able to handle it." With her free hand, she poked Mikelos in the knee. "Fist. Now."

Mikelos clenched his jaw and did as he was told. With agonizing slowness, all of his fingers curled inward. "Good," Victory said again. "This I can fix."

Zhinu placed the first aid kit next to Mikelos and rummaged through it. "What do you need? It should probably be sterilized."

"Nah," Mikelos said. "Just need my girl."

"What you need is a smack upside the head," Victory said. "What the hell possessed Guy to fight with you?"

Mikelos listed to the side as he avoided meeting her eyes.

"You started it?" That temper would be the death of him one day. "Dare I ask?"

"He was disrespectful," Mikelos said. "To you. Wouldn't stand for it."

"Of course not," Victory said. She wrapped the ends of the handkerchief back around Mikelos' hand and hauled him to his feet. "You realize that every time you get into a fight over my honor, you end up on the losing side?"

"This has happened before?" Zhinu raised her fingers to her parted lips.

"At least he doesn't need surgery this time." Victory tilted her head toward the first aid kit. "Thank you, but we'll be okay." She wasn't about to explain the mechanics of it while Mikelos sagged against her and bled all over his tuxedo shirt, clutching his wounded hand to his chest.

"Are you sure?" Zhinu kept pace on Victory's other side as she led Mikelos to their room. "It looks like it needs stitches."

"No, it will be fine," Victory said. "I'll take care of it. Go to bed, it's late." Before Zhinu could argue further, Victory slid the door home.

Once they were alone in the blessed quiet, Victory pressed her forehead against the cool wood of the panel door. Then she faced Mikelos and presented him with her most disappointed look. "You are a moron."

He narrowed his eyes at her, but the effect was lost by the way he couldn't focus on her face. "Am not."

Mikelos let Victory help him peel off his jacket, shirt, and undershirt before he sank to the bed. "No, no. Up you go. We need to rinse off your hand." She slung his uninjured arm over her shoulders and led him to the bathroom, where they made quick work of the blood and rebound his hand in a clean cloth. Washing off the clotted blood reopened the wound, and the white cotton soon turned scarlet. Victory would apologize to the woman who collected their laundry later.

"It does hurt, you know," Mikelos said.

"I bet it does," Victory said. "How did this even happen?"

"Put my hand down on a broken wineglass stem," he said. "Reynolds pulled it out. His handkerchief."

Victory finished undressing Mikelos, pulling off his shoes and socks. "Well, I'm sure he considers it yours now." Miracle of miracles, she'd managed to keep her own clothing free of blood. "What the hell am I going to do with you? Brawling at a ball essentially held in your honor? What were you thinking?" She stripped off the rest of her clothing and stood naked over the bed, glaring at Mikelos in the low light of the bedside lamp.

"I told you. Guy insulted you."

"Guy is an idiot kid," Victory said. "You know better."

"C'mere," Mikelos said. He held out his good hand.

"No." Since she knew Mikelos wasn't severely hurt, and as she contemplated the situation more, her anger grew. "Seriously, love. What possessed you?"

"I may have had a bit to drink." He let his arm flop back onto the bed.

"All you've done since we got here has been rehearse with the orchestra and drink with Rob and Guy," Victory said. "Now that the show is done, am I to expect the drinking to increase?" She wasn't being fair, and she knew it. But she also didn't want Mikelos to cause an international incident.

"Why are you yelling at me?" Mikelos asked. "Reynolds already yelled at us enough, trust me. My hand hurts."

"Good!" But even as she said it, Victory sank onto the bed. She crawled over Mikelos so that she braced above him on hands and knees. "Maybe if you hurt enough, you'll think before you punch next time."

Mikelos pushed a lock of her hair behind her ear, finishing the movement with a caress of her cheek. "I'm not your responsibility," he said. "I don't need protecting. I'm not your client."

"That's because you're more important than a client, you idiot." Before he had the chance to respond, she lowered her face to his.

He tried to catch her in a kiss, but she avoided his lips. Instead, she tilted his face to the side with one finger and licked across the cut on his cheek. Most of the slice had already closed, thanks to his enhanced healing as her daywalker, but one small portion still leaked a pinprick of red.

She hadn't done it for him. The hair on the back of her neck raised as his blood touched her tongue. Fresh blood was better than bottled, and the fresh blood of her bonded daywalker was more potent than the strongest liquor. She dropped her head onto the bed next to his and let his breath ghost across her cheek as her entire mouth tingled with the taste of rice wine and precious life.

He lifted his good hand and cupped her breast, thumb brushing across her nipple. "I'm not your client. I'm your partner." Turning his face to her, he caught her earlobe between his teeth and bit down.

She jumped in surprise and sat up, straddling his stomach and bracing both palms on his shoulders. Mikelos continued to toy with her nipple, so she grabbed his arm and pinned it to the bed above him. "I'm still mad at you," she said. Keeping him immobilized with her legs and arms, she leaned down to nip at his neck, brushing his chest with her breasts.

He gasped and canted his hips up. "You going to heal me or not?"

"You're lucky you're cute," Victory said. She let go of his arm and brought the inside of her wrist to her mouth. With a practiced swipe across one of her fangs, she opened a small cut. Blood the color of deep burgundy welled up from her sensitive skin, burning where it touched the cool air. "And that you've ruined me for other men."

Mikelos caught her wrist and brought it to his lips. First he licked a stripe across her skin, catching the blood that emerged. Then he latched his mouth over her wrist and sucked deep. The sharp pain changed to a different sensation, and Victory gasped. Delicious fire swept through her body from the point where Mikelos' lips met her wrist.

Sparks burst in her vision and she ground against Mikelos. She bit her bottom lip against the moan that threatened to escape, in case the girls still lurked in the main room of the suite.

Mikelos pulled away from her wrist after seconds that felt like hours. His chest heaved, and she collapsed atop him. She listened to the comforting murmur of his heartbeat for a spell before pushing herself up again. She pulled his left hand to her. When she unwrapped the towel and wiped away the excess blood, his skin was clear. Not even a scar marred the face of his palm.

This was what made the daywalker bond unique. A vampire was made when someone on the brink of death was drained and then fed the blood of a vampire. They came back healed, more than human. A daywalker, however, drank the blood of a vampire while whole. They could heal from major wounds, even mortal ones, and come back human, with a bit extra.

Victory didn't understand the genetics or magic or whatever caused it. All she knew was that once upon a time she had saved Mikelos from a gunshot wound to the stomach, and with regular infusions of her blood, he had been by her side ever since.

She tossed the dirty towel off the bed and licked the rest of his hand clean. Her blood had even cleared all of the alcohol from his system, so this time she tasted pure blood. It was better this way. Vibrant, alive.

Energy coursed through Mikelos' body, almost shaking within his skin. With two strong hands, he gripped her shoulders and rolled them over on the bed. Now he straddled her, and she didn't resist when he captured her lips against his.

When Mikelos came up for air, he said, "You've ruined me for other men, too."

"What? Goofball." She raked both sets of nails down his back in retaliation before surging up to capture the side of his neck. She sucked against his carotid artery, drawing the blood to just beneath the surface, then nipped with her top fangs and opened two tiny wounds.

Mikelos was a lot less quiet than she had been.

She found that she didn't much care.

ACT II

When Victory and Mikelos emerged from their room past noon the next day, the handmaids exclaimed over Mikelos' healed hand and Zhinu favored them with a wicked grin. Mikelos blushed, but Victory didn't let the young woman get to her.

After they joined the ladies for a light lunch, Mikelos pecked Victory on the cheek and said, "I should go apologize to Guy."

"I think you should apologize to Tan and Reynolds, but that's just me." Victory had curled next to the unlit fireplace with her Qin textbook once more while Zhinu, An, and Yi-Ting embroidered on the sunlit patio outside the suite. One of the daytime guards was with them, and Victory was content to be in earshot.

"They will be my next stop, I promise." She and Mikelos exchanged a deeper kiss, then he crossed to the main door of the suite. Before he could unlatch it, however, a heavy knock sounded.

At Victory's affirmative finger twitch, Mikelos slid open the door a crack. As Rob's cologne drifted into the suite, Mikelos scrubbed a hand over his face and opened the door further. "Good afternoon," he said.

"Good day, Mikelos!" Rob clapped a hand on Mikelos' shoulder and brushed past him into the suite. "How's the hand doing?"

Mikelos lifted it to the earl. "Much better."

Rob examined his intact palm with interest, then turned to Victory. She didn't bother to rise. "Good afternoon, Lady Victory!"

"Can we help you, Earl Wallace?" The return to his formal title wasn't weird when she was still too perturbed for familiarity.

"I have come to invite Lady Zhinu for an afternoon stroll about the gardens," Rob said.

"Not happening," Victory said. Behind Rob, Mikelos escaped while he still could. She didn't blame him.

A bit of the wind deflated from Rob's sails, but not for long. "What chaperoned activity would meet with your approval?"

He wasn't even being sarcastic. It was obvious that letting the two converse over tea the previous evening had been a major tactical error on Victory's part. Now Rob expected things. She set aside her book and stood. She resettled the long sleeve of her shirt over the stiletto strapped to the inside of her wrist, not bothering to hide the action—or the weapon.

He made no outward sign of fear or nervousness, though his pulse quickened. Victory said, "Perhaps—"

"Robert!" Zhinu's face lit up as she slipped past the heavy drapes into the suite. "How nice of you to call upon me." She shot Victory a glare of defiance as she crossed the room toward the werewolf.

Rob caught one of her hands in his and bowed over it, pressing a light kiss to her knuckles as Zhinu giggled over the unfamiliar gesture. "How could I stay away from such a beautiful lady for long?"

Some situations called for a person to look to the sky and pray to all the gods in existence for patience. This was one of them.

But the gods wouldn't provide the answers Victory needed, or tell her which choice to make. That was on her. Who did she owe her allegiance to in this scenario?

Well, that answer was easy. To her own conscience.

It was Victory's job to protect Zhinu's life, not police her actions or protect her heart. Zhinu was an adult who could make adult decisions and experience adult hearthbreak, if it came to that.

Perhaps familiarity would breed contempt, as Zhinu and Rob came to the realization that their lives were too different, and that they truly had nothing in common. In the meantime, the only way out was through.

Over the next few evenings, Victory felt less like a bodyguard and more like a maiden aunt. Though she managed to keep Rob and Zhinu inside the suite during the daylight hours, as Rob stopped by for a few moments here and there between trade negotiation sessions, nighttime was a different matter. They shared private dinners. Evening strolls through the gardens. Card games in the palace salons.

Xian had to have gotten a whiff of this by now, but though Victory expected a summons at any moment, none ever came.

While Zhinu had the time of her young life, Victory's nerves drew tighter and tighter. Rob was a perfect gentleman, but he hadn't given up on Operation: Marry a Qin Princess.

The other shoe was bound to drop soon.

Victory just had to figure out which direction to block.

Though Mikelos had apologized to Guy days ago, the young man had been cool to him the two times they had crossed paths since. According to Rob, he spent more time at the rented townhouse in the city proper than at the palace.

Mikelos was well aware he had gone too far the other night, and he was prepared to wait it out. Instead, he filled his new free time with private *erhu* lessons with Tan and a few members of the Jiang Yi Yue Provincial Orchestra he had bonded with. In return, he worked with one of the palace librarians on a basic instructional booklet for reading Europan-style sheet music.

Not drinking his days away, as Victory had feared.

He did not deny, however, the pleased warmth that spread through him when Yi-Ting stepped out onto the patio to pass along a note delivered by a servant. He set down his violin and accepted it with thanks.

Written in a careless scrawl: *I'm tired of listening to Rob talk about his princess. Come to dinner with us tonight and share in my misery. —Guy*

Rob's slight obsession had been enough to finish the thaw. Victory was elsewhere in the palace, accompanying Zhinu as she attended afternoon tea with her mother. Mikelos had not been invited, but he hadn't been too put out. He left the note on her pillow and changed for dinner, then lurked outside the meeting room until the afternoon session ended.

He latched onto Rob when the British and Qin delegations spilled into the hall. "I have been invited to join you for dinner," he said.

Rob clapped him on the shoulder. "Excellent. I told Guy to get over himself."

Mikelos did not enlighten the earl as to the real reason for the invitation.

Reynolds had not held a grudge against Mikelos and appeared delighted at his sudden appearance. The three men headed for the palace garage and caught a ride into town in another ethanol-fueled vehicle. On their original trip through the city, Mikelos had been focused on Victory's fascinated reaction to a sun-dappled world. This time, it was his turn to gaze upon the seaside views and enjoy the trip through an elegant part of the city. This was where nobles and high-level bureaucrats who didn't warrant rooms in the palace lived, and where Rob had rented a house from a bachelor spending the season in Shencheng, back on the Qin mainland.

The chauffer dropped them off before an unobtrusive front gate, and Rob led the way through the entrance and into a large single-level dwelling that surrounded an interior courtyard. Guy lounged in the sun, already enjoying a pre-dinner cocktail next to a pond filled with large orange and gold fish. Spring was coming, south of the equator, and the air around them was cool and inviting, with none of late summer humidity that would have been prevalent back home in Limani.

Guy jumped to his feet upon seeing them. "Right on time."

"Right on time for what?" Rob asked as Guy led them to one side of the garden. There they found a grouping of low tables, surrounded by cushions. A taller counter had been set up to one side, and as they approached, an older man in plain blue robes emerged from the house carrying a covered tray.

"We are having a traditional dinner from one of the smaller Qin territories," Guy said. "I asked around and found the best chef who would agree to a private catered meal."

The chef gave them a short bow, but otherwise kept himself occupied with the various trays and platters already covering his cooking space. The first thing Mikelos noticed was the lack of heating element. This would be interesting, since Guy didn't strike him as the type to enjoy a meal of raw vegetables.

Reynolds had his nostrils flared. "Fish?"

"Yes!" Guy said. "*Raw* fish."

Mikelos looked back at the counter. "What."

"That sounds atrocious," Rob said. He checked himself, and said to the chef, "Your pardon, sir."

That was about Mikelos' take on the whole concept as well. But he was a guest, and not about to ruin the gesture of friendship Guy had extended by inviting him along. He sat with the others and stayed quiet.

"Hanamura doesn't speak any Loquella," Guy said. "We're supposed to eat what we're given." As a maid from within the house served them water and hot tea, Hanamura chopped and rolled and performed other arcane actions with sticky rice.

Finally, he presented the four men with bite-sized rolls of fish, vegetables, and rice wrapped in—was that seaweed? Mikelos exchanged a "what have we gotten ourselves into?" face with Rob before popping the first into his mouth and chewing with care.

"Wow," he said, after he swallowed.

"Exquisite," Reynolds said. "Well done, Guy. We shouldn't have doubted you."

The rest of the meal was half sustenance and half performance art as they watched Hanamura concoct more fancy rolls. He even handed them pieces of straight-up raw fish balanced on a thin ball of rice and flavored with a hint of spices. Mikelos received tuna at first, but later traded for Rob's mackerel. While the tuna tasted fatty and smooth, the mackerel had more of the "fishy" taste he'd expected, but the flesh was firm and a nice contrast against the sticky rice.

When they finished the meal and none of the men would eat another bite, Hanamura packed his supplies and disappeared without a word. "Not a chatty fellow, is he?" Rob asked.

"Don't have to be chatty when you're a bloody miracle worker," Guy said. "I'm stuffed. Shall I call for wine?"

"Don't bother," Rob said. "I can't move anyway."

A snore shuddered in the air next to Mikelos, and he found Reynolds fast asleep in his own nest of cushions. He and the other two men tried, and failed, not to burst into laughter.

"Old man deserves a rest," Rob said. "We did good work today."

"How are the talks going?" Mikelos asked. He hadn't done much to keep up with the details of the negotiations, but he knew better than to believe every rumor that passed through the palace complex like wildfire.

"Very well, I think," Rob said. "We're getting a little, the Qin are getting a little. How these things go, apparently." He cupped his tea and sipped. "I did manage to have lunch with Zhinu."

"Oh gods, here we go again," Guy said. He tossed a dramatic arm over his face. "Tell me, good sir, what special and amazing thing did you learn about the good lady today?"

Rob tossed a pillow at his friend. "I'm playing a slow game," he said. "You know that. Breaking down her walls. Breaking down Victory's." He arched an eyebrow at Mikelos. "Speaking of—she has seemed more inclined to give us time together lately. Did I wear her down?"

Mikelos bought a few seconds before responding by draining his water glass. He knew every detail about Rob and Zhinu's "dates" because Victory bemoaned them to him each morning before bed. "Keep being the perfect gentleman, and you'll be okay."

Rob groaned. "It's been torture. A fleeting touch of the hands. Not even so much as a single kiss."

"You sound like your sister's romance novels," Guy said, throwing the pillow back.

"Well, here's the odd thing," Rob said, his tone sobering. "We've actually been talking, Zhinu and I. Getting to know each other. And I think I'm falling in love with her."

Mikelos gripped his empty glass at Rob's proclamation, not paying attention to Guy's immediate spurt of teasing. He was serious. Rob wasn't making a political play anymore.

How the hell was he supposed to tell Victory this?

Zhinu flopped onto the chaise opposite Victory. "I'm bored."

"I'm sorry," Victory said. "You don't have after-dinner plans tonight?" The previous three evenings had involved strolls through the gardens trailing after Zhinu and Rob, and she had been more than relieved to find the note from Mikelos indicating the earl would be otherwise engaged that night. At this point, she didn't even care whether Mikelos came home stinking drunk again.

Okay, she would care a little bit if he was bleeding and wounded. But drunk she could handle.

"Not tonight," Zhinu said. She stroked a petal of the purple orchid displayed on the table between them. "Robert sent this as an apology that he had other plans."

"How sweet of him." Victory's tone was dry, but Zhinu already knew her thoughts on the entire Rob situation.

"I know," Zhinu said. She giggled. "That's why I'm going to marry him."

If Victory had had a functioning heartbeat, it would have stopped. She checked the suite for backup, even though she already knew the handmaids were all gone on evening errands and activities of their own. "Say that again?"

Zhinu leapt from her seat and paced, vibrating with energy. She waved her hands as she spoke. "I'm going to ask Earl Wallace to marry me. I will abdicate all claims of my heirs to any seats of power in the Qin Empire and move with Robert to Britannia. After we wed, I will establish a private household in Oxenafor and attend school while he works in Londinium for the family business." She bent to sniff the orchid. "I'm sure we can come to some sort of suitable arrangement once I graduate."

This was not good. Xian would kill her. "Wait," Victory said. "So this isn't because you're in love with him?"

"He's fantastic," Zhinu said. "But let's be realistic. I've known him for less than a month."

"Exactly," Victory said. "None of this is realistic. This seems like a pretty major commitment in order to get an education." It tore at her heartstrings. That a young woman with this much potential thought such a drastic decision for the sake of an education was necessary went against the grain of Victory's entire worldview.

Or maybe it was because she would never stand in her own daughter's path the way Zhinu's family had.

"What other choice do I have?" Zhinu asked. She threw up her hands and collapsed onto the other chaise once again.

Victory opened her mouth to respond, then closed it again before speaking. Zhinu was right. They'd had this conversation before, and nothing had changed. Lady Jinghua still pitched a fit whenever she learned her daughter had been in the library. Victory had never managed to give Zhinu the promised combat lessons. Her days were too packed with other social engagements and handicraft projects, and Zhinu had been clear on the fact that what little free time she did have was prioritized with visits to the library for another stash of the books she read late at night and in the bath.

Time to focus not on the basic idea of marriage to Earl Wallace, but on what it might mean to the grander scheme of things. Ideas neither Rob nor Zhinu could have considered due to their ages and life experiences, despite their intelligence.

"Let's operate on the assumption that I agree with you," Victory said, drawing out the words. Zhinu kept her focus somewhere on Victory's face, giving every cue she might at least consider what Victory had to say. "Can we look at the bigger picture this time? Beyond the effect all of this will have on your angry family and Lord Reynolds, Rob's mentor?"

"Are you going to tell me something I haven't already thought of yet?" Zhinu asked.

"Maybe," Victory said. "Tell me what you know about the Last War."

"Our people and the British clashed over shipping rights to the Magnus River on the New Continent," Zhinu said, as if reciting an answer to a teacher. "Direct land combat escalated to nuclear war when the British bombed Wan City, and then we destroyed Nacostina, the former capital of the British colonies, with a hydrogen bomb."

She recited this as if by rote, and Victory had to acknowledge that it was a good basic summation of some of the worst years of her life. "And do you know why this is important?"

"Are you worried my running away with Robert will cause another war?" Zhinu asked, her voice incredulous. "That's a bit extreme."

"It is extreme," Victory said. "But you're both political figures. You're both nobility. You need to think about more than yourselves. You need to consider your people."

"Robert thinks a marriage between us will solidify the bonds between our empires," Zhinu said.

"Sure. Or it could lead to another war when the Qin demand their princess back," Victory said.

Zhinu sat in silence for a beat before jumping to her feet again. "Would you like some tea?"

"I would love some tea," Victory said, leaning back in the chaise.

Quiet descended upon the suite as Zhinu set the kettle on and prepared the loose-leaf tea she knew Victory favored. With any luck, the girl was considering Victory's words and not making an excuse to avoid finishing the conversation.

Once Zhinu brought a cup to Victory and resumed her seat, she asked in a small voice, "Was the war very terrible?"

Victory paused for a moment, unsure of how to respond to such a question. War was brutal, and she'd been through more than her fair share. Before the Last War, she'd fought for the Roman Empire during the invasion of Aragonia. Before that, it had been for the British during the Germanic expansion. And that didn't even include all of the smaller-scale mercenary contracts she and Asaron had taken for centuries as petty nobles fought amongst themselves. "I'm sure you've read books about it."

"A few basic history texts," Zhinu said. "I made it most of the way through one memoir, but it was when I was still young and it gave me nightmares. But even it had been written by a higher-ranked officer who never saw actual combat."

Victory stared into the moss green liquid of her tea, studying the way the lamplight reflected across the drink's surface. "It's a hundred times worse."

"Obviously," Zhinu said. "Tens of thousands of people died in Nacostina alone. Even the Qin leadership at the time mourned the decision."

"I was almost one of them." The words slipped out before Victory could stop herself, and Zhinu's unblinking eyes widened in shock. Victory had left Nacostina on a mission mere days before the hydro dropped, and in her mind, she could still see the explosion that had turned night into day and been heard for hundreds of miles.

"But you... knew people? Who died?" Zhinu asked. Her voice was a whisper and she clutched her teacup with white-knuckled hands.

"Yes," Victory said. "Both in Nacostina and Wan City."

"Okay," Zhinu said. "I won't pretend to understand, but I do get what you're trying to tell me."

"Promise me you'll think more before making such a crazy decision," Victory said. "Especially angles you might not have considered yet. I'm just the hired muscle. I can lend you my expertise, but I can't make your choices for you."

"I promise," Zhinu said.

"Thank you."

"We should get married, Robert."

Victory stopped in the middle of the garden path, looked at the starry sky, and did not bother to muffle her groan of dismay. Next to her, Mikelos gaped at the couple ahead. At least no one was anywhere around them, as far as she could tell with her enhanced hearing. The only witnesses to this fiasco were herself, Mikelos, and a few marmosets lurking in a nearby palm.

The words had burst out of Zhinu in a rush as she meandered through the trees with Rob, on yet another chaperoned not-date. Victory did not miss the glare Zhinu shot back at her.

"I'm sorry, lady?" Rob did an admirable impression of a fish, wide-eyed.

Setting her shoulders, Zhinu clasped both of Rob's hands in hers. "We should get married."

Rob brought her hands to his lips and kissed the backs of them, one by one. With a solemn voice, he said, "I accept." He leaned down to kiss Zhinu's forehead.

He aimed for her lips next, but she pulled out of his grasp to face Victory and Mikelos with arms crossed. "Well? I know you have something to say."

Helpless, Victory shrugged at Mikelos. Like she had told Zhinu the night before, she was just the bodyguard. She wasn't in charge of Zhinu's life, and the girl could choose what advice to heed.

Mikelos shrugged back at her, then stepped forward. He bowed to Zhinu, then shook Rob's hand. "Congratulations to you both."

Zhinu's face radiated satisfaction as she allowed herself to be tucked under Rob's arm.

Victory covered her eyes with both hands. This bodyguard contract had been open-ended, but now the end might be sooner rather than later.

Though one evening per week of personal time was in Victory's contract, this was the first night she had taken advantage of it. Personal time had never been a thing a few centuries ago, so she was unused to taking the benefit afforded to her. Now was the time to change that.

She called an intervention in Rob's suite, summoning Mikelos, Guy, and an unsuspecting Lord Reynolds after depositing Zhinu back at her suite into the care of her handmaids and Sergeant Soon-ja.

Victory knew Reynolds was in for a rude surprise, but she hoped he could talk some sense into the idiot. She had not expected the red-faced bout of screaming, accompanied by the musky scent of werewolf that indicated the older man was a hair's breadth away from shifting shape in fury.

Rob stood in silence, back ramrod straight and arms stiff at this side. He maintained better control of his form, but Victory noted that he made no submissive motions. Didn't look to the ground, didn't hunch to a lower height than the older werewolf. Didn't look repentant in the slightest.

Victory, Mikelos, and Guy stared from their seats in the suite's formal room, waiting out the storm.

After raging about propriety and responsibility for close to five minutes, Reynolds whirled away to the suite's wet bar and poured himself a large glass of amber liquor. He sank into a seat of his own, jaw clenched. "Sit, Rob."

The earl sat across from Reynolds, leaning back and crossing an ankle across his opposite knee. He might try to act casual, but Victory did not miss the way his hands fidgeted until they came to rest on his thighs. The tension in his shoulders also showed that he knew this wouldn't be a pleasant conversation.

Reynolds glanced over at Victory and the other men. "Did you three know anything about this?"

"I knew Rob had the crazy notion of marrying the girl," Guy said. "Didn't expect her to beat him to the punch."

"And I don't suppose you thought to talk him out of it?" Reynolds asked.

"I find I'm better at talking him into things," Guy said.

Reynolds took another large sip. "True." He pointed the glass at Rob. "And what about Maria?"

At the sound of the name, Rob deflated and sank back in his seat. "Yeah, that's an issue, I guess."

If Rob thought that was the only issue in this whole mess, Victory had a bridge in Parisii to sell him. "Who's Maria?" she asked.

"His fiancée," Guy said.

Mikelos yelped in laughter. Victory clutched the seat cushion in a desperate attempt not to throttle Rob. "Your *fiancée?*" She bit off the word with a snap of her teeth.

"Sort of?" Rob said. "It's not like I proposed to her. Our families have expected us to marry since she was born. It's more of a financial issue. Something about bank investments and land deals. Nothing to do with love. We're barely acquaintances, and I haven't even seen her for over a year." He was babbling, but he didn't need to justify anything to Victory. "Hell, my family will be happy to break the arrangement if I manage a better match on my own. This qualifies."

The only way this could get any more ridiculous would be if Victory next learned that Rob and Guy had already married each other in a drunken college escapade. She did have one weapon in her arsenal, though.

"This isn't a love match either," Victory said. "You might think you have the innocent girl wooed, but she has a separate agenda as well." She folded her hands in her lap. Rob would learn eventually, so she might as well clue him in now before he got too used to the marriage idea.

Reynolds perked up at this news. "Interesting," he said. "What are you referring to?"

Victory pointed at Rob. "You want to marry Zhinu because you think it will lend legitimacy to the current trade negotiations and enhance your political standing back home in Britannia. Zhinu proposed to you because here in the Qin Empire, her political standing rests in her ability to breed the next generation of weredragons. She wants to continue her education and thinks you'll allow her to enroll at one of the colleges at Oxenafor and maintain a separate household."

She sat back and waited for the outraged declaration to follow. That Rob wouldn't let his wife have such independence. That she would have her own political and social obligations to fulfill as his spouse. Instead, Rob tapped his lips with a finger and said, "Huh. I'm okay with that."

"Brilliant," Guy said. "Let her do what she wants, and you can still live the bachelor lifestyle. Then get her knocked up after she graduates."

Reynolds broke in here. "What if you two aren't even genetically compatible? How are a werewolf and weredragon supposed to produce an heir to the Wallace line?"

"Welcome to the modern world, Ben," Rob said. "If it turns out we can't have kids, the title will pass to any nieces or nephews my little sister has."

"Here's an even scarier thought," Guy said. "What if you do have kids, and it's a dragon?"

"There's little chance that the queen will allow your title to pass to a weredragon," Reynolds said. "If human offspring can't inherit—"

"Those are always illegitimate pairings," Rob said. "And isn't that the point of this? To bring our empires together? Can you imagine the first non-werewolf with a seat in the House of Lords?"

"I can imagine riots in the streets," Reynolds said, muttering into his glass. Clearing his throat, he said, "You're taking advantage of a poor girl's emotional immaturities."

"He's really not, Lord Reynolds," Victory said. "Like I said, she can't be in love with him either. Infatuated with the exotic? Sure. But not in love."

"Don't be preposterous," Rob said. "I've seen the way she looks at me. The girl is smitten."

"I just said that there's a difference," Victory said.

"Of course there is," Rob said. "But Lady Zhinu is just a young lady. Whatever ambitions she has, her love for me is the catalyst."

Victory grit her teeth as Mikelos placed his hand atop hers in a calming gesture. This was not the time to give Rob a lecture on feminism and the full spectrum of emotion possible across every sentient species. "So you're a hundred percent fine with her coming to Britannia and focusing on her own life?"

"Yes!" Rob said. "I support the rights of all women to pursue their own educations and careers." He cocked his head at Victory. "What is her career going to be once she's finished school?"

Good question. "I believe she fancies herself a bit of a historian," Victory said. "Education may be the end goal in itself for her."

"Perfectly acceptable," Rob said. "There's nothing improper about a noblewoman being a lady scholar in her free time. Not all women are content with balls and cocktail parties."

This was it. Victory had run out of plays to make. Even Mikelos appeared to have drawn a blank. Reynolds, however, stared into the distance, and Victory knew gears turned in the diplomat's head. "Lord Reynolds?" Perhaps he had come up with an argument Victory had not yet considered.

Before he could respond, a knock at the door interrupted them. After Guy answered it, he pushed the door wide and invited in Tan. The weredragon entered the suite and bowed to Rob and Reynolds before turning to Victory.

"My apologies for the intrusion," Tan said, his poker face on full display. "Lady Victory, Lord Xian requests the pleasure of your company."

"Right now?" Victory asked.

"At your earliest convenience," Tan said. His façade cracked, and from the pointed look he gave her, her earliest convenience was right now.

So late at night? But a summons was a summons, so Victory bid farewell to the men and followed Tan out of the suite.

She had the feeling her old friend wasn't requesting a social call, and that there would be nothing pleasurable about it.

As Tan escorted Victory to Xian's suite, he kept his hands balled at his sides and his breathing steady. But away from the other men, Victory heard the rapid patter of his heartbeat.

"Tan," she said, lifting a hand to touch his elbow. She didn't try to grab him, but he reacted as if she had by whirling away and raising his fists.

Victory dropped into a defensive pose, and for a tension-filled moment, she wondered whether they were about to come to blows in the middle of the palace hallway.

With a shuddering breath, Tan lowered his hands and drew himself straight. "Do not touch me," he said, voice thick with suppressed emotion. The sudden flush in his cheeks showed his anger as if he screamed it at her. "Do not talk to me."

He turned his back on her and continued down the hallway. What could Victory do but follow?

By the time he left her at the entrance to Xian's rooms, Victory's mind whirled with possible scenarios. Xian knew Victory had not blocked Zhinu's visits to the library. Jinghua had complained about Mikelos residing in her daughter's suite. At this point, the whole palace knew about Zhinu and Rob's burgeoning friendship, but perhaps word of the proposal had already gotten out?

If she'd been human, her heart would have raced. Instead, Victory steeled herself into the perfect image of calm professionalism and knocked.

Kyo-Young allowed Victory inside Xian's suite, but disappeared into one of the back rooms right away. Xian resided behind a desk to one side of the room, but no other chairs sat in front of it. Victory approached at a steady walk, making sure her boot heels made sound across the wooden floor, and presented herself. *"I came as requested, old friend."* She did not bother bowing.

"Are we?" Xian said. *"Friends, I mean."* A chill permeated his words, and he kept his hands placed flat on the empty desk in front of him.

"Yes, Xian," Victory said, keeping her voice steady. *"I still believe we are."*

"The friend I knew, the mercenary Moon, would never have broken the terms of a contract," Xian said. *"Yet I have been led to believe that the Lady Zhinu has developed a relationship with one of the visiting British wolves. I trust you will assure me this is baseless palace gossip, the stories of bored serving maids."* He stared past Victory's left shoulder.

"I wouldn't call it a relationship," Victory said. *"But they have become friendly acquaintances."*

"Friendly acquaintances do not share moments in the garden," Xian said. *"Friendly acquaintances do not make eyes at each other across the dinner hall."*

"You are overstating things," Victory said. That was utter bullshit, of course. Xian was right on the money.

"I am not paying you to allow my granddaughter to be influenced or manipulated by the British." One of Xian's hands drew closed in a fist. *"Please keep that in mind from now on. Good night."* Without another word, he rapped his knuckles on the desk once, and Kyo-Young darted back into the main room and to his side.

Xian ignored Victory, instead directing Kyo-Young to assist him to his room. Victory showed herself out and, once alone in the hallway, sagged against the wall. But the tension in her neck didn't release, and a headache built behind her forehead.

If she wanted to get technical, Xian wasn't paying her at all. The funds for her contract came from Zhinu's trust, at the discretion of Governor Yu, since Xian could not afford her through his stipend alone.

But on the other hand, Xian was the official holder of the contract.

On a third hand, Zhinu was her direct client. And if she was honest with herself, she had bonded much more with the girl than she had expected and found herself genuinely wishing for the girl's happiness. Perhaps she should have done more to reconnect with Xian over the past few weeks, but she had assumed there would be time for that once a routine with Zhinu was established.

Victory set off down the hallway and spent the next few hours roaming the palace grounds, needing space to ponder these developments. This used to be so easy. Do the job, get paid, move on to the next job. But as she stood above a pond and watched the large ornamental koi snatch night insects from the surface of the water, a calm swept through her.

She didn't care about the job this time. She cared about the girl. The girl who reminded her so much of her daughter. The girl who wanted more out of her life than to be a wife and mother, which Victory could not help but admire.

This was all getting muddled. Centuries ago, Asaron was the one she went to with these dilemmas. Though her sire was out of reach, she was fortunate to have someone even better on hand. Mikelos would be an excellent sounding board tomorrow.

Mikelos slipped out of bed and escaped the suite before noon, while Victory still slept, and before Zhinu and the girls returned from their luncheon. With violin case in hand, he meandered through the palace complex, searching various parlors and secluded courtyards until he found a spot both out of the way and already deserted.

Normally, he had no problem with an audience. It had even become a bit of a game for various courtiers to hunt him down and listen to his daily practice sessions. Today, however, he intended to focus on fingering drills and other exercises essential to maintaining his skill level but not so exciting to listen to.

Rob managed to find him anyway within the first twenty minutes. Probably that werewolf nose of his. He entered the intimate parlor with a Qin man dressed in plain homespun robes, and they both took seats as Mikelos transitioned from finger exercises to a popular British ballad.

"Bravo!" Rob applauded with gusto when Mikelos finished with a flourish. His companion stared at Mikelos with luminous orange eyes that should have seemed out of place, but fit the man well.

In fact, something about the way the man lounged in his seat reminded Mikelos of Rob.

"Thanks," Mikelos said. "To what do I owe the pleasure today?"

"I wanted to introduce you to someone," Rob said. "Mikelos Connor, this is Father Hisato."

"A pleasure to make your acquaintance," Mikelos said, bowing to the other man.

Hisato inclined his head in return, and said in halting Loquella, "And… you."

He stared at Mikelos, almost as if trying to intimidate him. But Mikelos lived with two vampires and two teenagers and didn't fear much. Instead, he stared him down until the priest looked away first. Mikelos twirled his violin bow the way Victory limbered up her wrists with blades. Rather than sit in the last remaining seat in the parlor and relinquish his position of dominance, he leaned on the edge of a table and braced his violin on his hip. Power plays were silly, but he still knew how to dance with the best.

"Father Hisato is a member of a religious order with a temple in Jiang Yi Yue proper," Rob said. "Guy stumbled across it during his meanderings the other day and brought me to visit. Father Hisato and I got to talking, and he offered to officiate Zhinu's and my marriage right before it's time for us to leave the city."

"Make it legal here," Hisato said. "To appease family and ancestors."

"Well said," Rob said. "One less obstacle in our way."

"Makes sense," Mikelos said. He wasn't comfortable with encouraging more of this crazy plan until he had a chance to speak with Victory about why she'd met with Xian the night before. He kept his tone innocuous and hoped Rob would interpret it as annoyance at having his practice interrupted.

"We'll be off, then," Rob said. "Please tell Lady Zhinu that I look forward to joining her in the gaming parlor tonight after dinner." He waved to Mikelos and escorted Hisato out the garden entrance.

Hisato glanced back at Mikelos before they disappeared. Mikelos stared after him as they crossed the sunlit courtyard toward a different part of the palace. There was something weird about the guy.

Starting with one important fact: As far as he had been aware, Qin religious officials were all vampires. So where the hell did Rob find this guy?

Victory stepped out of the shower as she heard Mikelos return to their room. She allowed him to kiss her cheek, then batted him out of the way when he ruffled at her damp hair so she could brush and braid it in peace. "Have a good practice?" she asked.

Mikelos stowed his violin case in the wardrobe and perched on the edge of the bed while she dressed. "Practice was good. The surprise visit I had during my practice was more interesting," he said. "How did your meeting with Xian go? I'm sorry I fell asleep before you got back."

"You can't drop a teaser like that and change the topic," Victory said. Hair done, she finished dressing and joined Mikelos on the bed. She leaned against the wall and tucked her bare toes under Mikelos' thigh.

"It's relevant," Mikelos said.

"Okay. It wasn't great." It could have been much worse. "Says he isn't paying me to let Zhinu make friends with the foreigners. The trouble is, he's not the one paying me. And he didn't used to be this paranoid and xenophobic."

"That's a bit harsh," Mikelos said. "Don't say that just to make me feel better."

"Not the reason I said it," Victory said. "But it rings true, based on the way he acted last night. Accused me of not being the person I once was."

"Well, that part is true. Two hundred years have passed since he last saw you. People change. Even immortal people."

"I imagine you're not the same person as you were two hundred years ago, either."

Mikelos laughed. "Two hundred years ago, I was a spoiled snob leaving a trail of broken hearts behind me."

"I bet you were," Victory said. "So what did you have to tell me?"

Mikelos described the supposed priest Rob had appeared with. "Not a vampire, that much is certain. Saw the man in sunlight."

"Definitely a disqualifying feature," Victory said. She combed her memory for what other religious sects Father Hisato could represent, but once again, her information was hundreds of years out of date. "What if he's not a priest at all? Rob doesn't know anything about Qin religions. Someone could be scamming him."

A babble of feminine voices swept through the suite as Zhinu and her handmaids returned from a charity luncheon hosted by Lady Jinghua. Victory lifted one finger. "Hold that thought."

Victory debriefed Zhinu's daytime guard, but Sergeant Soon-ja reported nothing amiss before departing. She and Mikelos waited as the women changed out of their formal robes, and Zhinu, as if sensing their intent, dismissed her ladies for an afternoon stroll about the gardens.

Zhinu settled on one of the chaises and Victory and Mikelos sat side-by-side on the other. "You two look serious today."

"A concern has arisen, lady," Victory said. "Earlier this morning, Rob introduced Mikelos to a priest, and said that he has chosen this man to officiate your wedding before the two of you flee Jiang Yi Yue. However, this man was not a vampire."

Zhinu clapped her hands in delight. "Oh, what a perfect idea! I would never have thought of that."

This had not been the expected response. "I'm sorry?" Victory said.

"He must be a *kitsune*," Zhinu said. "Many people don't approve of them taking vows. Cousin Yu will not allow any of them to lead services in the palace, unfortunately. How lucky of Robert to make contact with the temple in the city."

"A *kitsune*?" Mikelos asked, stumbling over the pronunciation.

"It makes sense," Zhinu said. "And how appropriate. For a long time, they remained secluded in the islands of Nippon. It's only in the past few decades that they have expanded their territories."

Mikelos nudged Victory with an elbow. "What did you think the priest was?"

"Not a member of the political faction against Zhinu's family, that's for sure. He must have managed to con Rob into palace access," Victory said.

"You're all doom and gloom these days," Zhinu said.

"My happiness is not required to keep you safe," Victory said. "And remember, neither is yours."

A flash of hurt crossed Zhinu's face, and she folded her arms.

"That was a bit harsh," Mikelos said. "You know how to take care of an entire person's well-being. You did a pretty good job with Toria."

"Toria also had you," Victory said. "And Kane, and the rest of our extended family."

In a low voice, Zhinu said, "Well, right now all I have is you."

That couldn't be right. "What?"

"Technically, An and Yi-Ting and the others are my servants, paid to ensure my happiness," Zhinu said. She pulled in her legs and wrapped her arms around her knees. "You've been here almost a month. You can count on one hand how many times I've seen my mother. And all of those have been as a decorative object at some function she's hosted, like the lunch today."

"What about that first lunch here in the suite?" Victory asked.

"She wanted to get a good look at you, which is why I insisted you join us," Zhinu said. "I know you didn't want to, but it seemed like the easiest way to appease her curiosity and get her to back off." She picked at her nails, then continued, "I know you think I'm being stupid these days, but I'm not an idiot. I'm just a womb to my family. Why do you think I'm willing to risk so much for the chance at something more?" A tear streamed down her cheek.

Mikelos entwined his fingers with Victory's and squeezed. She squeezed back.

Damn it. She'd already raised one daughter to be a young woman capable of thriving on her own.

Now a second had crept her way into Victory's heart.

Victory trailed Rob and Zhinu as they left the large room of the palace where people gathered to play tile and card games. She'd allowed Rob to rope her into partnering him for one of the tile games that gambled with small change, then shocked him by raking in a tidy sum. Zhinu had partnered with Reynolds, amusing herself with teaching the British men how to play and updating Victory on rules that had evolved since the last time she had tried her hand at the game.

Reynolds called it a night, reminding Rob of an early meeting the next morning with representatives of some of the city's trade guilds. Rob offered to escort Zhinu back to her suite, ever gallant, and it would have been rude of the young woman to turn him down.

All attention in the room was on the three as they left. Victory placed mental odds on how long the gossip would take to get back to Xian, with double or nothing on whether she would be summoned to his rooms for another lecture on contract terms.

She tuned out Rob and Zhinu's whispered conversation ahead of her and dropped into a particular mental state. Senses open, attuned to the environment around her, with a broad focus that still allowed a portion of her brain to mull over a different issue. She needed to read her copy of the contract again and figure out negotiation tactics. She didn't want to break the contract, but Mikelos had been right. She wasn't a true mercenary anymore, and on the off-chance that they did return to this life for real again, she wouldn't need long to work off the breach penalties and return to her former status.

She heard two sets of familiar laughter before they turned the final corner to the hallway that housed Zhinu's rooms. As much as she thought Guy an immature idiot, he was one of the few people here in Jiang Yi Yue who Mikelos could call a friend, and it pleased her that no issues had lingered after the brawl the night of the performance. In a way, they had all united in the common cause of supporting Zhinu and Rob, attempting to keep the would-be lovers from doing irreversible damage, whether political or social.

When they turned the corner, Guy and Mikelos stood laughing with an unfamiliar Qin man Victory had never seen before. His robes were plain cotton, not common in the palace during the evening hours, but not the dress of a servant. As they drew closer, Victory noticed his bright eyes, the color of a freshly minted copper coin, and her nose picked up a wild scent that contrasted with Rob's wolfish aura.

This must be the *kitsune* priest. She touched Zhinu's arm and drew her to Victory's side as Rob approached the gathered men. Zhinu stayed back, though her own face danced with excitement to meet the unfamiliar priest.

"Hisato!" Rob called out as they approached. He extended a hand, as if out of habit, but pulled it back to instead exchange bows with the priest. "Thanks for coming tonight!" He half-turned to Zhinu and gestured her closer. "I'd like you to meet the Lady Zhuanxu Zhinu, my fiancée. Zhinu, this is Father Hisato, of the Shirubafokkusu Monastery." He stumbled over the pronunciation, but the priest nodded with approval at the effort.

Mikelos coughed. "Let's move this inside, shall we?"

Victory braced herself, but motioned Zhinu to approach. The young woman darted forward and bowed low to the priest. *"It is an honor to meet you, Father Hisato. Please, join us for evening tea."*

Mikelos slid open the door to the suite, and Victory hung back as everyone filed in. Zhinu babbled questions to Hisato in a steady stream of Qin while Rob smiled in indulgence, a pleased expression on his face. Victory made a final visual sweep of the hallway. She blinked as a shadow beneath one of the hall's wall sconces seemed to elongate and then snap back into place. But when she looked again, she caught a flash of black silk disappear around the corner. That made much more sense than twisting shadows.

She dashed down the corridor and swept around the corner to see a familiar profile vanish through a garden entrance farther away. Tan had been the one lurking around the bend.

For a split second, she considered chasing him. But as a weredragon, he could match her speed. And tracking someone would be difficult in the floral-scented gardens that saw the passage of dozens of people a day.

With a heavy heart, she returned to Zhinu's suite and shut the door behind her.

Rob, Guy, and Hisato gathered around the low table as Zhinu and Mikelos prepared tea and evening desserts. Victory stretched her hearing, relieved to find none of the handmaids in the suite. At first, she had been concerned when Zhinu had allowed them more freedom in the evenings in order to spend private time with Rob, but it was to their advantage tonight—though she knew Zhinu was smart enough not to invite so many men into her rooms otherwise.

Mikelos acknowledged her first, as if sensing her worry. "What's wrong, love?"

"We might have a problem," she said. "Tan overheard the conversation in the hallway. Which might include Rob calling Lady Zhinu his fiancée."

"And Tan speaks Loquella," Guy said. "Bollocks."

The room descended into tense silence as dismay crossed each face. Except one.

"Is no problem," Hisato said. He kept his hands folded before him in the sleeves of his robes. Victory wasn't sure how to describe the peculiar expression on his face—part amusement, part expectation. The lamplight glinted in his bright eyes, coloring them gold.

"We should leave, just in case," Rob said. He touched Zhinu's cheek. "Sweet dreams, my love."

Zhinu bowed her head, and a delicate blushed colored her cheeks. "And you."

The other men left, and for lack of anything better to do, Mikelos finished the tea and served Victory and Zhinu. Victory sipped the smooth green tea and warmed both hands around the cup. Her usual habit was to disarm within the suite, but tonight, the weight of her hand-and-a-half sword was comforting on her hip.

"I am not well-versed in the ways of other cultures the way you two are," Zhinu said, "but something was off about what Father Hisato said before they left."

"There's something off about Father Hisato, full stop," Mikelos said. "And not because I've never met a werefox before." He drained the rest of his tea and placed the cup on the table with a low *thunk*. "He tried one of those dominance tricks werecreatures like so much with me when I met him earlier today. Your pardon, Lady Zhinu."

"No offense taken," she said. "The weredragons are much too civilized to resort to such childish tactics."

"Rob is solidly alpha," Victory said. "He's not about to let someone else jerk him around. Especially not an animal a wolf would view as prey."

"But the *kitsune* are known to have other tricks," Zhinu said. "Not much is known about the culture, and it is said they are not a genetic offshoot the way the wolves and other mammal werecreatures are. Legend says they are touched by the gods the same as the weredragons." She sniffed once. "Well, not quite the same."

"So there might be something else going on there," Victory said. "Mikelos?"

"Yep," he said. "I'll snag Rob in the morning and speak to him."

"Thank you." Victory placed her cup back on the tray to be collected in the morning by the housekeepers who serviced the suite. "Hopefully Tan doesn't make all hell break loose first."

Act III

Guy let Mikelos into their palace suite the next morning. "Thank hell you're here."

Mikelos followed him into the room and handed over the extra pastry he'd snagged on his way through the main hall. "What's wrong?"

Spraying crumbs through a bite, Guy said, "Rob wants to run away with Zhinu and get married tonight before the treaties can be signed."

"That's a terrible idea!" Mikelos said. "How far away are they from finalizing everything?"

"Old Ben says two or three days at most," Guy said. "There's going to be another ball to celebrate. I'm trying to convince him that stealing away during the chaos of the ball is the best bet, but he won't hear of it."

"Where is he now?" Mikelos asked. He set his unfinished stuffed roll on a side table, appetite vanished.

The door to the suite slammed open, and Mikelos whirled around as Guy reached for a sword that did not hang at his side. Tan stood in the entrance, anger burning in his gaze.

Mikelos' stomach sank. Instead of his usual impeccable robes or silk suits, Tan wore simple drawstring pants, with feet and chest bare.

The weredragon's fists clenched at his sides. "A good question," Tan said. Despite his obvious ferocity, he kept his voice steady. "Where is Earl Wallace?"

"I'm right here, boys," Rob said from behind them. Mikelos glanced back over his shoulder and saw the earl emerge from his private room as he pulled a T-shirt over a pair of ragged jeans. Though he acted jovial, Mikelos saw the pointed look on Rob's face that told him the man had heard every word.

Rob padded across the suite on his own set of bare feet and faced Tan. With another intentional step, forcing his way into the weredragon's personal space, he said, "Do you have a problem you wish to speak with me about, sir?"

"Confronting you last night in the presence of the ladies would have been inappropriate." Tan did not back away from Rob as he stared up at Rob's greater height. "And the ancestors counsel us not to act on our anger."

"You seem pretty damn angry at the moment," Guy said. He also stood with legs wide and arms held out, as if bracing for something.

Mikelos had the sudden urge to back away. And leave the room. And the building.

"I bring complaint against Earl Robert Wallace for his familiar treatment with Lady Zhuanxu Zhinu," Tan said. "You are not worthy of a woman of her standing."

Rob snorted. "And I suppose you think you are instead?"

Tan did not take the bait. "Though my blood ran pure, I am the product of an unapproved match," he said. "The Lady Zhinu deserves to bear sons who will have proper places as rulers amongst the Qin people. Not halfbreed mongrels."

Mikelos had wondered why Tan was not much more than a servant instead of a figure with real political power. According to conversations he and Victory had had with Zhinu over the past week, the ruling weredragons still operated under a stricter class system, despite the meritocracy that dictated the upward mobility of the Qin Empire's human inhabitants.

Rob didn't flinch at the insult, though his voice grew icy. "I will have you know, sir, that I can trace my family back to the original gathering of the clans to force the Romans from Albion. My blood is as pure as yours."

"You parade around as if you are our equals, but you are no more than animals," Tan said.

He and Rob stood nose to nose, shoulders thrown back and fists tight at their sides. Mikelos stepped back from the proceedings, putting the table between himself and the two werecreatures. But Guy approached, parking himself right behind Rob's left shoulder.

People might dismiss Guy as a sycophant, grasping at the favors of Rob's prestige, but in this moment, Mikelos saw him as a true friend to his earl. He had already earned a knighthood for protecting Rob once, and man didn't hesitate to support the nobleman again.

"I will not fight you for the lady's honor," Rob said. "Because we should be beyond this conflict. I don't remember the Last War, but I know I have spent the last few weeks working with your people to prevent another. I believe marrying Lady Zhinu will cement our alliance and bring our peoples from uneasy truce to lasting peace."

"I don't remember the Last War, either," Tan said. "But I know a whole pack of wolves is no match for one dragon."

One of Tan's hands flashed out, and by the time it wrapped around Rob's neck, his dark green nails had elongated into emerald talons. Before he could squeeze, Guy forced his way into Rob's place and knocked the other man aside.

As Tan swiped his other hand low, the knife-blade talons scraped across Guy's stomach instead of Rob's. Guy clutched his abdomen and doubled over with a scream as blood seeped between his fingers. With a snarl of rage, Rob dropped to all fours. His body rippled.

Mikelos had seen werewolves shift before and averted his eyes. But that did not shield him from the sounds of bones breaking and reforming, the snap of tendons, the growl of pain. When Mikelos looked back, Rob kicked out of his ripped clothing and stood over Guy's body and snarled. His tawny fur was a shade darker than his hair, with golden highlights at the snout and paws.

But this time, Mikelos' attention was caught by Tan. Back in Fort Caroline, he had shifted from dragon form to human as if hidden behind a shadowy magical mirage. The effect was just as startling the other way. Tan's entire body shimmered once. Then, without a trace of ruined clothing, a sinuous reptilian form stood before Rob, opened a mouth with fangs the size of daggers, and screamed.

Mikelos wanted to run to Guy and help the young man curled in a fetal position, staining the wooden floor beneath him with blood. But he lay between the wolf and dragon who circled warily.

Tan darted his long neck forward and lunged for Guy's prone form, but Rob dashed between them, snapping his teeth at Tan's tender nose. He stalked back and forth, not giving Tan an opening to finish the job.

Instead of backing off, Tan dove again—this time, for Rob's flank. The werewolf twisted and lashed out with a front paw, catching Tan's neck. Claws dragged down scales with a metallic shriek.

Mikelos would not have been surprised to see literal sparks fly. But now Guy lay behind them, so Mikelos darted in to grab the man's shirt and pull him away. He rolled Guy on his back and went light-headed at the scent that hit his nose like a punch—the distinctive sickening smell of guts that meant breached stomach or intestines. If Guy didn't get help soon, he was in danger of a painful death.

The sound of splintered wood echoed through the room as Tan and Rob rolled through the suite. They traded swipes, dodging each other and slamming into furniture. Tan's reach was longer, but Rob was more dexterous. He jumped back and twisted his body away as Tan screamed again, missing his shot at Rob's neck.

A howl echoed through the suite, and another wolf slid around a corner and into the room. The large grey wolf's nails scrabbled for purchase on the slick wooden floor, and he launched himself onto Tan's back before the dragon could whirl to face his new opponent. With jaws that could snap the neck of an elk, the second wolf clamped right above Tan's shoulder blades.

Where wolf claws found no purchase on dragon scales, teeth sank deep. Tan reared back on his hind legs and tried to heave off the wolf. But he left his front open, and with a high lunge, Rob fastened his own jaws around Tan's throat. After a single mighty shake, Rob ripped his mouth away. Blood and scales sprayed the room.

Tan tried to scream again, but a painful gurgle emerged from his ragged throat instead. He lashed out at Rob a final time as the energy drained from his other three legs and the weredragon collapsed under Ben's weight.

Ben held on tight with his jaws for another heartbeat. After a final *snap* echoed through the room, he stepped off the still body.

Rob didn't stick around to ensure Tan's death. As Mikelos pressed his hands over Guy's leaking stomach, the younger werewolf paced next to them, whining low in his throat.

"You have to get help," Mikelos said. Guy had sunk into unconsciousness, and Mikelos didn't like the gray cast to his face, or his bloodless lips.

With a single bound, Rob headed for the suite entrance, only to be forced back as palace guards spilled into the room, wielding swords or pistols. Captain Huang stormed in and absorbed the scene with a sweeping look. He narrowed in on Mikelos and snapped a question in Qin.

Mikelos kept his hands pressed to Guy's stomach. "I'm sorry, I don't know. Please send help for this man."

The wolves allowed the guards to crowd them into a corner. Rob's attention was still on Guy, and he emitted a low whine. In contrast, Ben's focus darted from guard to guard, and he was poised as if to lunge at any moment.

Huang snapped a series of orders, and while one guard left the suite at a run, two others sheathed their weapons in order to assist Mikelos. He backed away and allowed the guards to take over. When he stood, he tried to ignore the blood soaking the front of his shirt and the knees of his pants.

In slow Loquella, Huang said, "What happens here?"

It wasn't only Rob and Ben's lives at stake, but all the work they had done in the past few weeks. No one else had to know about Rob and Zhinu's ill-fated plan. As the only one with a voice, no one could argue with Mikelos' version of events. He took advantage of that, and the words poured out. "Tan and Earl Wallace had a disagreement that escalated. Sir Olivier was caught in the crossfire when Tan attacked, and Lord Reynolds—"

With a cutting motion, Huang motioned Mikelos into silence. "Too fast."

"It was self-defense," Mikelos said, raising his bloody hands.

"Quiet," Huang said. "Come."

Mikelos allowed himself to be escorted from the suite with the werewolves. When Rob tried to stand his ground to stay with his friend, Ben snapped at his ear. A trio dressed in medical garb rushed past them into the suite, but over his shoulder, Mikelos saw one of the guards already shaking his head.

They left the shambles of the suite behind them. The wolves had to be able to hear with their sensitive ears what Mikelos already knew. Guy was dead.

The entire court was in an uproar. Victory had been awakened by the distant dragon screams and wolf cries too early in the morning. Mikelos was nowhere to be found, but right after Victory was about to use the servant passages to search for him, Xian sent word that Zhinu was confined to her suite until further notice. When Zhinu's daytime bodyguard never arrived, Victory had no choice but to stay with her.

Her mind raced. She wondered if there had been an attack, either on the palace or against the British delegates.

Mikelos had planned to visit Rob that morning. Had her daywalker been caught in the crossfire?

A tense few hours passed while An tried to distract Zhinu and Victory with card games. Yi-Ting even offered to go in search of Mikelos. As morning shifted to noon, and then to afternoon, Victory's nerves drew tighter. A brief interrogation of the servant who brought luncheon told her none of the meetings with the British had occurred that morning. Xian had been cloistered with Governor Yu and Captain Huang since a mysterious ruckus involving the palace guards a few hours ago.

Victory dismissed the nervous man and resumed pacing the suite. Zhinu perched on a chaise, but she hadn't turned a page in her book in over ten minutes. The two handmaids played a quiet game of cards at the table, but An jumped up when a harsh rap sounded at the door.

Victory beat her to the door and held the girl back as she slid the panel open, one hand ready to draw her weapon. Sergeant Soon-ja bowed low. *"I am here to escort you and Lady Zhinu to Governor Yu."*

"What's going on?" Victory asked, not backing away. *"Where is Mikelos Connor?"*

Soon-ja had now known Mikelos for weeks, and despite the language barrier, they had become fast friends. Today, however, her face remained stony. *"Come with me, please."*

Zhinu brushed past Victory and out into the hallway. *"Let's get this over with."*

Sergeant Soon-ja led them through the back passages of the palace, away from sunlight. Servants watched them pass, whispering behind hands and robe sleeves. But Victory wasn't sure whether the whispers were directed at her or Zhinu, and the worry was driving her up the wall. Each time she found her hand resting on the sword hilt, she moved it away, but it always found its way back. She didn't want to approach the governor on the offensive, but she had to know what was going on.

And where the hell was Mikelos?

Victory followed Zhinu into a small receiving room. The décor was grander than anything else she had seen in the palace so far, and the seat in which Governor Yu reclined could have doubled as a throne. Precious stones sparkled against the black lacquer, and silver thread glinted in the embroidered drapes covering the windows.

But the wall of scent that hit Victory as she entered the room distracted her from the display of ostentatious wealth. Werewolf musk and old blood. After a quick scan of the entire room for any threats to Zhinu—Governor Yu, Xian, and Captain Huang included—she zeroed in on the figures to the side.

Mikelos was between Rob and Reynolds, and the three men stood behind a phalanx of palace guards. The two British men wore simple Qin garments of plain cotton, but her daywalker wore his own familiar clothing. Dried blood covered his front.

Victory forced herself to take a deep breath and exhale, examing the full scent, before she jumped to any conclusions. The blood was at least a few hours old. Human. It did not belong to Mikelos.

Zhinu had stopped to gape at the apparent prisoners, so Victory took the lead. After a curt bow to the governor, she asked, *"What is the meaning of this?"*

"We shall speak Loquella, for the convenience of our guests," Yu said, inclining his head toward the men under guard. "There was an incident this morning."

"Why are these men being held prisoner?" Victory asked.

"It is for their protection." Yu gestured, and the guards broke apart. Mikelos grabbed Rob's arm and pulled him to Victory's side. Reynolds followed at a slower pace. Both of the werewolves had bare feet, adding to the evidence that they had been taken into custody while in wolf form and provided clothing after they shifted back.

Mikelos tapped Victory's wrist twice with the side of his pinky finger. He was fine, physically. Any other communication between them would have to wait.

But she didn't like the way Rob's eyes were dull, and she didn't miss the muscle jumping in Reynolds' cheek as he grit his teeth.

"Tan and Sir Guy Olivier are dead," Yu continued. Zhinu gasped, and only years of experience allowed Victory to keep her face inexpressive. "We believe Tan was an undercover representative of a political faction who does not approve of increased relations with the British Empire. He attempted to assassinate Earl Wallace, and Sir Olivier perished protecting his master."

Except Victory could tell Yu was lying. Anger laced his voice, but it was directed at Rob, which didn't make sense. Yu should have fallen over himself with apologies for the failure in his security, for not protecting his guests. Rob and Reynolds should have been garbed according to their station, not provided clothing that looked like servants wore it to perform the most menial tasks. And Mikelos should have been allowed to change, at the very least.

She held her own counsel, waiting.

"Since the safety of our guests can no longer be assured here," Yu said, "they will move to their rented house in the city until such time as they can travel home. Mr. Connor will return to his rooms here in the palace."

Yu stood and left the room through a back entrance, leading Xian by the elbow. Her old friend had not given any outward indication the entire meeting, but he had always had an excellent game face.

Captain Huang approached their small cluster. *"I will escort Wallace and Reynolds out of the palace while my sergeant accompanies you back to your rooms, Lady Zhinu,"* he said.

"You will address Earl Wallace and Lord Reynolds by their proper titles," Zhinu said as she faced off against the captain. *"And the only escort I need is my faithful bodyguard, the Lady Moon."*

He pursed his lips together, but made no argument.

Mikelos touched Rob's shoulder, and after a short delay, the young man gave Mikelos his attention. "It's going to be okay," Mikelos said. "I'll come as soon as I can."

"It's too dangerous," Reynolds said.

Huang cut off their conversation. "We leave now." Backed by his guards, the two British men had no choice but to accompany the captain, leaving Victory alone in the room with Mikelos and Zhinu.

Victory grabbed Mikelos' hand. "What the hell is going on?"

"Not here," Mikelos said. "Let's get back. I need to get out of these clothes." He stalked out of the room.

Tears welled in the corners of Zhinu's eyes. When Victory touched her arm, she visibly pulled herself together. They followed Mikelos back to her suite.

Ignoring the gasps from the handmaids, Mikelos stripped off his ruined shirt the moment he entered Zhinu's suite. Once in the privacy of their own room, he kicked off his pants and boxers and aimed straight for the bathroom. Victory turned on the shower, and Mikelos entered the stall without even waiting for the water to warm.

Using the cover of the running water, Victory said, "I know what happened back there isn't the whole story. Where were you all day?"

"Getting grilled by Huang and his minions," Mikelos said, lathering a cloth with soap and scrubbing it over his arms. The blood had soaked through the sleeves and stained his skin. At some point earlier in the day he must have been allowed to wash his hands, but blood caked his nails as well. "They didn't believe me when I said we were attacked by Tan."

Victory reeled as if struck. "Rob attacked first?"

"No, no," Mikelos said. "He was defending himself. Tan did overhear Rob call Zhinu his fiancée last night. But instead of going to the governor, he decided to confront Rob himself first. Guy got in the way when Tan attacked, and it took both Rob and Reynolds to overcome Tan in his weredragon form."

"So I wasn't imagining the howls this morning," Victory said.

Mikelos sagged back against the tile wall, letting the water wash over him. "Gut wound. Guy bled out under my hands."

Ignoring the water, Victory touched Mikelos' cheek. "I'm so sorry, love."

"By the time the guards arrived, Tan was dead, Guy was dead, the other two were in wolf form. I did some quick talking and spun the story about Tan being one of the terrorists." He smacked his hand against the tile and a wet slap echoed in the bathroom. "Dammit, I liked him. I hate sullying his name like that."

"You're protecting the living," Victory said. She leaned against the opposite wall in the small bathroom and toyed with the brush she'd left on the sink that morning.

"For what?" Mikelos dumped shampoo into his hand. "For two idiots who think getting married against the wishes of everyone around them is a good idea? We've all been fools."

"At least this explains why the Brits have been banished from the palace," Victory said. "I'd have expected the opposite reaction if the governor thought the attack had been legitimate." She almost cracked her brush by squeezing it too hard. "How were they interrogating you?"

Even over the running water, Mikelos heard the growl in her voice. "Just questioning me. Trying to rip apart my story. Don't worry."

"I'll always worry," Victory said. She set her brush down before she did it permanent harm. "If Rob and the others are being sent away as soon as possible, I guess this means all the work on the treaties is for naught."

Mikelos finished rinsing his hair and shut off the water. "That's a price I'll pay if it keeps you all alive."

Victory handed him a towel. "Me, too."

Victory left their room while Mikelos finished dressing in clean clothing. She found the rest of the suite deserted. No Zhinu, no handmaids. She suppressed her immediate panic and listened instead. One other heartbeat besides Mikelos', accompanied by frantic footsteps and the rustle of clothing.

She pulled open the door to Zhinu's room and saw the girl tossing various articles of clothing on her bed. An open bag sat next to the pile, already half full with books and the antique jewelry box that had held a place of honor on Zhinu's nightstand. Victory knew what was going on, but asked anyway, in the gentlest tone possible. "What are you doing, hon?"

"I sent the girls away," Zhinu said. "It's not safe here anymore. And I'm packing to leave with Robert. I know some ways out of the palace."

Mikelos stuck his head over Victory's shoulder and also saw the whirlwind Zhinu had made of her room. "Good, you can tell me about those ways so I can go see them."

"I'm coming with you," Zhinu said. She rolled up a silk overgown and shoved it into the bag.

"No, you're not," Victory said.

"I can take a message for you if you want," Mikelos said. "But Victory's right. You need to stay here."

"You're not even taking a message," Victory said. "This whole situation is out of control."

"I need to make sure Rob is okay—"

"People are *dead*." Victory raised her voice, and Zhinu stopped in her tracks, clutching a pair of slippers to her chest. Even Mikelos backed away a step. Victory prayed for sanity. "I'm not risking either of you."

"But the danger has passed," Mikelos said. His voice was quiet now, as if to counter Victory's outburst. "Tan was the only one who knew what was going on."

"But Xian and the governor know there's more to the story," Victory said. "And they will be watching us that much closer. They didn't buy the 'Tan as terrorist' story, otherwise they would have kept Rob and the others in the palace with extra security, not sent them into the city with no protection at all."

"I'm going to check on my friend," Mikelos said. "Whose side are you on right now?"

She could have smacked him, but would never raise her hand against him in anger. Mostly Victory wanted to shake sense into all of them. "I am on the side of protecting both of you. I'm sorry, Lady Zhinu, but this whole thing has failed. You won't get to run away and live happily ever after."

If Mikelos' jaw tightened any further, his teeth might crack.

"I guess you're in charge, *Moon*." He all but spat the name at her. He turned around and stalked back into their room, slamming the door closed.

Zhinu compared two robes and discarded one in a pile on the floor. She refused to acknowledge Victory.

Victory left Zhinu to her self-imposed task. If it made her feel better to be active, Victory wasn't about to rip the clothes from her hands and put them away. She backed out of Zhinu's room and put the kettle on. Tempers were high, and tea would soothe them both.

As she set out cups, Mikelos burst from their room and ran across the suite. He pulled on a battered jacket as he darted across the floor. Before Victory could ask what the rush was, he flicked away the drapes covering the garden patio doors, pulled aside the door for enough room to slip through, and disappeared into the daylight.

Victory froze in her corner of the suite until the curtain settled and bits of sunlight stopped sparkling across the room.

"Damn it."

Escaping the palace was easier than Mikelos had anticipated, which should be worrisome. On the other hand, the security was designed to keep people out, not in. He slipped through the servant passages until he made it to the garages. As he'd expected, the lower echelons of the British delegates and their belongings were still being packed and loaded into trucks to be moved to the house in Jiang Yi Yue proper.

Mikelos strolled over to Adam, who supervised two Qin stewards hoisting trunks into the back of a truck. "Hey," he said.

The man jerked in surprise. "I don't suppose you have any idea why everything has been called off like this?"

"I know a bit," Mikelos said, wondering how much he should hedge. "Mind if I catch a ride out of here with you?"

"Not sure I could stop you," Adam said. He thanked the stewards in Qin before gesturing for Mikelos to follow him to the cab of the truck.

Mikelos piled in next to Adam and the driver, and they were off. No one searched the truck, and the palace gates stood open at the bottom of the mountain where daily traffic continued uninterrupted. More evidence that Yu and Xian did indeed know his spun story had been a farce, even if they didn't have any way to negate it.

When the truck arrived in front of the rented house, Mikelos jumped out with a shout of thanks over his shoulder and headed inside. He ran into Lord Reynolds at the entrance.

"What are you doing here?" Reynolds grabbed his arm and pulled him into the cloak room inside the front doors. "How did you even manage to get here?"

"Hitched a ride from the palace," Mikelos said. "I came to see how Rob is doing."

Reynolds ran a hand through his mussed gray hair. He'd found time to change, but his suit was wrinkled and he wore no tie. "Not well, I'm afraid. He won't talk to anyone except that damn priest."

"Hisato is here?"

"They're shut up in one of the back rooms. Rob told me to supervise the move from this end and make sure we had all our people and at least most of our things."

"I'll go check on them," Mikelos said. Reynolds slapped his shoulder and exited the front door, calling for Adam.

Mikelos crossed the courtyard, avoiding the spot where Guy had arranged for the amazing seafood dinner, and hunted through the back rooms. He didn't have Victory's enhanced senses, but he had patience. He explored each room, greeting the members of the British delegation as he came across them. Half of them were trying to settle into the house while the other half were packing things to leave the city, and he hoped Reynolds set them straight soon.

In the back of the house, he found an island of peace. Without bothering to knock, he slid open the door to what must have been the master suite. Rob sat on the edge of the bed, his head bowed, still wearing the ragged Qin clothing. Hisato kneeled on the floor in front of him and broke off whatever he had been saying to glance at Mikelos. His face darkened.

Rob glanced over as well, but seemed happier to see Mikelos than the werefox did as he pressed his palm to his heart. "I'm glad to see you."

Mikelos chose to accept that as an invitation. He entered the suite and closed the door behind him. Ignoring Hisato, Mikelos perched on the bed next to Rob and gripped his shoulder. "How are you?"

"What's going on at the palace? Is Zhinu alright?" The gleam in Rob's eyes was almost manic.

Not missing the fact that Rob hadn't answered his question, Mikelos said, "Zhinu is fine. She sends her love."

Rob tilted his head back and looked every bit the inexperienced young man he was. "I don't know what to do anymore, Mikelos."

Mikelos knew the pain of losing his best friend all too well. He wasn't about to dismiss Rob and Guy's handful of years compared to the two centuries he had spent with Connor.

But Hisato spoke before Mikelos could respond. "Need to leave city. Soon. Without lady."

"But you were in favor of this marriage," Mikelos said.

Hisato gave an expressive shrug. "Plans fall apart."

Rob's laugh was devoid of humor. "Whereas Ben wants us to stay and try to salvage what we can of the treaties. I have no idea how we're supposed to do that when it was made clear Governor Yu no longer wanted anything do with us." He rose from the bed and stood at a large window overlooking another section of the courtyard. After a few seconds of staring out at the intricate landscape of shrubs and flowerbeds interspersed with winding paths, he said, "I've fucked things up, haven't I? My grand plan to bring together the nations has ruined everything instead."

"You couldn't have known Tan would overhear us," Mikelos said. He rose from the bed and meandered around the room, examining the delicate orchid set on a plinth in the wall. He wanted to give Rob space, but also show his friend that he was there if needed.

"I got lazy," Rob said. "And stupid."

"Watching me," Hisato said, pushing himself to his feet in one lithe movement. "Not you."

Mikelos and Rob whirled on him. "What?" Rob said, with a hint of snarl.

Hisato spread his arms. "Am *kitsune*. Lower than mighty dragons. Not trusted." He bowed low to Rob. "Should not have been in palace."

Biting off a growl, Rob said, "So why the hell did you risk it? Straighten up, man."

He rose with care. "See how other side lives?" Hisato kept his gaze downcast. "Find weaknesses in palace."

A growing fear dawned over Mikelos. "You're one of them," he said. "The separatists. Did you ever have any interest in helping Rob and Zhinu? Or was it all a ploy?"

"Path for all things," Hisato said. "Openings and secrets."

"That doesn't even make any sense," Rob said. He flexed and fisted his hands at his sides, but though the anger rolled off him in waves, Mikelos didn't think he was in danger of shifting. "Get out. Now."

Before Mikelos could interject, Hisato bowed low once more and swept from the room, robes billowing behind him. "We could have used him," Mikelos said. "Gotten more information."

"Information about what?" Rob said. "I no longer care what happens to the Qin Empire. As far as I'm concerned, Hisato's side won. I'll send Ben to the docks to arrange passage home as soon as possible."

Mikelos hadn't been sure what he had expected to accomplish when he came to find Rob, but watching the destruction of all Rob and Reynolds had worked for over the past few weeks wasn't it. "It's hard to think this was all for nothing. I have to admit I got a bit invested."

"In the treaties?" Rob asked. "This wasn't an epic ceasefire. It was basic tradescraft. We didn't even get everything we wanted, because Governor Yu missed the memo that this was a first step, not the be all and end all of goods exchanged between the Brits and the Qin."

Mikelos dreaded this necessary next step, but the words had to be said. "I don't trust Hisato. I was surprised to find him here, and he's more involved than he needs to be."

"Of course you feel that way," Rob said. "Your lady has always been in deep with the dragons. I'm sure she had her fill of fighting the *kitsune* during the years she spent with Lord Xian and the other Qin royals."

A laugh escaped Mikelos before he could stop it. "You think this is a racial thing? That's precious, coming from a scion of British royalty as yourself. I'm surprised you manage to be civil to me and Victory, considering the current views on vampires in your homeland."

"Oh, please." Rob flapped his hand in dismissal. "Those policies are the remnants of institutionalized racism. My peers and I will do away with those laws as soon as our generation achieves majority status in parliament. It's only a matter of time."

Mikelos liked Rob, he really did. The kid was smart, if at times too smart for his own good. But he always had a glib response to everything, and right now, Mikelos didn't have the time or energy to argue semantics with him. Rob was set in his position, and if he wanted to believe Mikelos was prejudiced against the werefox priest because of Victory's tangled history with Xian, that wasn't a debate worth having right now.

The sun had dipped low in the courtyard, dimming the room. "I have to get back soon," Mikelos said. "I know Victory is waiting to come after me as soon as she's able. She must be furious."

"I'm coming with you," Rob said, as if he hadn't recently accused Mikelos of abject racism. "I owe Zhinu an apology."

"How the hell do you expect to get close enough to her to do that?"

Rob encompassed his thin cotton tunic and pants with one wave of his hand. "I'm already dressed for the occasion. Just get me inside the palace walls." He pulled a fresh set of clothing from a trunk next to the door and bundled it into a cloth bag that he shoved into Mikelos' arms. "Keep these for me, will you? Not sure the princess will appreciate an apology on all fours."

"This is a terrible idea," Mikelos said, mostly to himself, as he followed Rob through the house. With sudden clarity, he imagined how Victory must feel. Time to ratchet up the quality of his upcoming apology.

Rob pulled aside one of his aides to pass along his instructions for Ben. They avoided Lord Reynolds himself, who must have been elsewhere in the sprawling house. And they were in luck—one of the palace trucks still idled out front as a steward carried a final load inside. Mikelos and Rob jumped into the back and pulled the doors closed after them. They sat against opposite sidewalls, peering through the dim light that entered through the wooden slats.

Unbidden, a stir of excitement flashed through Mikelos. This was still a terrible idea, but at some point, the nontraditional love story between British earl and Qin princess had passed from the illogical to the dramatic. The composer in him already played with melodies in his head, assigning instruments to represent Rob's idealism, Zhinu's longing for a better future.

Huddled across from him, Rob's jaw was set and he stared ahead without seeing the other side of the truck.

The summons came within moments after Mikelos' dramatic disappearance. Victory's chest tightened when Captain Huang entered the suite without permission, and she wondered whether this was what an anxiety attack felt like.

Her hand clutched so tight on the hilt of her sword that her fingers must be blue. Mikelos had been captured, his lies had been revealed—

Captain Huang bowed to her, a shallow nod that almost didn't merit the term. *"I am here to escort Lady Zhinu to a meeting with Lord Zhuanxu Xian. The presence of her bodyguard is not required while she is under my care."*

Zhinu emerged, robes immaculate and not a hair out of place, as if the bedroom she left didn't look like it had been struck by a tornado. *"Thank you, captain,"* she said. *"But in the absence of my handmaids, it would be inappropriate for you to escort me alone. Lady Moon will accompany me."*

Huang did not appear pleased by this turn of events, but court customs trumped whatever desire he had to keep Victory away from this meeting. He bowed once to Zhinu, much lower this time. After she closed the door to her bedroom, Zhinu motioned for Victory to follow her out of the suite.

They traveled through the palace in silence. Zhinu led the way with her head held high, and Victory pretended not to notice the glares Huang shot her way. She kept her face impassive, wrapping herself in cool professionalism.

Kyo-Young waited outside Xian's suite and let them in at once. As before, Xian sat behind his imposing desk. His aide whispered into his ear, but Victory's senses heard the words as if they had been spoken at a normal volume. *"Zhinu and the captain are here. The vampire came with them."*

Xian gave a sharp nod, once. Kyo-Young moved to the back of the room, keeping her gaze lowered.

Zhinu approached the desk while Victory and Huang maintained positions inside the door. *"Grandfather! What a pleasant surprise. Am I to join you for a private supper tonight? We have not done this in so long."*

"No," Xian said. *"As the eldest in the family, it is my responsibility to tell you a husband has been chosen for you."*

Victory could not see Zhinu's face, but the entire line of her back jerked in surprise, as if she had been struck. But when the girl spoke, it was in a tone that could have been used to describe the weather on a pleasant day. *"What good news, Grandfather. Who is my betrothed to be?"*

"I have decided your cousin Yu will be an appropriate choice."

This time Zhinu did step back. *"My cousin?"*

Shock even crossed Huang's face at this revelation.

"Yu has the position and bloodline necessary," Xian said. *"The two of you will continue the line of leadership for this province and ensure succession of rule in Jiang Yi Yue."*

"But he is family!" Zhinu's nervous energy overwhelmed her and she paced before Xian's desk. *"This is unheard of! We were supposed to be matched with dragons from the mainland."*

"Events have transpired that necessitate an acceleration to the timeline," Xian said. *"The line of succession must be assured as soon as possible."*

So this wasn't about Zhinu at all—except that everything revolved back to the girl. The governor could not prove Tan had not been a member of the rival political faction, nor could Xian prove anything untoward had occurred between the earl and his granddaughter. The men were covering their bases and Zhinu had gotten the short end of the stick.

Victory bit her tongue before she could make a comment about the lot of women through the ages.

"You have spent my whole life telling me I am destined to marry a man from one of the other four great families," Zhinu said. *"What if I do not want to marry a man I grew up with?"*

"You are a daughter of this house, and will do what is best for the Zhuanxu line," Xian said. *"Right now, the integrity of the Zhuanxu line is more important than the idealistic fancies of a young woman."*

"But Grandfather—"

"I will not discuss this further."

Zhinu bowed low. *"Yes, Grandfather."* She spun on her heel and sailed out of the suite, spine stiff. But Victory could see the brightness in her eyes of unshed tears.

The journey back to Zhinu's suite was also made in silence, but the moment Huang left them at the entrance, Victory slid the door shut and opened her arms. Zhinu collapsed against her, burying her face in Victory's shoulder.

Victory held her close, petting Zhinu's hair as the young woman's body shook with sobs. She whispered platitudes in both Loquella and Qin against the top of Zhinu's head, but even she knew nothing was certain.

Victory's bedroom door slid open, and Mikelos peeked out. He put his finger to his lips before Victory could snap at him, and a tawny brown wolf padded out of the bedroom toward Victory and Zhinu, his nails clicking against the wood floor.

Zhinu was too wrapped in her own internal agony to notice anything. "It's not fair," she said through her tears. "All I wanted to do was escape. Now I'm stuck in this city forever, with no way out and no life beyond this."

Rob sat at Zhinu's feet and leaned his entire body against her, whining low in his throat. She gasped, pulling away from Victory, and stared at the large wolf who had appeared from thin air.

Victory waited for the scream of fear at the large carnivore inside the palace, but once again, Zhinu surprised her.

"Robert?" she asked in a hesitant whisper.

He dipped his head once and whined again. With a grunt, he kept his balance as Zhinu dropped to her knees and wrapped her arms around his furry body. He tucked his muzzle over her shoulder and let her hold him close.

Mikelos wrapped his arms around Victory from behind, and she settled against his warm chest. "I'm still mad at you," she said.

He kissed her temple. "I know."

"How did you get a wolf into the palace?" Victory asked. The cozy scene below them was sweet, but better to know ahead of time whether palace security hunted for a rogue werewolf as they spoke.

"Carefully," Mikelos said. Victory swatted his arm, and he laughed. "Stowed away in one of the trucks returning to the palace after bringing the rest of the British into the city. Rob shifted and we made our way through all of the connected gardens and servant passages. He can be pretty stealthy for being so big and... blond."

After a few minutes, Rob pulled out of Zhinu's embrace and loped back into the privacy of the bedroom. Zhinu tried to go after him, but Victory grabbed her arm. "This isn't something you want to see," she said, as the sickening sounds of bones breaking and fluid skin shifting reached her ears. "It's not like one of your people changing."

Zhinu remained silent, with a pale face still streaked with tears. Victory led her over to one of the chaises and settled her into it. She and Mikelos took the one across and waited for Rob to emerge.

The shifting noises stopped, followed by the rustle of clothing. Soon after, Rob emerged from the bedroom on bare feet, dressed in casual clothes. He paused by Zhinu's seat, but when she held a hand out of him, he cuddled in close with her.

The two couples stared at each other while Zhinu maintained a white-knuckled grip on Rob's hand. He didn't seem to care or notice. "So," Rob said. "I guess this is where we need to talk."

"They're going to make me marry my cousin," Zhinu said in a burst. "I want to run away with you."

"We can leave tonight," Rob said, pressing a kiss to her temple. "Say the word, princess."

"Before we get too hasty," Victory said, "perhaps this would be a good time for you to both talk about what you want out of this scenario." When Rob and Zhinu avoided each other's gaze, Victory pointed at each of them in turn. "You both know this isn't a love match either. So better to be on the same page."

"Like some sort of pre-nup?" Rob asked. At Zhinu's uncomprehending stare, he said, "A prenuptial agreement. A contract some couples sign before marriage, in regards to issues like financial matters."

Zhinu glanced back at the closed door of her bedroom. "I will have no money," she said. "Beyond what I can make from selling my jewelry in Britannia."

"That won't be necessary," Rob said. "I have more than enough to support us."

"But Lady Moon is correct," Zhinu said. "If this is not a love match, I do not wish to be beholden to you."

"Sweetheart, I'm a scion of one of the four clans of Britannia," Rob said. "I was never going to get a love match. And if my partner is going to be beholden to me, or vice versa, I would rather it be something to benefit both of us. My wife and I should choose our own future, not have one picked out for us by our respective families."

Mikelos squeezed Victory's hand, and she squeezed back. It was refreshing to listen to the kids have a frank conversation instead of spouting idealistic future plans. Getting them on the same page was the first step. After, Victory could figure out whether she would let Zhinu walk out of here with Rob.

That gave her a momentary pause. When had that happened? When had she tossed the all-mighty contract to the wind and thrown her lot in with the princess?

Probably when Zhinu had lost her future and cried in her arms. It appeared that Victory's primary loyalty to the Zhuanxu family had shifted from Xian to his granddaughter.

Continuing, Rob asked, "You wish to study in Oxenafor, correct?"

"Yes, history and business," Zhinu said. "In order to help my family rule." She sniffled once, and Mikelos handed over a handkerchief. "I guess this will no longer be an issue."

"I think it sounds fantastic," Rob said. "Mikelos, can you please fetch pen and paper?"

Mikelos heaved himself out of the chaise and did as requested. Rob scribbled out a short paragraph. "This isn't official by any means, but it should be a good start," he said. "How is your written Loquella, lady?"

Zhinu plucked the paper from his fingers. "Perfect, sir." She read what Rob had written and snapped her fingers for the pen. With an indulgent smile, Rob handed it over. In a neat print, she added an additional sentence before signing it with a flourish in both Loquella and Qin. "If this meets with your approval, Robert?"

He accepted the pen and paper again, read the addition, and also signed it. "Perfect, my dear." He handed the items over to Victory. "If the lady and gentleman will sign as witnesses?"

Victory scanned the sheet as Mikelos read over her shoulder:

Earl Robert Wallace hereby agrees to support Lady Zhuanxu Zhinu during the full course of undergraduate and graduate studies at the college of her choice at Oxenafor University, to include both tuition and household expenses. Upon graduation, Lady Zhuanxu may remain wed to Earl Wallace or have the marriage annulled in order to follow her own path.

Lady Zhuanxu Zhinu hereby agrees to support Earl Robert Wallace politically and socially to the extent that it does not interfere with her studies in order that a more natural bond may develop between the two. Upon graduation, Earl Wallace may propose to Lady Zhuanxu again so that they may see what the future holds.

This was both straightforward and the most romantic thing Victory had ever read. Without hesitation, she signed it also in Loquella and Qin, and Mikelos did the same in Loquella. "And with that, my contract with your grandfather is broken," Victory said. "I am yours now, Lady Zhinu."

Zhinu looked stricken. "I can't afford you either."

"Consider it an early wedding present," Mikelos said. "Victory's protection of you is now on my dollar."

"That's not how it works," Victory said.

Bumping his shoulder against hers, Mikelos said, "I don't really care."

Laughing, Rob slid off the chaise. Bent on one knee, he held out his hands to Zhinu. "Lady Zhuanxu Zhinu—I have no ring for you now, but with a heart full of friendship, will you do me the honor of giving me your hand in marriage?"

"Dear Robert," Zhinu said, "with a heart full of hope, it is my pleasure to accept. Now let me finish packing." She pressed her lips to his once and then twice, quickly, before pulling him to his feet and tugging him after her to the bedroom.

"That was adorable," Mikelos said.

"I agree," Victory said. "But what's less adorable is that we also have to pack. And pack light. So pick which violin you're leaving here." She braced for the ensuing argument, but relaxed when Mikelos tossed his head back and laughed.

Instead, he wrapped his arms around her and spun her in the middle of the suite. "Love, we're about to kidnap a weredragon princess from the middle of a heavily guarded palace complex with the help of an overeager baby werewolf. As far as I'm concerned, both the violins and the *erhu* can be left behind. Now I'm just concerned that we didn't bring any guns."

Victory wriggled out of his grip and settled her sword-belt back into place. "If this gets to a point where we need guns, we're doing it wrong. I'll handle our things. Go make sure those two aren't too busy making out to finish packing a reasonable bag for Zhinu."

"She's leaving her whole life behind," Mikelos said. "How much do you expect will be reasonable?"

"Go!" Victory said, nudging him away from her.

Mikelos stole a kiss, and as it deepened, there was a knock at the door.

Victory and Mikelos froze, staring at each other. "Hide Rob," she said, hissing through her teeth. He ducked into Zhinu's room. Victory tidied her hair and pulled open the entrance to the suite.

Kyo-Young bowed once on the other side. *"Lord Xian to see his granddaughter alone."*

Victory backed away from the door, and Kyo-Young entered with Xian on her arm. She settled him into one of the chaises before taking up her customary spot by the wall. With a bow, Victory said, *"I will fetch Lady Zhinu."*

"You never thought I was an idiot, Moon, so don't treat me like one now," Xian said. *"I will see them both."*

Oh, hell. Xian's enhanced senses had picked up on Rob's presence, whether by sound or smell. But before Victory could move, Zhinu came out of her room with Rob at her side. Kyo-Young stifled a gasp.

"You are welcome to speak with us both, Grandfather," Zhinu said.

"I see," Xian said. *"What are you thinking, child?"*

"I am not a child anymore," Zhinu said, chin held high. *"I haven't been a child for a long time, but you and Mother never let me grow up. Declaring your intention of marrying me to Governor Yu means you no longer see me as a child either."* She caught Rob's hand when he held it out to her. *"I intend to marry Earl Wallace and accompany him home to Britannia. I give up all claim any of our children may have to the city of Jiang Yi Yue or any other Zhuanxu holdings within the Qin Empire."*

The blow-up Victory had expected did not come. Xian tapped his chin with a forefinger. *"You may do this on one condition,"* he said, his voice level. *"You must declare your intentions to Governor Yu and officially abdicate any claim by you or any descendants."*

"I agree to this," Zhinu said. *"Please inform Cousin Yu that I will see him shortly."*

With uncanny precision, Xian turned in Victory's direction. *"Moon, I believe the Loquella expression is 'you are fired.' Prepare to leave the palace at once."*

Now was not the time to announce Victory's plan to renege on her contract anyway. Instead, she said, *"I'm so sorry, Xian. But Governor Yu is the official holder of my contract to guard Lady Zhinu. He is the only one with the power to release me from the contract early."*

It wasn't possible for the temperature in the room to plummet further.

"Ever the mercenary, Moon." With a sharp motion, Xian summoned Kyo-Young to his side. He rose, and they stepped together to the suite's door. *"Someone shall be here to summon Zhinu and Victory to meet with Governor Yu. Alone."*

When the door shut behind them, Mikelos popped out of Zhinu's room. He and Rob began speaking at once, but Victory raised her hands for silence. "Zhinu," she said, "how safe will meeting Governor Yu be? Or do we need to leave at once?"

"It's still daylight," Rob said. "How—?"

"That can be handled," Victory said, her attention still on Zhinu.

"Grandfather did not try to kill you, Robert," Zhinu said. "Therefore, I think meeting with Yu will be okay."

"It's probably a trap," Mikelos said, leaning against the doorjamb. "Actually, it's more than likely a trap."

"Then it's a good thing Victory will be there to protect me," Zhinu said. "It would be political suicide for Yu to take me into custody against my wishes. All I would have to do is proclaim him my betrothed. When we do run away, no weredragon will ever agree to wed him."

"I don't see how that makes sense," Rob said.

"No, it does," Victory said. "Technically, female weredragons have the right to choose who they breed with, since keeping the lines pure is so important. Which is why Xian's plan to marry you to your cousin was so unexpected."

"My grandfather is an old man set in his ways," Zhinu said, her expression pinched. "An old man who fled to Jiang Yi Yue long ago in order to heal a broken heart. He doesn't want to see the city he put so much work into land in the hands of a governor not of the Zhuanxu line, which will happen if Yu doesn't get his act together and find a wife from the mainland soon."

Her words were like a kick to Victory's stomach. "A broken heart?" She'd had no idea. Xian had been the one to send her away rather than cause scandal.

"He couldn't marry you either," Zhinu said, sorrow in her voice. "And if he wouldn't sacrifice the Zhuanxu line for his own happiness, do you really think he would let a mere girl do it?"

"So this is going to be a trap," Rob said. He began pacing.

The similarity in mannerism both wolf and dragon expressed when nervous struck Victory. But they had to keep their focus. "Zhinu?" she asked again.

The girl nodded once, with finality. "I will meet with my cousin. I will sign an abdication. I am not going to make up for my grandfather's mistakes." She tucked herself under Rob's arm to stop his pacing, keeping her eyes on Victory. "But bring your sword in case."

ACT IV

An armed guard contingent waited to escort Lady Zhinu to the governor when she and Victory left the suite. Their procession through the back passages of the palace made an incongruous image, but the sun had just touched the edge of the horizon.

Captain Huang had eyed Victory's sword, but made no comment. In return, Victory refrained from making a snarky remark about requiring men armed with rifles to escort a single woman and her servant.

With a sharp pang, Victory knew she would not get a chance to say goodbye to any of Zhinu's handmaids. The girls had grown on her over the past few weeks, and if it saddened her, Zhinu must be devastated.

But the young woman held her head high as the company emerged back into the formal areas of the complex. They found themselves across the hall from the private audience chamber Governor Yu had received them in earlier that morning.

It already seemed like a lifetime ago, but this day would only get longer before it ended.

A guard pushed aside one of the large panels blocking off the room, and Captain Huang announced them.

Victory followed Zhinu inside and stood behind her right shoulder. Governor Yu once again sat in his almost-throne, but a surreptitious scan showed he was alone in the room. Neither Xian nor any of his other advisors were present. This could bode well for the conversation to come, but it was more likely that Yu wanted no witnesses to the unwinding scandal.

"Leave us," Yu said to Captain Huang, confirming Victory's assessment.

"But Governor—"

Yu's golden eyes flashed in the lamplight and his voice rumbled with the echoes of a growl. *"I have nothing to fear from my cousin and her trusted servant. We will speak in private."*

Captain Huang bowed low before backing out of the room with the rest of his guards. The door panel slid shut with a resounding *thud* that echoed through the audience chamber.

Victory tensed when Yu rose to his feet and approached them. She prepared for yelling, for arguments, even for Yu to attempt to strike his cousin. But to her surprise, he stopped a few feet away and dropped on both knees before Zhinu. He touched his forehead to the floor at her feet three times in succession before sitting back on his heels and clasping his hands in front of him. But the expression on Yu's face was closed off, unreadable, and he said nothing.

They froze in an uncomfortable tableau for almost a full minute before Zhinu responded. "I will speak Loquella," she said, "to avoid confusion if Lady Moon is questioned later about the events that happen in this room." She glanced over her shoulder at Victory before turning back to Yu. "Though you come to me with all the proper motions of supplication, I must reject your marriage proposal. I'm sorry."

Victory braced again for anger, but instead sadness tinged Yu's voice. "We are a people touched by the gods, Zhinu," he said. "You would reject all I can offer you and our children for one of the shapeshifters created out of the earth?"

"I reject you for a better future for myself, and a man I view as a friend," Zhinu said. She dropped to her knees and clasped Yu's hands in hers. "We deserve so much more than this, cousin. Don't let our grandfather manipulate us into a match that will only harm both of us in the long run. If you marry me, the Zhuanxu line will have no new blood. Any son or daughter we have will have the same fate, stuck in Jiang Yi Yue with no way out, expected to breed more heirs."

"Is that such a bad thing?" Yu asked. He dropped Zhinu's hands as if they were hot coals and rose to his feet. He collapsed into his ornate throne and rested his head back against the wood. "This city has given much to our family. We owe nothing less than to do our best for it in return."

"Just because Grandfather ran away does not mean our family should be stuck with the dregs of Qin lands forever," Zhinu said. Now she bowed to him. "Let me have more, Yu. If I leave, you will be free to marry into one of the mainland families. Your sons could serve in the court of the Emperor himself!"

Yu slammed a fist onto the arm of his seat. "Don't pretend you are doing this for my benefit. And I could even understand if you were in love with the mongrel. But to run away from your home and your people just because..." His voice faded away as some sudden realization crossed his face.

Yu's focus shifted at once to Victory. She squeezed her right hand into a fist at her side. The alternative was to grip the hilt of her sword, but she wouldn't risk such an aggressive move.

"The source of this entire problem lies with you," Yu said. "Stories you've put into the girl's mind. Encouraging her friendship with Wallace. Encouraging her to abandon her responsibilities to her family."

"She tried to prevent our friendship!" Zhinu stood and stamped one foot. "She tried to do what you and Grandfather wanted!"

Yu was fast, but Victory moved faster. Before he could reach Zhinu, hand raised to strike, Victory slid between them with sword raised. Zhinu yelped in surprise, and Yu drew back. "How dare you," he said, with more of the echoing snarl.

"My job is to protect the client at all costs." Victory balanced on the balls of her feet, keeping the sword angled before her. "Even if it means protecting her from the men who hired me."

"But there are certain things I can still order," Yu said. "Return the girl to her suite and keep her there. Our betrothal will be announced at dinner tonight. There will be no more discussion."

Victory sheathed her sword and bowed. "Yes, governor." Zhinu would have to forgive her for this later.

Zhinu gasped and clutched the back of Victory's shirt. "You can't!" She pushed away from Victory, and her wild gaze scanned from her to her cousin and back again.

"Come, lady," Victory said. She held out a hand to Zhinu, but the girl stepped back again. Victory tried not to take the betrayal in Zhinu's face to heart. This only had to last long enough to get back to the privacy of her suite. Then they could figure out what to do next.

Choking back sobs, Zhinu almost ran to the door of Yu's audience chamber. She surprised Captain Huang, who backed away from the door and tried not to act like he eavesdropped. Ignoring Victory, Zhinu said, *I am ready to return to my rooms.*

Huang glared at Victory and offered an arm to Zhinu. *Right away, Lady Zhinu.* They set off down the main hallway. Zhinu didn't look back.

Victory refused to be offended by the actions of an angry teenager, instead ducking into the servant passage on this hallway. She startled two maids in her haste to beat Zhinu back to the suite.

By Victory's measure, they had less than an hour until dinner was called and Zhinu was expected to be present in the main hall. An hour to convince Zhinu that Victory was still on her side, pack any necessary belongings, and figure out a way to smuggle all four of them out of the palace.

She would have to tell Zhinu to stop referring to her as "Moon." Moon never had these sorts of problems. Moon would have followed the contract to the letter, living by her sword and not by her heart.

But Moon was the reason they were in this mess. She'd had no idea that when Xian sent her away all those years ago, he never recovered. Scandal had been averted, and from the outside, it looked like he'd married and moved on. He'd lived a good and full life, with Jiang Yi Yue as proof of his legacy.

Love hadn't been enough to make Xian sacrifice everything, and it wasn't why Zhinu faced the same decision. But a better future was worth the sacrifice.

Moon hadn't known the difference. But she had been a hired sword, whereas Victory was now a leader. She had spent the past hundred years of her life seeing the bigger picture, and she couldn't put the blinders back on.

Zhinu returned to the suite less than two minutes after Victory, but it had been enough time for Victory to give Mikelos and Rob the run-down. "Zhinu, wait," Victory said, as the girl brushed past her toward her own bedroom. She didn't even look at Rob, who had jumped from the chaise when she entered the room.

"I have nothing to say to you," Zhinu said.

Mikelos blocked her passage. "No, you should hear her out."

"Hear what?" Zhinu crossed her arms in defiance. "I thought you supported us in this! But instead you're willing to do what my cousin wants."

"That's not precisely true," Rob said. "Otherwise she wouldn't have warned us that we have less than an hour to run."

"So you don't intend to deliver me on a platter to my cousin?" Zhinu asked.

"Of course not," Victory said. "But going against him right then wouldn't have worked out well for either of us. Safer to get back here as soon as possible so we can figure out what to do next."

"Running is what we do next," Rob said. "We can make it back to the house in the city and leave with my people."

"It will be too easy for them to accuse you of kidnapping Zhinu, especially since Xian knows you're in the palace right now." Victory shook her head. "He and Yu will never allow word to spread that Zhinu left of her own free will."

"We need something else," Rob said. "Something to divert attention from me and my people."

Zhinu bowed to Victory. "I'm sorry I doubted you."

"It's alright, hon," Victory said. Better doubt than avoidable conflict.

"We could kidnap you," Mikelos said. They all stared at him. "No, hear me out. Victory could hear that the governor isn't planning on paying out the full amount of her contract, so she and I kidnap Zhinu instead in retaliation."

"That won't work either," Victory said. "Contract disputes must be made with the nearest Mercenary Guild representative first. And my reputation would work against us, because no one would believe I'd go to that extreme instead of going through proper channels first."

"Not to mention the expectation would be that you'd kidnapped her for ransom," Rob said, "and that you would return her once you were paid your due." He crossed the room to Zhinu and wrapped an arm around her waist, though whether for her comfort or his own was unclear.

"I have to die."

They all froze at Zhinu's pronouncement.

"What, turn you into a vampire?" Mikelos asked. "That's a little hardcore, and Victory wouldn't go for it. Wait, can weredragons even become vampires?"

But Victory was already a few steps ahead of her daywalker. "No, it's brilliant." She waved away Mikelos' surprised expression. "I'm not going to turn her. But we can fake her death. Qin death ritual then works in our favor."

"Until one of us gets accused of her murder!" Rob's metaphorical hackles were raised, and he'd be pacing if Zhinu hadn't gripped his hand in hers.

"Not if it's a suicide," Zhinu said. "I know where Yi-Ting keeps her headache medicine, and I know the prescription is recent. Enough of it will take out even a dragon."

"Talk about a breach of contract," Victory said, laughing. "This would destroy my reputation if I can't even protect the client from herself."

Zhinu's face shone with nervousness. "Should we come up with something else?"

"Your life is more important than my reputation," Victory said. "And this is so ridiculous it might work."

They scattered to finish packing and make preparations. Because if this didn't work, Victory would find herself alone in a palace filled with armed guards and two angry weredragons.

Sounded like fun.

Victory and Mikelos glanced at each other from across their bedroom when a knock sounded at the suite's main door. Victory tossed the shirt she had been about to fold to Mikelos and darted out of the room, beating Zhinu to the door before she could open it.

Hand on sword, Victory called, "Who is it?"

"Reynolds. With an escort."

The voice was right, but it was still an unexpected answer. Victory cracked open the door.

Reynolds did indeed stand there, wearing a formal suit and carrying a garment bag. Behind him followed two palace guards, but they positioned themselves on either side of the suite door when Victory waved Reynolds inside.

Rob stepped out of Zhinu's room once Victory had closed the suite door again. "Reynolds? How did you get in here?"

"I was invited," Reynolds said. "Governor Yu sent a formal invitation to the house and made it clear our presence was required at dinner tonight. Inside was a note from Lord Xian's girl saying I would find you here."

"They're sending a message," Mikelos said.

"More like a slap in the face," Rob said, accepting the garment bag from Reynolds. "If I'm in the audience when the betrothal is announced, I can't make a scene without damaging formal relations further."

Reynolds looked around the suite, probably for a drink. He sank onto one of the chaises. "What the hell is going on, son?"

"We're packing to leave, Lord Reynolds," Zhinu said. "Robert and I are eloping. *Before* dinner tonight."

"Of course you are." Reynolds faced Victory. "Weren't you supposed to be here specifically to prevent this sort of thing from happening?"

"Lord Xian hired me to protect Lady Zhinu from rogue political elements," Victory said. "And it doesn't matter anymore, since I've broken contract."

Reynolds gaped at her. "That's a serious move to make for a mercenary of your standing," he said.

"Good thing I'm not a mercenary anymore," Victory said. "This isn't the way I make my living, so the pay cut I'll take on my next contract for fines to the Mercenary Guild and reparations to Governor Yu don't bother me." She paused, and gripped Zhinu's hand. "I have more important things to worry about now."

Zhinu's expression of happiness made all of this ridiculous drama worth it. Almost.

"Well," Reynolds said, "the trade negotiations are in shambles at this point. I suppose a marriage will be the best thing we can hope for. Come home with a proper love story, at least." He narrowed his eyes as Rob and Zhinu exchanged furtive looks. "And you've both figured out this isn't a love story, haven't you?"

Rob pulled their "contract" out of his shirt pocket and passed it to Reynolds. "We have this instead."

Reynolds finished scanning the paper. "May your mother have mercy on your soul." When worry flashed across Zhinu's face, he said, "Don't worry, girl. Lady Wallace will adore you, and I imagine you'll make a lovely daughter-in-law. But she's going to skin her son alive."

"She's done worse," Rob said, pecking Zhinu on the cheek. "Let me change into the clothes you brought me. If we're both at this dinner, it lessens the chances we can be accused of kidnapping."

"Zhinu and I will sneak out together," Mikelos said. "Dress her as a servant, and she can be helping me run an errand before dinner."

"Wouldn't it be better if Victory stayed with you for protection?" Reynolds asked.

"I'm the diversion," Victory said.

Reynolds bared his teeth in frustration. "I'm too old for this." When Mikelos laughed and Victory smothered a smile of her own, he pointed at them each in turn. "And this is why both of you should know better."

Rob pounded Mikelos on the back. "But I'm ever so glad they don't."

While Mikelos finished condensing their belongings into what he could carry with comfort and Reynolds helped Rob change into his formal suit in the main room, Zhinu and Victory ducked into Zhinu's bedroom for their own final preparations.

"You're still too tall," Zhinu said, fussing with the drape of Victory's robes.

"I'll be lying on the bed," Victory said. "It will be fine." When Zhinu kept messing with the fabric across Victory's shoulders, she grasped the young woman's hands in her own. "It's okay to be scared right now."

Zhinu stilled. "Is it that obvious?"

"I'd be worried if you weren't," Victory said. "This is a big step for anyone to take, even without all the added danger of this situation."

"I know what you and Mikelos have is different," Zhinu said, "but have you ever gotten married?"

"Once," Victory said. "It was a long time ago, and frankly, a big mistake on my part." Zhinu's mouth fell open. "No, no, don't let that scare you off. I was young, in the grand scheme of things. I was tired of following my sire around, and

I was given an opportunity that would give me great power—or at least I thought it would."

"Who was he?" Zhinu asked.

"A Roman lord, over five hundred years ago," Victory said. "Keep in mind, I was nobody. Progeny of a common mercenary. This was my way to proper power, the realm of the great vampire lords of the Roman senate. He was a widower who already had heirs, and thought marrying me would assure him prestige."

"I'm guessing it didn't go as planned?"

"That is a hell of an understatement." Victory tucked a strand of Zhinu's hair behind her ear. "Marrying into a noble family gave Leto the esteem he wanted from his human contemporaries, but to the vampires of the Roman senate, I was still nothing. A sword-for-hire of uncertain lineage, whereas the Roman vampires were all bred for the change. Educated from birth to know they would be inheriting immortality."

"But you're beautiful," Zhinu said. "And smart. What more could they ask for?"

"Legacy," Victory said. "Some vampires can trace their heritage back almost ten thousand years. My sire never knew who created him." She released Zhinu's hands and allowed the girl to pin her thick hair into the stylized braided knots Zhinu favored. It didn't need to be an exact match, but the silhouette had to pass for what they planned. "So I refused to turn any of Leto's children to elevate them to the senate, mostly because they were all spoiled brats, and my dear husband never forgave me for it. And since I wouldn't make him my daywalker, he claimed I hadn't fulfilled my end of the contract and divorced me."

"Europa seems to place much faith in its marriage contracts," Zhinu said. "Does no one marry for love?"

"Not any more than the great Qin families do, breeding for weredragon sons," Victory said. "Love is for people who have nothing to lose."

Zhinu stabbed Victory in the scalp with a pin. "Sorry. The texture of your hair is not what I'm used to."

"That's okay," Victory said. "No one has done my hair for me since my daughter was in middle school. She's always kept her hair short, so she used to play with mine instead."

"I hope to meet your daughter one day," Zhinu said around a mouthful of pins.

"You two would get along like wildfire," Victory said. "I'll make sure she looks you up if she and her partner ever find themselves in Oxenafor."

"You are a good mother, I think," Zhinu said. "Much better than mine."

Victory tried to turn, but Zhinu jerked her head back into place. "What makes you say a thing like that?"

"Who have we not seen in weeks?" Zhinu said. "Who have we not seen since she decided you were an appropriate chaperone for her daughter, and she could forget about me once again?"

"You had lunch with her two days ago."

Zhinu emitted an unladylike snort. "I attended a luncheon she threw for the Jiang Yi Yue Arts Council, so she could show off the fact that her family carried enough recessive genes to spawn a weredragon daughter. That's the reason I bear the Zhuanxu name. My line of the family is descended from one of Lord Xian's concubines." She pinned the last braid into place, and smirked when Victory turned in surprise. "You thought Grandfather cared about me because I was his beloved descendent? Hardly. I'm a fluke. A status symbol. At least in Britannia, I'll be worth more than my womb."

Of all the things Victory had thought to check on, Zhinu's actual lineage had never been one of them. Obviously Xian had wed and had at least one child, but she had not bothered to track the connection between Yu and Zhinu beyond the fact that they were cousins a few times removed, with Xian as a common ancestor.

Unlike the mammalian werecreature strains, which were an aggressive dominant gene, the weredragon lines were a pickier recessive. It was why the family matches were that much more important, to ensure the head of the empire and all of the major governorships could be held by male weredragons capable of shifting and that there were enough female weredragons to provide healthy heirs.

There were many things Victory could say to this news, but only one Zhinu needed to hear. "You will be an asset to Rob's clan, even without providing him with an heir."

"Thank you, Lady Moon."

"You should call me Victory," she said. "Moon was the woman who fell in love with your grandfather and apparently caused this whole mess without realizing it. Victory is Zhinu's friend and supporter."

"Thank you, Victory," Zhinu said, with a half bow. "And you look as good as I can make you. Remember to keep your legs tucked up so you don't seem so tall and your hands in your sleeves. The blue polish will fool at a glance, but not on inspection."

"I imagine my callouses will give me away if anyone checks too close," Victory said. "And I only need to cover my face?"

"Your whole head," Zhinu said. She pointed to the white silk scarf folded on her bed. "I'm sorry the hairstyle won't be comfortable to lie on, but it will be better to avoid having loose hair you'd have to worry about covering."

"I'm sure I can handle a bit of discomfort," Victory said. "Do you have everything?"

Zhinu hefted the laundry bag. "The things I can't bear to leave behind. How do I look?"

Where Victory wore a set of Zhinu's fanciest robes, Mikelos had been dispatched to raid the laundry facilities for a set of servant's clothing. Zhinu was wrapped in shapeless cotton, with her hair tucked into a plain scarf. Her nails had been covered in pink polish, a cosmetic available to a woman of even low station. Keeping her face bowed should shield her distinctive blue eyes from view.

"Utterly unremarkable," Victory said.

After a perfunctory knock at the door, Mikelos entered. "Time to say goodbye, ladies."

"We'll be out in a second," Victory said. She turned back to Zhinu. "Be careful. Do what Mikelos says. And I promise I will catch up to you soon."

Zhinu threw her arms around Victory's shoulders, hugging her tight. "Thank you," she said. "Be careful, too."

Victory squeezed her back. "It will all be fine."

She hoped she wasn't lying to the girl.

Mikelos examined them both when they entered the main room of the suite. He redid the kerchief covering Zhinu's hair and shifted the layers of robes Victory wore so that the weight of the fabric did not pull on her neck as much. "There," he said, stepping back. "I think we're ready."

"You make a good lady's maid, Mikelos," Zhinu said. "Perhaps I should take you to Oxenafor with me to join my household."

Mikelos offered her a short bow. "My apologies, but I am spoken for already."

"I will find you the best maid in all of Britannia," Rob said.

"I hate to rush this," Reynolds said. He tapped the face of his wristwatch. "But if we want to stagger our departures, the earl and I should leave for dinner now."

Rob and Zhinu embraced and shared a few quiet words. Even Reynolds pretended he wasn't capable of listening with his enhanced hearing. Zhinu pressed kisses to Rob's cheeks, followed by a chaste one to his lips. "If we don't make it tonight," she said, "leave with your people. I will make it to you in Britannia eventually."

"You'll make it," Rob said. "And I will be waiting."

Reynolds bowed low to Zhinu, clicking his heels together. "Your servant, Lady Zhinu."

"Thank you, Lord Reynolds." Zhinu curtsied in the British fashion, handling the edges of her loose servants pants as if they were a skirt of the highest fashion.

Rob followed Reynolds out of the suite, and they overheard the two men waving off the noises of surprise made by the waiting escort at Rob's appearance. Within moments, the group had passed down the hallway and out of hearing range.

Mikelos ducked into their bedroom and returned with two more laundry bags. He slung one over his shoulders and left the other on the floor while he and Victory exchanged an embrace of their own. "I'm sorry I doubted you before," he said, whispering.

Victory stepped back and held his face in both hands. "I'm sorry I ever gave you reason to, my love." When they kissed, she nipped at his bottom lip. "I'll see you in a few hours."

"Don't traumatize anyone too badly," Mikelos said. "And I'm still nervous about leaving you here unarmed."

"I've done more with less," Victory said. "Don't worry." She wore three knives of various lengths strapped to her legs and hidden in the many layers of her robes. But even unarmed, a vampire's strength would be more than a match for most of what the palace guard could throw at her. The vampire religious culture of Qin worked in her favor—the armaments here topped out at rifles and pistols, with no older-style crossbows bearing wooden arrows for her to worry about. It would take more than a few well-placed gunshots to overwhelm her, and her focus would be on escape, not combat.

They kissed once more, and Mikelos gathered the second laundry bag in his arms. Victory stood well away from the garden entrance as they departed out into the rays of the setting sun.

After Zhinu pulled the drapes back into place and closed the patio door, Victory found herself alone in the suite. Showtime.

She allowed herself the indulgence of a last sweep of the bedroom she had shared with Mikelos these past weeks. The packs he carried contained her sword, the two knives she wasn't wearing, and a few changes of clothes for her. In the end, she had convinced him they could spare the room for one of his violins. As she drew a finger down the *erhu* case he hadn't hesitated to leave behind, she resolved to make all of this up to him somehow.

Xian had manipulated Mikelos in order to tempt Victory into accepting this ill-fated bodyguard contract, and she thought he had received the worse end of the bargain through all this. She left the room without looking at the second violin case, sitting in the center of the bed. Mikelos had asked Zhinu to write a note for him, asking that the instrument be given to one of the friends he had made in the Jiang Yi Yue Provincial Orchestra. Victory hoped it made it to the musician, and that no one smashed it in a fit of pique instead.

She returned to Zhinu's room and picked up the empty medication bottle and white scarf. The pills had been flushed down the toilet already, so she crawled into the bed and laid down. She arranged the robes around her in an artistic flare and twisted her hips enough to tuck her slipper-clad feet under the hems.

She plumped two pillows and settled her head into the crack between them, easing a bit of the pressure from lying on her bound hair. With a flick of her wrists, she snapped open the scarf and let it drift over her face and shoulders. The thick weave blocked her whole view of the room, limiting her senses to hearing and scent to warn her of any arrivals.

Victory curled one hand around the empty pill bottle and slipped the other inside her long sleeves. She closed her eyes and waited.

Patience had been a learned virtue over the centuries, though she was more used to being the hunter than the prey.

Unbidden, her mind drifted to Mikelos and Zhinu's escape from the palace. Worst-case scenarios flitted across the inside of her eyelids, one by one. Guards caught them out in the gardens before making it back inside through the servant passages. Mikelos' presence was questioned: why would an honored guest assist a mere serving girl with laundry? They weren't able to slip out of the palace complex with the rest of the workers who lived in the city proper.

The main door to the suite slid open, dragging Victory's attention back to the here and now. Footsteps crossed through the suite, female feet in court slippers. *"Lady Zhinu?"*

Victory stifled a groan. Not An. She had grown close to all of the handmaids in the past few weeks, and she had hoped that it would not be one of them to discover Zhinu's "body," though she knew the odds were against her.

"Zhinu," An called again. She slid back the door to Zhinu's room. *"I came to help dress—"* Her scream cut off the rest of the sentence.

An dropped to her knees next to the bed, babbling in Qin too fast for Victory to decipher. Her light fingers touched the hand clutching the medicine bottle, but she drew back in haste at Victory's cool skin.

Back home in Limani, and in many other places in the world, the scarf would have been drawn back and Victory's true identity revealed. In Qin tradition, however, only the dead should look upon the dead. Qin soldiers wore helmets and masks into battle, and suicides intentionally covered their faces the way Victory had. Her face would not be revealed until she was moved into the palace temple and one of the vampire priests arrived at nightfall to tend to her body.

Victory banked on that sweet spot in between.

An murmured a prayer for her mistress through her tears, and Victory held back her own sympathetic tears through sheer force of will. Staining the white cloth with crimson would give up the game too soon.

An pressed a gentle kiss to the cloth over her forehead, then the girl left the suite. Next, servants would arrive to move her body. The first step of this plot was successful. Time to wait again.

Mikelos might be having a heart attack. One of those gradual-onset heart attacks, where a person clutched his chest and wheezed and complained about numbness in the left arm.

He had a lot of respect for Victory, but in the past thirty minutes, his respect had grown exponentially. Bodyguarding wasn't playing glorified babysitter. It was having someone's life in your hands.

Mikelos hadn't been this stressed since they had adopted Toria and he'd been responsible for the needs of a helpless infant. At least he didn't have to carry Zhinu out of the palace.

They timed their escape during the dinner rush, which had worked in their favor so far. Once they left the gardens and main hallways of the palace and entered the servant passages, no one glanced at them twice. As long as they walked with purpose, no one had time to question their presence.

Mikelos had been a feature in the palace long enough that while he drew some questioning expressions, no one stopped to try to chat with him. His habit of finding out-of-the-way places to practice over the past few weeks benefitted him now—he'd never chased away any servants who stole a few minutes to listen to him, and since he occupied that strange place between nobility and servant, they had adopted him as almost one of their own.

More important, if they looked at him, they weren't looking at the maid assisting him in whatever errand he ran before dinner.

Soon enough, they arrived at the lowest physical level of the palace complex and slipped into the back of the queue. With the rest of the daytime servants—gardeners, handymen, general maids—they left the palace through the footpath gate and stayed with the mass of people walking toward Jiang Yi Yue proper. Even their baggage garnered no specific attention, since Zhinu had assured Mikelos that nobles donated discarded clothing and bedding to palace workers all the time.

This should have been where Mikelos allowed himself a moment to relax, but as he led Zhinu to the trolley stop that serviced the palace, his nerves grew tighter. This had all been too easy.

The sun had dropped below the mountains that towered over the city, casting the world in shadow. It would be safe for Victory to move soon. Zhinu's death was bound to be discovered by now. When she didn't arrive for her own betrothal dinner, the governor or her grandfather would be sure to send for her. But no alarms had been raised, and it appeared none of the exiting workers had heard any gossip before Mikelos and Zhinu made their escape.

Zhinu gripped Mikelos' hand as they approached the waiting trolley with the others. "We don't have any money," she said, pitching her voice low.

"It's okay," Mikelos said. "Guy and I rode the trolley all over the city a few weeks ago. I've got it sorted." As he pulled out the small coins that were enough for two people's fare, he ignored the new pangs echoing in his chest. It had been less than twenty-four hours since Guy had bled out under his hands and started this endless day unfolding. The only thing they could do right now was keep moving.

True to his word, Mikelos fed the correct change to the stand by the trolley operator and led Zhinu to a two-person bench. She slid in closest to the window and kept her head bowed, though Mikelos caught her staring out at the city around them.

This might be the first time she had ever been out in the city with less than a retinue of handmaids and palace guards. Instead, she had a daywalker much more adept at wielding a violin bow than the ankle knife Victory had insisted he carry.

Once servants packed the trolley, it shuddered to a start and trundled along its tracks into the city. The nearest neighborhood was the fancy one where the Brits had rented a house, but it wasn't odd for people to get off at these stops. Some nobles who kept rooms in the palace also maintained homes in this neighborhood, and a few palace servants had families also in the serving class who lived in these grand homes. Mikelos and Zhinu left the trolley with half a dozen others who each went their separate ways. They traveled through streets lit by electric lamps, though up in the mountains, the slums flickered with candlelight and outdoor kitchen fires.

A figure emerged to impede their exit from the alleyway between two grand houses when they were still a block away from their destination. Mikelos stopped, keeping Zhinu behind him with an outstretched arm. It would be their luck to be mugged at this stage in the game.

He greeted them in Qin, but Mikelos understood none of it. He tensed when Zhinu shrank back at the man's words.

The man stepped into a pool of streetlight and pushed back the hood of his robe. "Father Hisato?" Mikelos asked.

"Yes," Hisato said. He spoke more Qin to Zhinu, then bowed to Mikelos. After, he turned on his heel and loped back up the street, disappearing once more into the darkness.

"Oh, gods," Zhinu said, her voice barely above a whisper.

"What?" Mikelos asked. "What did he say?"

Zhinu shook herself all over, as if collecting herself. "He knew it was me, but didn't care," she said. "He had a warning for us." Her face had darkened with fear. "The princess is dead, and those responsible would be punished."

"Who?" Mikelos asked. "Did he say who he thought was responsible?" Depending on the rumors spreading, Hisato could mean anyone from Victory to the British delegation to the governor himself.

"No," Zhinu said. "We are all in danger now."

Time passed in interesting ways when you could do nothing but lie still. When the main entrance to the suite opened again, Victory had no idea whether it had been moments or minutes since An left.

She braced for multiple people to descend upon the princess's body, but to her surprise, it was a single set of footsteps. Heavier, this time. A man, or a large woman.

Victory hoped it was not Lady Jinghua. Despite what Zhinu had said before, Victory knew her mother cared for the girl in the only way she could. And no mother needed to see their child after death.

The person stopped at the entrance to Zhinu's room, probably studying the scene. The exasperated huff had a distinctive male tone. *"This was your grand plan? I expected more from a famous mercenary."*

Governor Yu. His enhanced weredragon senses had pierced the thin veil of disguise with ease. It could have been anything from the blue polish on her nails that lacked the shimmer of dragon scales to the innate difference in scent between a living creature and a vampire.

She started to rise, but Yu placed a gentle hand on her ankle. *"Do not move. We will speak again."* He departed the suite, and more people entered afterward.

With great deference and respect, many hands lifted Victory onto a waiting pallet. They tucked the silk covering her face around her head and shoulders and covered her entire body with a heavier cloth. Despite the fact that they arranged her limbs straight, no one noticed or commented on Lady Zhinu's sudden growth spurt. And luckily, the nail polish fooled them all.

Victory had no idea whether these were common body servants summoned for a distressing task or religious aides who worked for the vampire priests. And though Victory had expected to be brought to the palace chapel and make her escape from there, they carried her body much farther than anticipated.

At one point, people loaded her into the back of a vehicle and drove her body out of the palace itself. But she wasn't about to complain—she would prefer making her way through the unfamiliar streets of Jiang Yi Yue this way to the daring palace escape scenario they had anticipated.

After a short time, the vehicle drew to a halt. The servants or aides lifted the pallet out and carried her a short distance. A wave of incense followed the sound of a door opening, and heavy scents assaulted her nose even through the layers of cloth. The servants bore her through a vast space where their footsteps echoed, then transferred her body to a hard surface. They retreated, and a heavy door clanged shut behind them.

"You can get up now," Governor Yu said.

Victory shot up, dragging the layers of cloth away from her face in the dim light of the cavernous temple. She coughed once to clear her nose and throat of the cloying incense. Governor Yu leaned against the wall near the dais where she sat, and he shrugged when she finished surveying the room and faced him.

"I don't know how the priests handle the smell with their senses either," Yu said. He straightened and balled his hands into fists. Switching to Loquella, he continued, "Is Lady Zhinu safe?"

Victory swung her legs off the dais and dropped to her feet. "As safe as we could make her," she said. "She's not in the palace anymore, as far as I know."

Yu cracked his knuckles, an action that had all the signs of a habit born of stress. "I assumed as much. Why go through all this trouble?"

Hell of a question. "You have to ask?" Victory said, stifling a laugh. "The girl doesn't want to marry you. She wants her own life. We're making sure she gets it."

Yu slammed one fist against the chapel wall, denting the plaster. "You had no right."

"We have every right!" Victory divested herself of the heavy robes, stripping to the cotton pants and thin tank top she'd worn underneath, collecting each knife along the way. "Zhinu is a person, not a political pawn. Don't tell me you actually wanted to marry her." The slippers weren't her first choice, but there had been no way to smuggle more appropriate shoes out with her. They would have to do for now, at least until the silk shredded on the rough city streets and she was reduced to bare feet.

"I will do what is best for my family," Yu said. The echoes of a growl tinged his words.

After stringing the dagger sheaths on the cord wrapped around her waist and tying it off again, Victory crossed her arms and propped her hip against the dais. "Do you honestly expect me to believe marrying your cousin is best for the Zhuanxu line?" She didn't have time for this conversation right now, but she wasn't about to pass up the opportunity to talk some sense into the man.

Yu lunged forward. Victory had just enough time to draw one of her blades before he bent her back over the dais. One hand wrapped around her throat, and the other caught her wrist and squeezed until she dropped the dagger. Sharp points touched her neck. He wasn't trying to cut off unnecessary oxygen, but his talons had lengthened. With one move, he could rip out her entire throat, and that would be a pain to recover from.

"I obey my elder," Yu said. Even a weredragon had trouble meeting a vampire's eyes, and he kept his focus somewhere on her forehead.

"Xian is—" Victory was cut off when the door to the chapel opened. Probably a good thing, since what she had been about to say wasn't flattering to Yu's elder in the least.

Captain Huang narrowed his eyes at the tableau he found on the other end of the chapel. *"Governor?"*

Yu shoved away from Victory and turned to Huang, his robes swirling around him. *"What? Speak."*

Huang bowed once and reported with his gaze downcast. *"Sir. My people have received word from the Jiang Yi Yue city police that a crowd is gathering outside one of the manor houses in the Chou Hu neighborhood. We believe it is the house occupied by Earl Wallace, and the reports say the false fox priests are involved."*

While Yu focused on Captain Huang, Victory edged away from the dais. She made no move toward the dropped dagger, afraid Huang would mistake it for an attack on the governor. But when she heard the news about Rob's house, she froze.

"Thank you," Yu said. *"Leave us now."*

Keeping his expression schooled, Huang bowed again and retreated, closing the chapel door behind him.

Yu turned golden eyes back to Victory. "Zhinu is with the British?"

"She left the palace with Mikelos Connor," Victory said. "We were supposed to reconvene at the city residence leased by the earl before leaving the city tonight."

"You heard what Huang said?" Yu picked up Victory's dagger with loose fingers.

"I did. The *kitsune* priests are dangerous?"

"We believe they are behind the faction who have performed terrorist acts in the city in protest of the negotiations with the British." He skimmed his fingers against his jawline. "You have broken your contract, but you still seem to care about Lady Zhinu," Yu said. He presented the dagger to Victory, hilt first. "If that is true, she needs you now more than ever."

Victory accepted the dagger and sheathed it at her waist. "I will do my best." Her respect for Yu grew by leaps and bounds in that instant, and she honored him with a short bow. Without waiting for a response, she sprinted through the chapel and burst out the front doors. She heard the gasps of Captain Huang and his men as she blew by them. She kept to the shadowed side of the street.

Once around the first corner, out of the palace guards' sights, she braced herself against the side of a shop and let the sounds of the city overwhelm her. She ignored the stares and whispers of the people who passed by, commenting on the crazy pale woman running about the city half-dressed. She pulled out hairpins and dropped them to the ground one by one as she oriented herself based on the smell of sea and forest and on light striations in the darkening sky.

There was the palace, perched on Tang Mountain and peaking above the rooftops. The house should be at the base of the mountain, and according to Captain Huang, might be under siege. All she had to do was go in that direction and listen for the shouting.

And pray Mikelos and Zhinu hadn't been caught by the separatists.

In the stories and expansive mythology about vampires, the connection with a daywalker was said to be the most powerful force in existence. Stronger even than the magical link that joined two mages into the famous warrior-bond pair, another duo sprinkled liberally through history and epic. Only death could sever that which joined the warrior-mages. Though there had been epic romantic tales between both warrior-mage pairs and vampires and daywalkers, a single strong thing could keep the latter bond going—friendship.

Trust and friendship were necessary to maintain the vampire-daywalker link, because that relationship was as necessary as the regular exchange of blood.

Through the vampire-daywalker bond, it was said, a vampire always knew the exact location of her daywalker. She could always find him, despite distance, homing in on some sort of metaphysical scent. In the end, nothing could keep them apart.

All mystical bullshit, of course, perpetuated by popular fiction that loved to feature epic bonded romances. The stories usually put the characters through trials and tribulations that could only be solved by magical connections that didn't actually exist rather than through anything resembling a real relationship. But on occasion, Victory wished it was true.

Instead, she would have to find Mikelos the old-fashioned way.

The stares and gasps became more common as Victory neared the fancy neighborhood where Mikelos and Zhinu were supposed to be, but she ignored them all. As predicted, the slippers had given up the ghost half a mile ago, but the minor scrapes and cuts her feet suffered from the rough city streets healed almost as fast as she received them.

So now she was a barefoot half-dressed crazy lady. It didn't help that her hair fell in thick tangles around her shoulders, brunette flashing with red highlights in the streetlamps, in contrast to the hues of black and almost-black hair of many Qin.

She did her best to avoid the tea houses patronized by upper-class women and bars and clubs overflowing with men, for two very different reasons. However, though she passed them on the opposite side of the street, she still heard conversations held within their walls.

"—shame about the princess, really. She had such a bright future."

"Those British bastards are going to get what's coming—"

"—about time someone did something about Yu and his cronies!"

Victory ran faster. She was a blur on the pavement, dodging between people and leaving a trail of bloody footprints.

The shopping district around the temple gave way to suburbs, then the houses grew larger and the surrounding gardens more expansive, all peeking out behind plain wooden walls hiding the beauty within.

The crowds around her grew thicker as she approached the rented house. A few vehicles inched through the masses of people, traveling in the opposite direction. Noble and higher-class residents fleeing the encroaching mob.

The whispers grew louder, into shouts and exclamations.

"*—the princess must be avenged!*"

"*It's a takeover by the Brits!*"

"*—the fox priests killed Lady Zhinu—*"

These disparate groups of people would soon converge on the house and realize they weren't all on the same side. Then all hell would break loose.

Victory ran faster.

ACT V

Victory came across the first street brawl about a block from the rented residence. She wasn't sure which faction fought which, and she didn't much care. Despite stretching her senses to the fullest, she picked up nothing of Zhinu's light voice or Mikelos' cologne. It made sense that they would not have passed this way, but she didn't have time to deal with a mass of strangers on top of it all.

Making a split decision, she jumped straight up, caught the top of the nearest wall, and hauled herself into the quiet gardens of one of the large manors. She ignored the yelps of shock that followed her. Time for a shortcut.

She bypassed the crushed gravel pathway in favor of grass that soothed her feet. Keeping to the shadows, she avoided the residents and servants of each of these opulent homes as she crept through gardens and scaled the walls between.

It was obvious she had found the right place when she dropped into a garden not quite as groomed as the others. Flowerbeds had not yet been replanted with spring plants, and a few piles of leaves collected in random corners.

The sounds of frantic Loquella from within the building before her confirmed that fact.

Victory slid open a patio door and entered an empty back bedroom. It was devoid of personal belongings, except for a lone tie crumpled at the foot of the bed that had been lost in hasty packing. She crossed the room and slipped into the hall, surprising the two men heading in her direction.

Reynolds clutched his chest, gripping Adam's arm to stay upright. "Gods, woman. You're going to kill me yet."

"Have Mikelos and Zhinu gotten here?" Victory asked. Something on her foot itched, and she lifted her leg to pluck a piece of mulch from between her toes.

"They're in the front room, ma'am," Adam said. "They got here before Lord Reynolds." He licked his lips once, as if unsure whether to continue. "Do you need to borrow some clothes?"

British bathing suits covered much less, but Victory had always found it odd that the mere idea of undergarments screamed nudity to men of all cultures. "No, thank you," she said, as if she paraded around in a tank top and

162

linen pants all the time. Which she did, back home in Limani. "Mikelos should have my gear."

"Wait," Reynolds said, as Victory brushed past them. "Rob's not with you?"

A knot twisted in her gut. Victory had been waiting for the first hitch in their plan. This was one she hadn't expected. "He didn't come back with you?"

"Governor Yu never made it to dinner, so we left before the first course," Reynolds said. "We were faster in the chauffeured town-car than Mikelos and Zhinu were by trolley. Only beat them by a few minutes, but Rob panicked and set off to find them. I was hoping he'd run into you."

Victory pushed her windblown hair out of her face and gripped it with both hands. "Ugh. Okay. Let me change and put on real shoes, then we'll figure something out."

"I'm not sure it's going to be safe here much longer," Reynolds said. "The crowd growing outside sounds ugly."

"It's going to get ugly, based on some of the things I was hearing," Victory said. "You already have passage out of the city tonight?"

Reynolds glanced at Adam, who said, "It's not the biggest boat in the world, but it will get us back to Fort Caroline. We'll be able to get passage back to Britannia from there."

"Get everyone together to leave," Victory said. "You'll be safer in numbers."

"I would ask whether you thought contacting the palace for an armed escort would be worthwhile, but I'm not sure Captain Huang is too fond of us after his interrogation this morning," Reynolds said.

"I wouldn't bet on it, and he and Governor Yu aren't even at the palace currently," Victory said. "They already know Zhinu isn't dead. I'd hate to see Jiang Yi Yue implode, but the mess outside will benefit us right now."

"Okay, we'll get ready to go," Reynolds said. He pinched the bridge of his nose. "I don't suppose you're willing to go back out there to find my wayward pup?"

"If we leave without him, he's done," Victory said. "Either by the mob's hands or by Xian's. Whatever happens, it's a surefire way to get the conflict your entire mission was to avoid. So I don't think I'm going to have much choice."

"Thank you, Victory," Reynolds said. "We'll meet you at the docks."

He rushed away with Adam to finish their original errand, and Victory continued to the front of the house, searching unfamiliar hallways. But Mikelos had been in this house before, and his distinctive smell of spicy cologne and violin resin did much to buoy her spirits already.

She saw Zhinu first, and the girl gasped and covered her mouth. At least her feet no longer left bloody footprints over these nice wooden floors. Mikelos turned around next, and Victory didn't stop moving until she'd stepped into his warm embrace.

He squeezed her tight, then held her at arm's length to inspect her. "You're a mess. But you're here, and that's all that matters."

"I hope you managed to get out of there with our stuff," Victory said. "Because shoes are a creature comfort I've decided to be fond of for a while."

Mikelos pointed to a rucksack he must have appropriated from one of the Brits. "Along with hair ties, I imagine."

"Did you two have any trouble?" Victory asked. With no time to waste, she stripped in the sitting room and donned more familiar articles of clothing as Mikelos tossed them to her.

"No, but Robert is missing," Zhinu said. Her cheeks grew red, and she faced away from Victory. "I don't want to leave the city without him."

"That would defeat the purpose of all of this," Victory said as she tugged a pair of jeans over her hips. "Don't worry. I'll track him. You two go with Lord Reynolds and the others."

"No!" Zhinu forgot her embarrassment and turned to Victory, stamping one foot. "I will not risk leaving him behind."

Yet another thing she didn't have time for. "I'll move faster on my own," Victory said. "And you can't miss your boat. Your cousin already knows you're still alive. You need to be gone before he's done dealing with the mess outside." The shouts had grown louder, and it was only a matter of time before someone got the bright idea to knock down the gates using force.

"How did he discover it so fast?" Zhinu asked.

"He was the first person to come verify your death," Victory said. "And he saw right through me. Well, smelled, probably. He had my body sent to the temple in the city and confronted me there."

"He is trying to protect me, in his own way," Zhinu said. "He could have put out the alert at once, but he gave us time to escape the palace. If he doesn't catch me, he does not lose face."

Victory resisted the urge to slap herself. Of course. Yu wanted to obey his grandfather, his ancestor, but he didn't want to marry Zhinu any more than she did. It was still in his best interest, politically and genetically, to find a wife from one of the other major families. If Zhinu fled from Jiang Yi Yue, the failure to obey Xian wasn't on him.

"How well do you know the city?" Mikelos asked.

"Not well at all, I'm afraid." Worry cracked Zhinu's voice.

"I can track him by smell," Victory said. "We're less than ten minutes behind him. Wolf musk is so alien to this place that if we leave now, we shouldn't have too much trouble." She settled her sword around her waist and threaded her hands in her hair, twisting it into a braid through muscle memory alone.

"Did my cousin say anything else to you?" Zhinu jittered her fingers against her robe.

Oh, hell. The girl knew her family too well. "He told me to find you and protect you."

"Then I guess she has to come with us," Mikelos said.

Victory tied off the braid with the elastic Mikelos handed over. "It's cute that you think I was going to let you come, too."

An ominous creak echoed through the front area of the garden as the group assaulted the estate's gates. Without further conversation, they each shouldered a pack. "Never mind. I'm not letting you out of my sight," Victory said. "Let's go werewolf hunting."

Reynolds caught up to them as they crossed the garden to the back fence. Victory opened her mouth to comment, but Mikelos beat her to the punch. "You are not the werewolf we are hunting," he said.

"What?" Reynolds asked. He jogged to Victory's side. "I'm coming with you. I don't feel right leaving Rob like this."

"I don't have time to argue with you," Victory said. "As far as I'm concerned, you're another person to watch out for Zhinu." This was an awkward hunting party, but at least they all shared the same goal.

Victory pulled herself atop the fence, then reached down and caught Zhinu as Mikelos and Reynolds lifted her. In this method, they circled their way to the back of the growing mob that had appeared.

Once back on a residential street, far enough away that the noise of the mob was a dull roar, Victory and Reynolds both prowled the area. Sensitive vampire and werewolf noses both sought the distinctive scent of Earl Rob Wallace. Werewolf musk, expensive cologne, and the sharp smell of fearful anxiety.

Reynolds found it first. "Here!" The others clustered around him under the glow of a streetlamp as he pointed farther up the avenue. He pointed in the direction away from the palace, to the end of the neighborhood that bled into the busier urban areas of the city.

"That's the direction I came from," Victory said. She spun in a slow circle, examining the surrounding grand estates within view. "Hell, I literally came this way. He could be tracking me and got turned around."

"Might we accidentally do the same?" Zhinu asked.

Reynolds snorted. "I have decades of experience on the pup," he said. "The day I backtrack prey may as well be the day I'm laid in my grave."

"Lead the way, sir," Mikelos said.

Victory took the rearguard, staying behind Mikelos and Zhinu as they followed Reynolds through familiar streets. Though she hadn't paid attention to the landmarks during her sprinting progression earlier in the evening, Reynolds soon pointed out a bloody stain as they cut through a narrow cobblestoned alley.

"Vampire blood," he said.

"Mine," Victory said. The gash had most likely been a result of one of the shards of glass she saw glinting in the dim light from a bare bulb illuminating the back entrance to a tea shop. It must have healed before she made it to the next street.

He nodded once and requested no explanation, continuing on with his whole body leaning into the pursuit.

They heard the noise of another gathered crowd before they turned the final corner to see it. The large temple where Victory's "body" had been brought earlier towered above the street. The growing cluster of gawkers stood at the bottom of the temple steps, all watching the lone man who pounded on the doors of the temple.

"Let me in!" Rob slammed his fist into the wooden door again, and the panel shuddered under the impact. "I demand proof!"

"What the hell is he doing?" Reynolds asked, his voice rough with a frustrated growl. He and Zhinu both leaned in, but Victory and Mikelos held them back.

"No," Victory said. "We can't expose ourselves. Listen."

Reynolds struggled in her grasp, half-hearted at best. His attention was already where Victory had directed. He knew just enough Qin to get the gist of the dark mutterings.

"—dare he attempt to view the princess's body?"

"He may have killed—"

Reynolds allowed himself to be drawn into the doorway alcove of a closed clothier shop. Zhinu, of course, understood without problem, and though her face was pale, the steel in her spine had returned.

Zhinu touched Victory's sleeve. "The priests will not allow this commotion to continue."

"The priests are damn well aware there's no body in there," Victory said. "Hell, Rob should know the same."

"He might think you were unable to escape," Mikelos said. "This is a rescue."

"Poor timing for one," Reynolds said. "One of us has to go out there."

Zhinu took one step forward, head held high, but this time three sets of hands hauled her back.

"Look." Mikelos pointed as a figure stepped out of the crowd and ascended the temple steps. He pushed back the hood of his homespun robes to reveal the familiar profile of Father Hisato.

Rob's baritone rose above the noise of the crowd again, the Loquella words standing out from the Qin tones. "We demand entrance!" he said, slamming the door once more. "My priest will perform the final rites!"

"What the hell is he doing here?" Mikelos asked.

Victory didn't let go of Zhinu's hand, but the girl restrained herself. "Wherever that man goes, trouble follows," Zhinu said, her voice dark.

Transferring Zhinu's delicate hand to Mikelos' grasp, Victory said, "Time to rescue the rescuer."

With Reynolds close on her heels, Victory marched through the middle of the growing crowd. This was no time for subtlety or finesse. They needed to get in, grab Rob, and get out. They would reconvene with Mikelos and Zhinu in the sheltered alcove, then make a break for the docks.

Why could nothing ever be simple?

Father Hisato confronted Victory and Reynolds as they approached the bottom of the temple steps. As if waiting for his cue, one of the temple doors swung open, shoving Rob away from the entrance.

Governor Yu emerged, followed by a white-clad vampire priest. Both Rob and the surrounding crowd descended into silence. Even a human could have heard a pin drop.

Hisato's attention was divided between the two sets of newcomers. He picked at the sleeve of Rob's suit jacket, but the werewolf shook him off. That appeared to make his decision for him, and the *kitsune* crossed his arms to face Victory.

"Move, pup," Reynolds said, an echo of a growl through his voice.

"Yes, do not block our esteemed guests," Governor Yu said. "Are you finished assaulting Father Masaru's temple?"

Now that Victory drew nearer, she noted this was the same vampire who had given her wordless acceptance into the city of Jiang Yi Yue during the welcoming ceremony upon their arrival. Jiang Yi Yue's Master of the City. She tried to keep her attention on Rob, but met the other man's gaze by accident as she did an automatic scan to check for other backup behind him and Yu.

The vampire wrested her attention, keeping it on himself. Though there was no challenge in his gaze, his sharp chin lifted. A show of power nonetheless.

Victory looked away first.

Her heart couldn't beat out of her chest in fear, but it could drop into her stomach. She had zero desire to face off against another vampire, especially not one who had proven without a doubt he was older and stronger than her. What the hell was he doing in a city like Jiang Yi Yue?

That was like asking why a vampire like her lived in Limani.

Hisato tried to block her, but she hip-checked him out of the way, throwing a little added strength into the move. Yu and the priest wouldn't mind that sort of treatment against the belittled *kitsune*. He tumbled back in a sprawl of limbs and robes. Victory jerked Rob's shoulder toward her. "We are leaving," she said, ignoring Yu's smirk and the priest's raised eyebrows. "Now." Her next instinct was to reassure him that they had Zhinu, but she bit back the words. Yu would be forced to rescind his grudging support surrounded by so many witnesses.

"Thank you, Lady Moon," Yu said. "Remove this nuisance from my city, with my blessing."

That was as good as they were going to get. Braced by Victory and Reynolds, whose grip on Rob's other arm might be even firmer than hers, Rob did not protest being led away.

Father Masaru's gaze made the hair on the back of Victory's neck stand up, but neither he nor the governor made a move to stop them.

They were so close to making it out of this in one piece.

A piercing scream rent the air. Victory doubled over as the shriek blasted her sensitive hearing. Her vision whited out as pain stabbed through her temples. When she was able to stand, she dimly heard Rob retching next to her even as he tried to help Reynolds, who had stumbled to his knees.

Through the residual ringing in her ears, she heard a door slam behind her. With a quick check over her shoulder, she saw Father Masaru had chosen the better part of valor and evacuated to the safety of his temple. She didn't fault him for abandoning the foreigners to their fate.

Because the last time Victory heard a scream like that, the ground had been littered with corpses afterward.

Blinking the last of the blurriness away, Victory watched as an enormous dragon descended from the sky. People in the temple square shouted and scattered, buffeted by the wind created by the flapping wings, and Victory hoped Mikelos and Zhinu remained in their out-of-the-way spot. When the creature alighted in the center of the square, its shoulders topped the streetlamps and its large tail swept a food cart away like kindling.

The dragon was blue, and Victory's heart broke.

Weredragons weren't like the other werecreatures such as the wolves or *kitsune*. Beside their humanoid and smaller dragon forms, they had a third shape. The ability to summon this final epic form that could decimate armies and crush entire towns.

One they could never come back from. Even if Victory ever returned to Jiang Yi Yue, Zhuanxu Xian was lost to her forever.

Yu brushed between Victory and Rob and stopped midway down the temple steps. *"Grandfather!"* His back was straight, but Victory could smell the fearful pheromones that poured from his body, despite the pungent fear emanating from the brave onlookers who still remained in the square.

Beneath sapphire eyes burning with an inner flame, and lips rolled back over teeth the length of bodies, Xian lowered his head to be level with Yu.

Victory braced herself for another ear-wrenching scream, but none came. Instead, Xian stared into Yu's face in silence.

"She is alive, Grandfather, I swear it," Yu said, answering a question only he somehow heard.

Victory wasn't sure how final-form weredragons communicated. She'd never stuck around long enough to find out. Like she didn't plan to stick around now, since Yu had given up their last card. The two werewolves at her side stood gaping, Reynolds still rubbing his ear. But before she could grab them to bodily haul them away with her, Xian's head twisted on its long neck. Now he had Victory in his sights.

This was nothing compared to holding the gaze of the oldest of vampires. Pure, unbridled fear ripped through her body as the blue eyes seared into hers.

Xian opened his mouth with an audible gasp. Victory braced herself, turning her face away and shoving her hands over her ears in preparation for another scream.

But the noise never came. Instead, a body slammed her aside as a burst of heat seared the air above her. She saw stars as the back of her skull collided with the edge of a step. When her vision cleared, she stared into Yu's face as he sprawled over her. The governor had saved her life from Xian's dragonfire.

Yu's eyes flashed gold, and he leapt to his feet. Victory checked for Rob and Reynolds, but both men had also had the sense to duck and appeared unsinged.

The dragonfire had been for her. That thought shouldn't hurt as much as it did.

Yu once again yelled to the dragon, despite the rage that still emanated from Xian's burning gaze and bared teeth. *"All is not lost, Grandfather."*

Victory pushed herself to her feet and drew her sword. She stepped in front of Rob and Reynolds and brandished it across her body. "Be ready to run," she said. "This doesn't look good."

"This looks bloody awful," Rob said. He shucked off his suit jacket and dropped it to the ground, then unbuttoned his cuffs. Like Victory, he focused on the giant dragon in front of them.

As before, Xian's response to Yu was nonverbal. But whatever the dragon said caused all the blood to drain from Yu's face. He stumbled back, almost tripping on the steps, and Reynolds steadied him.

The governor faced the three of them. "Shift," he said, his lower body already fading out. "Now." With that order, Yu's human body changed, and a sinuous golden dragon reared on hind legs and whirled on Xian. Though his scales glowed in the shine of the streetlamps, he seemed so inconsequential next to the beast more than a dozen times his size.

"You heard the man." Reynolds' words faded into a pained snarl. He didn't bother to remove his shirt, which burst at the seams as he fell onto arms that sprouted fur and claws.

Rob followed suit, but Victory tore her attention away and stood guard over the defenseless men while they shifted.

With a scream of his own, Yu launched himself at Xian. But Xian batted him out of the air with one clawed paw. Yu slid across the ground, dragging himself to a stop with claws that shredded the pavement.

The temple doors banged open behind Victory. She heard gasps of shock and horror as Captain Huang's sharp voice ordered his people past the werewolves. He led a complement of men and women, all wearing the uniform of the palace guard and carrying rifles. Half of them dropped to one knee and raised their weapons while the other guards aimed above them.

"Fire!" Captain Huang's voice rang out over the now-deserted square, echoed by the roar of a dozen gunshots.

Most of the bullets ricocheted off Xian's plate-sized scales, but a few found marks in the more delicate skin of his wings, peircing holes in them. Xian roared in pain, and Yu used the distraction to leap for his back.

With a matched set of howls, one blond wolf and one gray streaked past Victory. As Xian twisted to bat at the smaller gold dragon on his back, the wolves launched themselves at the skin protected by smaller scales at Xian's neck.

Captain Huang gestured for his men to aim again, but Victory dashed in front of them. *"Don't shoot the wolves!"* she called over her shoulder. With a prayer that Huang listened to her, Victory dove into the fray.

There wasn't much she could do with a short-range weapon versus a creature taller than a house, but while Xian focused on snapping and swiping at the three werecreatures that crawled over his back, biting and clawing, Victory had a clear shot at other vulnerable areas.

She dodged a forelimb and slipped under Xian's stomach. Victory swung her bastard sword with both hands, putting her not inconsiderable strength behind the attack. The blade cut into the back of one of Xian's hind ankles, shearing the tendon and catching against bone. She ripped her weapon out with a spray of scarlet blood.

Xian howled again, this time a sound of pain, and lurched to one side. The blond wolf—Rob—crashed to the pavement next to her. Victory almost ran to his side at his body's stillness, but then he climbed to his feet, claws sliding on the slick blood. After a jerky head toss at Victory with a muzzle stained red, he leapt back onto Xian's back.

"Fire!"

Victory braced for missed bullets to strike her, but the guards were either lucky or all decent shots. Xian's large mass shifted to the side again, and Victory dove out from under him as his wounded leg collapsed under his weight.

She rolled to her feet, ducked under a swipe of Xian's tail that would have thrown her across the square, and found herself on the other side of the action. She took in the scope of the battlefield with a wide visual sweep. Captain Huang waved an arm in command from the steps, and his guards fired another volley. He didn't dare risk hitting Governor Yu, but it was nice to know that he had considered her position and the wolves when he attacked as well. Now both of Xian's wings, outstretched for balance, were shredded messes, riddled with bullet holes. His blood cast a dark shadow over sparkling sapphire scales.

Rob and Reynolds each braced on Xian's shoulders, raking the finer scales of his neck with claws and worrying at open wounds with snapping jaws. Blood streaked their pale pelts, but Victory couldn't tell how much of it was Xian's and how much was from Xian scoring his own bites against the men.

Perched on the back of the giant blue dragon, Yu used his smaller size to his advantage. His claws dug between the overlapping scales further down Xian's back, keeping his back legs stable as he slashed and bit with as much fury as the wolves.

Xian snaked his long neck, attacking the men from every angle, but his own jaw sported bloody claw marks. He couldn't use dragonfire against the bodies on his back without hurting himself, and he couldn't blast Captain Huang's people without leaving himself exposed. With the state of his wings, he wasn't leaving the square by air.

Xian was going to die here. Or they were all going to die here.

All she wanted was for Rob and Zhinu to get their happy ending. And to give Yu a chance for his.

Victory saw her opening.

Dodging a wide sweep of Xian's tail, she sprinted across the square. Another massive two-handed swing severed the ankle tendon of Xian's other hind limb. She spun out of the way as Xian's large body collapsed back, then reversed the grip on her sword and stabbed straight up. The tip of her bastard sword, maintained as carefully as its edges, slipped between two scales and skewered the base of Xian's neck. Xian heaved backward, groaning in pain and lifting Victory off her feet until the sword slipped out and she dropped back to the street. Her feet skidded out from under her on the blood-splattered pavement. A tawny wolf crashed half on top of her, yelping in pain at the impact.

Victory shoved Rob away. But before she could resettle her sword grip and strike at Xian again, Rob hurled himself up and chomped down on the open tear Victory had left at the delicate skin of the dragon's neck.

With a sickening wrench, Rob used his entire bodyweight to rip through Xian's neck. Blood poured through the ragged gash, dousing him and Victory.

Xian tried to scream again, emitting nothing more than a sickening gurgle. Yu and Reynolds leapt free as the giant dragon slumped over. Reynolds shouldered Yu out of the way before Xian's long neck slammed onto them.

His snout came to rest on the steps of the temple. The palace guards stumbled back, but Xian's eyes stared at nothing, and the blue fire in them had dimmed. Victory stepped toward him, but a hand clamped her shoulder.

"No," Yu said. When Victory looked back at him, she saw the governor back in human form, chest heaving with exhaustion and clothes as stained with blood as his golden scales had been. "They all saw what happened."

Victory followed the line of his stare. As the people of Jiang Yi Yue returned from where they had sheltered in the surrounding buildings, many carried weapons, real or impromptu.

With an order from Captain Huang, the guards surrounded Governor Yu, forcing him away from Victory. Rob and Reynolds sat on their haunches next to the dead dragon, leaning against each other as Reynolds licked at a wound on Rob's nape. They appeared oblivious to the encroaching humans around them. Victory stepped closer to the wolves, keeping her sword raised against the rage she saw in the townspeople's expressions.

She deciphered Yu's warning a split second before she heard the first angry yell. *"The wolves killed the ancestor!"*

But because nothing ever goes as planned, part of the crowd in the square charged for Victory and the wolves and others bee-lined for Governor Yu and his armed entourage. More shouts rang through the air, even as older people with visible tears prostrated themselves before Xian's felled body. But Victory's initial assumption that they converged on the governor as a show of support evaporated when she noted the equal amounts of anger and confusion on their faces.

After all, Yu had fought the ancestor, too.

The wolves huddled on either side of Victory, both looking to her for leadership. When did she become the alpha in this crazy group? They needed to find Mikelos and Zhinu and either hide or get the hell out, fast. Governor Yu could deal with his enraged constituents on his own.

Yu caught her attention between the bodies of his guards. "The temple."

When Rob whined low in his throat, Victory said, "Not without the others."

"Zhinu is here?" Yu bared his teeth in frustration, and a dull golden glow shimmered in his eyes again.

"Mikelos is with her," Victory said.

"So her safety is in the hands of that maniac musician. Fantastic." In low-voiced Qin, Yu directed his troops to bring Victory and the wolves into their circle of protection.

Victory opened her mouth to defend Mikelos as the group backed up the temple steps away from the approaching mob, but this was neither the time nor place. And in all fairness, most of what Yu had seen of Mikelos—brawling at the ball, lying about Tan's death—did seem pretty shady.

"I'm touched you feel that way, sir."

Speak of the devil. Mikelos and Zhinu emerged from the shadows. The guards snapped weapons in their direction until Huang ordered them back.

"You should have gone for the docks, cousin," Yu said. "None of us are safe here." He and Captain Huang beat on the temple doors, with no response.

"But the people saw what happened!" Zhinu dropped to her knees and wrapped an arm around Rob's shoulders, heedless of the blood matting his fur. "Grandfather attacked you!"

Yu pointed to two of the guards. *Get these doors open.* Switching back to Loquella, he said, "With all due respect, Grandfather was an old man used to getting his way. He didn't take well to being defied and he brought this on his own head." He loaned his enhanced strength to the two large men heaving at the temple door, to no avail.

No wonder Yu spoke Loquella now. Those words bordered on blasphemy. With time, Victory would mourn the loss of the man she had once known. But it appeared Xian hadn't been that man for a long time. "I don't think the priests are interested in letting us shelter here," she said. She raised her sword. "We could beat down the doors, but that would defeat the purpose of barricading ourselves in." The crowd that had gone for Yu milled at the bottom of the temple steps, as if unsure whether to come closer. It could have been respect for the governor, but a healthy fear of the guards' rifles was a more likely reason.

Yu gave one last shove, grunting at the force of it, then pushed away from the door. "And what would you suggest?"

"If I may," Mikelos said. Yu wrinkled his nose, but Mikelos pressed on. "Ditch the guards. Leave them here as a distraction. You need to get out with us."

Zhinu choked back a manic giggle at his pun.

Glaring at his cousin, Yu said, "I thought Moon was the mercenary?"

"I've picked up a thing or two," Mikelos said, voice steady.

Zhinu rose to her feet, hand resting between Rob's ears. "Are you with us or not, Cousin?"

"The priests!" Captain Huang's voice distracted them from the hushed argument. They all followed the line of his arm. Half a dozen white-robed figures emerged from an alleyway on the other side of the temple and approached Xian's body. The people milling about the square fell back in respect as the priests filed through, heads bowed in prayer.

"Looks like we're not finding safety here anyway," Victory said. "Let's go, kids." Reynolds huffed, then pawed at the ground. She would take that as an agreement.

Yu growled deep in this throat, more in frustration than threat. Without another word, he stripped out of his fancy embroidered robe and left it in a pile at the temple doors. Revealed beneath were simple pants and tunic, making him indistinguishable from the garb of the crowd they needed to escape—as long as no one noted the quality of the cloth or the eyes that still burned a steady gold. Yu snapped orders to the guards to remain in their holding pattern.

Captain Huang opened his mouth to argue, but any protests died on his lips at the determination on Yu's face. Instead, the captain glared at Victory. *"You are responsible for him now."*

"I'm pretty damn sure I can handle myself," Yu said.

As if the governor had not spoken, Victory bowed low to Huang. *"I will do my best."* It was the least she could do. He was Zhinu's family, after all. "Let's go."

Despite their best efforts, it was hard to conceal two foreigners and two wolves creeping out of the group of guards with two Qin. *"Run!"* Huang called over this shoulder before raising his rifle at the approaching crowd. *"Halt in the name of Governor Yu!"*

"The governor is a traitor to his people!" An angry roar of approval echoed this shouted jeer.

Yu turned back, but Victory and Mikelos grabbed each of his arms and hauled him into a run with them. The wolves ranged ahead, followed by Zhinu, and Victory trusted their noses to lead them to safety.

She did not loosen her grip on Yu, even when the sounds of gunshots echoed from the square behind them.

Rob and Reynolds arrowed through a maze of small streets and alleys, and Victory and Mikelos finally released Yu. She expected either Zhinu or the governor to balk at some of the refuse-filled pathways they traveled, but both nobles kept up without complaint.

They stayed away from any areas where people gathered, though Victory's sensitive hearing picked up the sounds of other roaming mobs. She had no idea what path the wolves led them down, but she hoped they neared the docks soon. Hours separated them from dawn, but she didn't fancy being pinned for the day and missing the ship with the rest of the British contingent. Getting out of the city would be that much harder, especially if Yu found himself ousted from power.

Rob darted out of the alley they followed and turned to the left. But when the rest of them stepped out into the street, bordered on either side by generic apartment buildings and dark storefronts, they found Rob stock-still in the middle of the avenue.

Father Hisato stood before them, surrounded by a pacing, shifting skulk of foxes. But intelligence shone in their sharp eyes, and Victory knew they faced more of the *kitsune* in Jiang Yi Yue.

Victory stepped between Rob and Reynolds, forcing Zhinu back with Mikelos and Yu. She pointed her sword at Hisato. *"Let us pass."*

Hisato ignored her. *"Governor Yu, you grace us with your presence."* His bow was short, mocking.

Rob growled, unable to follow the conversation.

Yu lifted a placating hand to the wolf as he stepped around Victory. He did not return Hisato's bow. *"Let. Us. Pass."* His voice resonated with echoes of his draconic voice.

Victory caught movement in the shadows of the buildings around her, but saw nothing when she shifted her focus to them. When she looked back to the tense tableau of werefox, weredragon, and werewolf, the movement returned, shifting and spreading out of the corner of her eye.

"The city has spoken," Hisato said. The *kitsune* continued to pace and twist at his feet. *"The Zhuanxu reign has come to a close."*

Yu took one step forward, disregarding Reynolds' warning growl. *"Why have you stirred up such trouble in my city?"*

As the foxes barked around him, Hisato laughed. *"What makes you think we are only in your city?"* His robes slipped from his shoulders, leaving him nude in the street. The streetlights painted his slim body in sharp shadows that shifted as red fur rippled across his skin.

Victory raised her sword. Yu deciphered Hisato's intention at the same moment. He blurred a moment, then his dragon form lunged for the priest.

But the other *kitsune* were ready. They mobbed Yu, protecting Hisato while he finished shifting. Their growls and yips, and Yu's snarls, covered the sounds of Hisato's bones breaking and reforming.

Though they were all exhausted, the two werewolves pounced and joined the fray. The werefoxes were larger than their natural brethren, thanks to conservation of mass, but still no match against the larger wolves. Rob sank his teeth into the neck of one fox attempting to flank Yu and ripped him away from the dragon. He shook the fox like a rag doll, snapping its spine and tossing it away. The fox slid down the street and stayed still.

But the *kitsune* outnumbered Victory's group.

Yu was dexterous, sliding through the mob on quick limbs and using his tail as yet another weapon to complement teeth and talons. Zhinu squeaked in fear as one fox snapped at Yu's rear ankle, almost accomplishing against her cousin what Victory had managed against their grandfather.

As if drawn by the noise, two of the *kitsune* peeled away from the fight and sprinted toward Victory and the others. The foxes were fast, but not vampire fast. Victory lunged with her sword single-handed at one, catching the sharp tip against its hip. Using the momentum, she spun around and caught the other fox under the chin with a solid roundhouse kick. *Kitsune* blood mixed with the dried weredragon blood that already coated her blade, and both foxes stumbled.

They regrouped and tried again, this time ignoring Mikelos and Zhinu in favor of the more immediate threat. Whoever these *kitsune* were, they weren't trained fighters. Victory dropped to one knee and let the first fox charge. She brought up her sword at the last second, putting her own strength into the blow that impaled the *kitsune* in the sternum. The fox slid down her blade, snapping its teeth a hairsbreadth from Victory's face before screaming in pain and collapsing.

She tried to wrench her sword out of the fox's body, but steel caught on bone and wouldn't shake free. Abandoning the trapped weapon, she twisted her body at the last second so that the second *kitsune* collided with her shoulder. They tumbled to the street in a tangle of fur and limbs. Sharp jaws closed around one forearm, but Victory ignored the pain screaming through her limb because it kept the fox's teeth away from her neck. Kicking her legs to get leverage, she twisted her body enough to wrap her free hand around one of the knives at her waist. In one move, she dragged the small blade from its sheath and stabbed upward. The teeth gripped tighter, worrying at the bone and muscle and spraying Victory's own dark blood over both of them. She squinted past the stinging liquid and kicked, rolling over onto the fox. This freed her other arm, and she stabbed again. This time she hit something more vital. The fox collapsed beneath her, releasing her arm with a pained yelp before going silent.

She pulled herself to her knees, cradling her wounded arm. Mikelos helped her to her feet, catching her as she staggered. She ignored his wordless query, the concern she could see in his face. The wound was bad—bone peeked out from shredded skin and muscle—but she would survive. Mikelos retrieved Victory's sword and knife while she checked on the others.

Snarls and growls, punctuated by sharp yelps of pain, continued from the other end of the block. Two more *kitsune* lay dead in the street, and Reynolds dragged one useless hind limb. Three werefoxes remained, evening the odds. But Yu and the wolves had begun at a disadvantage, already tired from battle. Victory's experienced eye saw slowed reaction times, and there was too much blood.

She shuddered as the scent of blood enveloped her. Blood would heal her wound, and she needed all her self-control not to wade into the fray. She couldn't chance that the werecreature she tried to drink from wouldn't be from her own side.

Reynold's bad leg hindered him, but he harried the *kitsune* as Rob and Yu tried to split the foxes. But true pack animals would have gone for the weakest prey, and foxes hunted alone. In a furious burst of action, all three convened on Rob the moment he was separated from Yu and Reynolds in an attempt to come from the rear.

The tawny wolf collapsed under a pile of burnished fur, howling in pain. Another wave of fresh blood, along with the sharp sound of cracking bone.

The scream that emerged behind Victory wasn't human. It raised the hair on the back of her neck.

A sinuous blue form darted past her and slid to an uncoordinated halt next to Rob. Though less bulky than Yu, with delicate whiskers and a fringe that cascaded the length of her neck, the blue dragon sported talons with wicked curves and hissed through long fangs. As lamplight glinted cerulean off her scales, she grabbed one fox at the neck and shook hard until the spine snapped. When the fox went limp in her jaws, the dragon released it and gagged at the blood coating her teeth and tongue.

Yu and Reynolds had both frozen, even as Victory and Mikelos stood gaping. Victory couldn't blame them. "Zhinu?" Yu asked, as Reynolds whined in confusion.

For a moment, Victory forgot the pain in her arm. This was impossible. Female weredragons couldn't change form. It was like a vampire standing in the sun.

"Help me, you idiots!" Tossing her head, Zhinu pulled a second fox off Rob's prone form by the leg, dropping the *kitsune* as it swiped with its other front paw.

As if seeing the *kitsune* strike at Zhinu spurred him into action, Yu used his larger form to block the fox. When it twisted around to pounce again, Yu gouged at its exposed belly with his talons, spilling intestines and other organs across the pavement.

Zhinu made quick work of the final *kitsune*. Though she seemed unwilling to use her jaw as a weapon a second time, she grabbed it with both forelegs and tore it limb from limb. She tossed the broken and bloodied werefox to one side, and with a keening wail, wrapped her own body around Rob's splayed and limp form.

In the sudden silence, broken by Reynolds' low, pained whine and Zhinu's whimpers, Victory could hear Rob's ragged breath.

In a blur of gold, Yu's human form returned. He staggered to one side on a bloodied leg before steadying himself and hobbling toward Zhinu. She had tucked her legs under her body and draped her long neck over Rob, still keening low in her throat.

Mikelos helped Victory to Yu's side, where they watched him touch a shaking hand to Zhinu's back before pulling it away. *"I can't believe it,"* he said, reverting to his native Qin in a stunned whisper. Shock was painted across his face when he looked at Victory.

"This is new to me, too," she said.

"I'm confused," Mikelos said. Without any of Yu's hesitation, he caressed a gentle hand over Zhinu's side, combing his fingers through the fringe at her spine. "I thought female weredragons couldn't—"

"They can't," Yu said. "This is unheard of."

Zhinu's whimpers resolved into anxious mutterings. "He's dead," she said. "He died for me. I never—I don't love him, but he was never supposed to die for me!" The volume of her voice rose until her wails echoed off the darkened buildings surrounding them. Her long neck whipped back and forth with the force of her panic.

Ignoring the searing pain that arched up her ruined arm, Victory grabbed the sides of Zhinu's snout. Where male weredragon scales formed hard sheets of armor with edges that could cut unprotected skin, Zhinu's scales flexed under her fingers and reminded Victory more of the flexible Kwolek armor some mercenaries favored that could withstand bullets. She drew Zhinu's face to hers and stared the girl down. "Listen!"

As the weredragon calmed, hopefully her sensitive hearing would pick up what Victory also heard. Rob's heartbeat—slow, but steady.

"Werewolves are tough," Victory said, keeping her voice calm and firm. She reeled with the same shock still etched across Yu's face, but they didn't have time to drown in it. "You're smarter than this, girl. He's alive!"

But Zhinu reared away from the touch, wrenching out of Victory's grasp and sending her staggering. Though still unbalanced and uncoordinated on four limbs, she galloped around the group, avoiding the dead *kitsune* but sliding through entrails. Her long tail whipped out of control behind her, smashing through the plate glass window of one storefront and tearing a streetlight from its foundation.

After cursing in Qin, Yu changed back to dragon form. But the blurred space between shapes lasted longer this time, more evidence of his exhaustion. "We have to calm her before she shifts again."

In Victory's own dulled state, temples throbbing in counterpoint to the pain in her arm, Yu's words needed a moment to sink in. Zhinu wasn't going to shift back to human form. She was in danger of letting her stress and strong emotions goad her into her own "final form," if such a thing was even possible for female weredragons. The final dragon form from which there was no return.

Yu tackled Zhinu. With the grinding screech of scales against scales, they rolled across the street. Despite his injuries, Yu was still the larger dragon, and he managed to wrap all four legs around Zhinu and pin her to the ground.

Victory sprinted to them, her path careening in a wide arc as her vision became hazy. Her arm no longer bled, yet another warning sign that she needed to feed soon. Dropping to her knees next to Zhinu, she once again grabbed the young dragon's head and twisted it around. This time, she forced Zhinu to face Rob's body. Zhinu flailed where she could, striking Yu with her tail and wrenching her long neck out of Victory's grip.

Victory gasped in pain as her injured arm lifted up and out with the familiar jerk of a dislocated shoulder. Pushing through the pain, she wrestled Zhinu back down. *"Look!"*

The familiar Qin jolted Zhinu, and she froze. This time, Victory was able to guide Zhinu's attention to Rob. Even as they watched, the fur on his body seemed to melt away. In a transformation much gentler in his unconscious state, Rob reverted to human form. The wounds on his body were already half-healed, though bright red lines marred his skin where both Xian and the *kitsune* had done their damage. His chest heaved, evidence of his deep breathing. Reynolds limped over to him and licked at his face, whining with relief.

Zhinu's head sagged, and she stopped struggling against Yu. With slow, cautious movements, as if ready to wrestle her into submission once more, her cousin released her and backed away. Victory kept her hand against Zhinu's cheek, this time for comfort.

"He's alive." Victory hoped the waver in her voice didn't betray too much of her pain. The last thing they needed was for Zhinu to panic again.

Instead, Zhinu's body shimmered and Victory found herself with an armful of human-shaped noblewoman. She ignored the stabbing pain in her shoulder and hugged Zhinu back with her good arm.

"I hate to rush this, but the clock's ticking," Mikelos said.

"He's right," Yu said. Though he still stared at Zhinu, this time with compassion instead of shock, he spoke in response to Mikelos' words. "The commotion we've caused is sure to bring unwanted attention soon." An even longer blur shifted him back to human, and Victory knew the gold dragon would make no more appearances that night.

Victory surveyed the street around them, littered with *kitsune* bodies and shattered glass. "Commotion," she said. Understatement of the century. "Right." She hauled herself to her feet and leaned against Mikelos for a second. But one second was all they could spare.

Mikelos handed Zhinu Victory's sword and dagger, and the girl accepted them as if on automatic. With practiced movement, Mikelos gripped Victory by the shoulder and her arm above the elbow, then twisted the joint back into place. Zhinu flinched at the sound of the bones settling, but handed over the weapons when Victory reached for them.

Yu stood over Rob and Reynolds and pointed at Mikelos. "Can you help carry them?"

"Guess I'll have to," Mikelos said. With Yu's help, he hauled Rob into a fireman's carry. Yu scooped up Reynolds and draped the wolf across his stocky shoulders. The older werewolf gave a perturbed grunt, but otherwise accepted the assistance without argument.

Victory prodded Zhinu, still pale and distant with shock, into following the two men before taking the rear behind their pitiful party herself.

Once the site of the slaughter fell behind them, the scent of blood was washed from Victory's nose and replaced with the salty tang of an ocean breeze. After slipping through another alleyway, they heard waves crashing against wooden piers. The end was near.

If the boat hadn't sailed.

They raced through Jiang Yi Yue's shipping district at a quick hobble. In the distance, glinting in the moonlight, Victory spotted the tower they had used to disembark upon their arrival in the city. But their destination this time was not as grand. A midsized vessel reeking of old fish and in desperate need of a fresh coat of paint awaited them.

Adam stood at the bottom the gangplank. He lifted his arms in a silent cheer when Mikelos came into view. But his face grew ashen when he saw the state of their procession. "My stars. The earl—?"

"Alive, but wounded," Mikelos said. Other members of the British delegation watched from the ship, and they thundered down the ramp to accept the daywalker's burden. Yu also knelt to transfer Reynolds to eager arms.

"Get them on the ship," Victory said. "And tell the captain we're departing as soon as possible."

"With five minutes to spare," Adam said. "I'm so glad you all made it."

Yu scrubbed at his face with his hands. "Good timing, indeed. I'm not sure what I'd have done otherwise."

Adam stepped back. After a nervous beat, he dropped into a bow. "Governor!"

"So I hope," Yu said. He stepped in front of Zhinu, still subdued from shock and gripping Victory's sword arm at the wrist as if it was the sole thing keeping her together. *"Cousin,"* he said, his voice gentle. He brushed a tangled lock of hair out of her face. *"Zhinu."*

Zhinu's glassy eyes cleared enough to focus on him. *"Cousin?"*

"You must promise me you will be well," Yu said. *"Show the wolves what it means to be Qin, and marry your earl, and live your dreams."*

"I don't know what happened," Zhinu said, her voice cracking on the words. *"I don't know what I am."*

"You are a gift," Yu said, holding her face in his hands. *"Our people's gift to the world."*

"Come with me," Zhinu said. *"You're not safe here."*

"My duty is here, to our people." He pressed a kiss to Zhinu's forehead, then released her to step back. *"I don't know what chaos Hisato's people have wrought, but I must help to restore order."*

"My duty—"

"Your duty," Yu said, interrupting Zhinu, *"is to yourself."* He bowed once to her, and turned and repeated the action for Mikelos and Victory.

Victory had sagged against Mikelos while the cousins talked, but she pulled herself to her full height and returned the bow. *"I will make sure she reaches Britannia in safety. You have my word."*

"The word of the Lady Victory is good enough for me," Yu said, switching to Loquella. After bowing once to Adam, who had taken Zhinu's arm and was ready to lead her to the waiting ship, Yu turned on his heel and disappeared into the darkness.

Two hundred years ago, Victory had thought she'd seen her last dragon when Moon left Xian on mainland Qin. Today, she would have thought the same once again.

But on the ship waited another dragon, a miracle dragon who shouldn't exist, and Victory—not Moon—had a duty to her.

"Come on," Mikelos said. He tugged her sword from her fingers and wrapped a strong arm around her waist. With a groan of mixed pain and relief, Victory leaned against him and allowed herself to be half-carried up the gangplank. "Let's go home."

EPILOGUE

Where the trip from Fort Caroline to Jiang Yi Yue had taken less than a week on the enormous *Xianfeng*, the return voyage was much more circuitous. The British contingent had found a long-range fishing vessel that usually hired out for corporate team-building events, but the captain and his small crew were just as happy to accept British money as Qin.

Rob and Reynolds healed both quick and clean thanks to a few hearty meals of fresh fish and Zhinu's careful fussing. Reynolds was left with a residual limp he claimed would add to his distinguished image, and Rob had a scarred knot on his shoulder, a battle wound that he wore with pride.

Victory, however, found herself in dire straits as they fled Jiang Yi Yue. Despite the increased strength and endurance afforded him as a daywalker, Mikelos could only spare so much blood. And what Victory was willing to drink from him wasn't enough to heal her arm, which she kept wrapped in a length of bandage even as she refused to leave the small cabin she shared with Mikelos.

Two days into the trip, Zhinu barged into the cabin and settled herself on the edge of the shelf bed where Victory curled around her injury. The girl thrust her wrist to Victory and huffed in annoyance. "Mikelos says you're being stubborn."

Through a pained gasp, Victory said, "You don't know what you're offering." She was in no danger of going berserk and eating everyone on the ship. She was too old for such nonsense. But she still hurt, and pain made people do stupid things.

"I know I'm offering to help my friend. In the history books I've read, the lore says werewolf blood is stronger than human, which is why the vampires of Roma wanted Albion so badly," Zhinu said. "So the blood of dragons should be of a quality for even your palate." She balled her other fist at her side, as if daring Victory to argue.

Mikelos knew how to keep her from taking too much blood. Zhinu's desire to help her friend might push her past any safe limits.

But the girl's attitude of gentle teasing, not anxious concern, reassured Victory. And it was true that one feeding of her more potent weredragon blood would erase all signs of Victory's injury.

And Victory was tired of being in pain. "Fine," she said. "But get Mikelos first." He could at least supervise.

Once she emerged from her sequestration, arm clear of even the smallest bit of scarring, the British contingent cheered. It was as if knowing Victory had helped protect Rob and Reynolds erased all lingering suspicion of the vampire, and they welcomed her into their midst the same way they had Mikelos and Zhinu.

The rest of the voyage passed without incident. They stopped at smaller ports to resupply, but skirted the larger city of Jiao. Though they passed at the height of noon, the smoke drifting from the city in giant plumes permeated even Victory's cabin, choking the air with ash and dust.

Father Hisato had not exaggerated when he told Yu that Jiang Yi Yue was not the only target of their displeasure. That night, Victory held Zhinu while she cried out of worry for her cousin, her handmaids, and even the mother she had left behind. She hadn't wanted to show Rob her despair and make the man feel guilty for pulling her away from her people, despite Zhinu's constant reassurance that it had been her choice.

It was a good thing that, once they arrived in Britannia, Zhinu would be settling in at Oxenafor and Rob would spend most of his time working in Londinium. Their relationship could develop naturally instead of going through the trials of too much togetherness, too soon.

Though she hadn't supported the match at first, by the time the ship left the group in Fort Caroline, even Victory hoped the couple lived happily ever after.

Under Reynolds' supervision, the majority of the aides and minor diplomats continued from Fort Caroline to Calverton, the southernmost British colonial city. But Victory had made a promise to Yu. Though she couldn't escort the couple all the way back to Britannia, they would travel with people she trusted. As Victory sheltered in Limani's customs house away from the early morning sunlight, Mikelos waved at the departing ferry with Rob and Zhinu.

The people she trusted were Limani's mercenaries, and she hoped two in particular would be available to accept a bodyguard contract.

Rhaavi, Limani's custom's master, was kind enough to drive the group back to the manor house rather than risk being stuck with Victory haunting his office until nightfall. When they arrived home, Victory's adopted daughter and foster son sprinted out of the house and sheltered her under thick quilts and magical shielding until she was inside.

Where entrusting her safety to Rob and Guy's whim back in Jiang Yi Yue had given her so much anxiety, she put the same faith in Toria and Kane without a second thought.

A flurry of activity followed. Introductions all around, greeting family members, and exclaiming over the piles of luggage that had beaten them from Jiang Yi Yue to Limani. Even Mikelos' second violin and the Qin *erhu* had made it intact.

"There was a note from some fellow named Yu," Asaron said, as they gathered in the kitchen for lunch. A tight squeeze around the table for seven, but Zhinu and Rob had been absorbed into the group with little effort. "Looks like all of the cases you two left with, along with some extra trunks labeled for Zhinu."

Zhinu sagged in her chair with relief. "I'm so happy to hear he's alive. And in some state of power, if he was able to manage this."

"Rumors are already spreading," Asaron said. "From both the colonies of Dongqu and mainland Qin. My contacts say the *kitsune*-led uprising is a symptom of a larger disease. Some cities are in better shape than others. But it's hard to separate fact from fiction when all the long-distance communications are still down worldwide."

"Here, too?" Victory exchanged a troubled glance with Mikelos. "We were told the Qin separatists were at fault."

Toria raised her hand. "That's, um, not exactly true. I can tell you with pretty much one hundred percent certainty no one in Qin had anything to do with it."

Asaron laughed as Victory and the others all stared at Toria and Kane.

Somehow, the idea her daughter was behind the global communications issue did make more sense than the explanation Yu had first provided in Jiang Yi Yue. Victory decided not to examine that idea further. "You'd better start from the beginning," she said.

Later that night, once Victory had settled Zhinu and Rob into one of the guest rooms on the second floor, she wandered back downstairs. She did her best to ignore the piles of luggage still blocking the entrance to her gym, knowing the laundry wasn't going to do itself. Instead, she followed the sounds of a pen scratching in the library.

She found Toria curled on a window seat, writing on a pad of paper propped on her knees. Victory settled next to her, waiting in content silence for her daughter to finish.

Finally, Toria capped her pen and set the stationary aside. "Hey, Mama."

"Hey, yourself," Victory said.

"Sounds like we both had adventures."

"If you can call kidnapping a Qin princess and escaping civil war an adventure." Victory rested the back of her head against the cool glass of the window.

"I'm pretty sure whatever Kane and I did to the world's magic trumps that," Toria said.

"From what Kane explained, it sounded to me like you saved it," Victory said. She brushed away the tear trailing down Toria's cheek. "Do you want to talk about Syri?" The news that her daughter's best friend had not survived their trip to Parisii had shocked Victory to the core, even more than the news that the world spell the elves had set to limit technology in the world might have collapsed. If civil war was in fact brewing in the Qin lands, the first side to discover that weapons creation was once again possible would end up on top.

"No," Toria said, her voice sharp. "But sit with me a bit?"

She didn't have to ask. Victory lifted her arm and allowed Toria to snuggle close on the window seat.

"I'm glad we saw you and Dad before we had to find another job," Toria said. "Max has some options for us."

That was right—the kids still had almost sixteen months left on journeyman status before being granted their full mercenary titles. The head of Limani's Mercenary Guild probably had a good idea where to send his protégés next since they had survived their first adventure. But he would forgive Victory for preempting him. She pressed a kiss to her daughter's hair and held her close.

Across the darkness of the library, lit only by the light above the window seat, Victory saw shadows twist around her desk. She should really mention those, but instead said, "How do you feel about being a bodyguard to a princess?"

"I guess that depends," Toria said, her voice muffled in Victory's arms but sounding more positive. "How much are you willing to pay us?"

Once the ink on the contract dried the following afternoon, Toria and Kane settled at the kitchen table with Rob and Zhinu to make travel plans. Victory had expected to join them to assist with details, but she had quickly felt extraneous as Toria and Kane debated the merits of leaving from Calverton or New Angouleme with Rob, which devolved into a discussion of how they all knew some werewolf named Earl Henry Delacour.

Zhinu sipped her iced tea in silence as the conversation swirled around her, happier than Victory had ever seen her. It was as if an invisible weight had lifted from the girl's shoulders, and she looked far more comfortable in a pair of leggings and large T-shirt borrowed from Toria than she had ever appeared in her formal robes.

As the conversation devolved into an argument between Toria and Kane about whether to wait for the assistance of someone named "Archer" in New Angouleme, Victory drifted out of the kitchen without notice.

Before accepting the contract from Xian, her biggest worry had been her children entering the world without her protection. But they were making the friends and connections necessary to make a mercenary career work for them.

Asaron had already made it clear to Victory he would be leaving the following night. For him, the news of civil war in Qin meant business opportunities, and he would be on the road south as soon as possible. She hoped he heeded her advice to travel to Jiang Yi Yue and offer his services to Yu. The governor would appreciate the assistance of the second half of the famed mercenary team. And pay handsomely.

She followed the strains of music into Mikelos' studio. He perched on a stool, plucking at the *erhu* with deft fingers. When he saw her, he picked up the bow. She braced herself, but as he drew it over the strings, the sound that emerged was smooth and fluid.

"Looks like Tan managed to teach you something after all," Victory said, leaning against the doorframe. "Happy to be home?"

Without pausing his playing, Mikelos grinned at her. "Happy to be where you are."

She entered the studio and curled in the armchair in the corner. Victory let the sounds of Mikelos' music play in counterpoint to the excited conversation drifting from the kitchen. Like Zhinu, she felt a million times lighter.

The mercenary Moon had been abandoned in Jiang Yi Yue. The Master of the City of Limani was home.

Acknowledgments

Since I have not yet had the pleasure of visiting space, this novel was not written in a vacuum. I am grateful for the support of so many people in my life.

My insightful beta readers and critique partners—Chris Stout, Breeanna Pierce, Chelsea Stickle, Alex Savage, Lana Ayers, and Faryn Black—who read all or parts of this novel. My work is better for your thoughts and assistance.

Everyone who cheered me on during National Novel Writing Month 2015, especially my local chapter in Columbia, Maryland.

Mrs. Locey, Mrs. Callaghan, and Prof. Charlebois, for fostering my appreciation of William Shakespeare through high school and college.

My editors and friends, Jennifer Barnes and John Edward Lawson, for their continued encouragement of this crazy series.

And always, my husband Erik, for his love and patience.

ABOUT THE AUTHOR

By day, J. L. Gribble is a professional medical editor. By night, she does freelance fiction editing in all genres, along with reading, playing video games, and occasionally even writing.

Previously, Gribble studied English at St. Mary's College of Maryland. She received her Master's degree in Writing Popular Fiction from Seton Hill University in Greensburg, Pennsylvania, where her debut novel *Steel Victory* was her thesis for the program.

She lives in Ellicott City, Maryland, with her husband and three vocal Siamese cats. Find her online (www.jlgribble.com), on Facebook (www.facebook.com/jlgribblewriter), and on Twitter and Instagram (@hannaedits). She is currently working on more tales set in the world of Limani.

www.ingramcontent.com/pod-product-compliance
Lightning Source LLC
Chambersburg PA
CBHW020636250626
47154CB00008B/2709